D1784396

# Mr Darcy's Struggle

A Pride & Prejudice Variation

By
Martine J Roberts

## Copyright:

Copyright © 2014 by Martine J Roberts

All rights reserve. No part of this book may be reproduced in any form, or by electronic mechanical means, including information storage and retrieval systems, except in the case of brief quotations embodied in critical articles or reviews - without permission in writing from the publisher, Martine J Roberts.

All the characters and events described in this book are fictitious or are used fictitiously. Any similarity to real persons, living or dead is purely coincidental and not intended by the author.

# Dedication

This book is dedicated to my entire family, for their forbearance with my obsession of all things Jane Austen, especially Mr Darcy. With a special thank you to Lady Lacey Brooks, whose enthusiasm and support was unwavering.

# **<u>Acknowledgement</u>**

Jane Austen has inspired many generations of writers to put pen to paper, including me. From the age of nine when I was first introduced to her baby, Pride & Prejudice, I have been in love with its characters, especially Mr Darcy. In my alternative version, have tried to follow her example, by adding a few twists and turns to the plot, whilst conveying the emotions, and desires of young lovers. I would like to thank her for bringing these people into our lives, for without Jane and her wonderful imagination, the world would be a sadder place. I hope you enjoy it.

Cover image by kind permission of Sandwell Museum Service.

# Table of Contents

# CHAPTER 1

As Elizabeth paced the room, her temper rose. How could she have been so foolish as to let Mr. Darcy get under her skin so? If only she had remained calm and acted in a dignified and ladylike manner, she would not be in this predicament. And now she could see no way out but the one offered by him. Stamping her foot in frustration she folded her arms and sat on the edge of her bed. When he had declared himself and offered her his hand in marriage, she should have just refused politely, and hoped he would leave. But oh no, she had to use the opportunity to vent her ire at him about Jane and Mr. Wickham. Stupid, stupid girl she chided herself. She rose and walked over to the window. It afforded her a clear view of Rosings, Lady Catherine De Burgh's stately home. With a sigh, she sat in the window seat, brought her knees up under her chin, and hugged them to her chest. Resting her head back, she closed her eyes and reviewed the events of the afternoon.

Unbeknown to Elizabeth, Mr. Darcy was also remembering their encounter!

Having received some shocking information from Colonel Fitzwilliam, namely about Mr. Darcy's involvement in the separation of Jane and Mr. Bingley, Elizabeth had begged off going to Rosings that afternoon. Instead, she had stayed at the parsonage to read over some of Jane's letters. Although they were full of accounts of outings and shopping, Elizabeth could detect no gaiety in the tone of the writing. It was clear to her that her sister was still suffering from a broken heart. Thinking of Jane made Elizabeth long to be home, so she might comfort her sister. Lost in thought, she was startled when she heard the doorbell and subsequently a male voice. Ruefully, she refolded the letters and put them on the table just before Mr. Darcy entered.

"Forgive me, you are feeling better?"

He enquired as he strode into the room. His presence seemed to fill the small parlour, and Elizabeth's eyes could not help but be drawn to the contours of his toned muscles, visible under his well-fitting jacket and trousers. She noticed his countenance, and thought how agitated he looked, distracted even, as he entered.

"I am sir thank you, will you not sit down," Elizabeth responded.

She tried to hide her displeasure at seeing him, as she took the seat by the window. She folded her hands in her lap, and waited for him to speak. He had invaded her solitude, and therefore she was not inclined to put him at his ease. He placed his hat and gloves on the table, and turned as if to address her. Instead, he walked to the chair by the fire and sat down. Elizabeth was puzzled, why had he come to call; he must know everyone else was at Rosings, having only just left there himself? Surely it could not be to scold her for missing tea with his aunt. Perhaps Colonel Fitzwilliam had informed him of their earlier conversation, and he had come to offer his excuses. She felt, rather than saw his piercing gaze, and when she cast him a sidelong glance, her suspicion was confirmed, he was studying her intently. It was most un-nerving. He rose from his chair and came to stand before her. It was clear something was troubling him, and she wished he would just say what he needed too, and then leave. Then he took up his familiar stance, with his hands folded behind his back, and finally began to speak,

"These many months I have struggled in vain, and I can bear it no longer. You must allow me to express my feelings, and to unburden myself, in telling you how ardently, I admire and love you."

He was making her an offer? He, who had declared she was tolerable, but not handsome enough to tempt him,

"By revealing the depth of my regard for you, I will of course court the displeasure and censure of my family, my friends, and possibly the whole of society. I hardly need add it goes against my own character too, but it cannot be helped," He continued.

She hoped the shock she felt had not registered on her face, but this was the last thing she expected from the proud, and arrogant Fitzwilliam Darcy. With her own thoughts in turmoil, she only caught a few of his words as he continued with his proposal,

"...alliance between us must be regarded as highly reprehensible.....regard it as such myself."

Noticing her raised brows he paused briefly, and then resumed.

"...which despite my struggle has overcome every rational objection, and I must beg you, most fervently, to relieve my suffering and consent to be my wife."

Elizabeth was speechless. The man who had purposefully separated her beloved sister from the man she loved, declaring her unworthy due to her lack of fortune and low social standing, was now making her an offering. He was certainly audacious! And if this was his notion of a proposal, it was sorely lacking in any inducement for her to accept. Insulting her family, and their position in society, was hardly conducive to receiving a positive reply. Drawing a breath, she took a moment to contrive her answer. Even through her anger at his interference, she was conscious of the honor he was bestowed on her. Speaking slowly, and with thought, she replied,

"In such cases as this, it is I believe the established mode to express a sense of obligation, for the sentiment avowed. If I could feel such gratitude I would now thank you," she paused before adding "but I cannot. I have never desired your good opinion Mr. Darcy, and you have certainly been most reluctant to bestow it. I am sincerely sorry that my refusal may cause you pain, but I hope it will be of a short duration."

She knew she had been curt in her reply, but the mode of his declaration had been quite insulting. The look of surprise and puzzlement on his face, as he tried to comprehend that he had been rejected, held Elizabeth, and she could not look away.

Darcy walked over to the mantle-piece then turned to face her again. No, he was not wrong; she was earnest in her rejection. This was not the reply he had been expecting. He was sure she had been aware of his intentions, and had indeed returned them. Clearly she had not thought about what such an advantageous marriage could mean to her, to her family. Fixing his eyes on her, he tried to give the appearance of composure, while inside he was feeling anything but. In a tone of forced calmness, he asked,

"And this is your answer? I might wonder why with so little *endeavour* at civility, I am thus rejected."

"And I might enquire why you thought insulting me would result in a positive reply. You just told me that you liked me against your will, your better judgement. That you have struggled for months, in an attempt to overcome your feeling for me, is this not motive enough for incivility, if I *was* uncivil?" She replied with a lift of her chin.

"Besides, I have good reason to think ill of you now, and even though I had thought favourably towards you at one time, you have driven such feeling away."

"How have I undone your affections? Have I not treated you with respect and courteously at all times?"

"Do you deny separating Mr. Bingley and my sister?"

His jaw tightened and his face grew pale, which made Elizabeth paused for thought. Had she had gone too far, been too outspoken she wondered? A man of Darcy's stature and rank was not accustomed to having a woman speak to him thus. She had no doubt that he expected her to accept his proposal at once, to even feel honoured. Indeed, had she not learned of his meddling in Jane and Mr. Bingleys courtship she would have given his declaration serious consideration? He was a far better prospect than Mr. Collins had ever been.

"I have no wish to deny it and rejoice in my success," Darcy responded, and then muttered "To him I have been kinder than towards myself."

Elizabeth drew a sharp breath at this admission of guilt, and rose from her seat. Ignoring all propriety of the distance that should be observed between a single man and woman, she entered Mr. Darcy's sphere.

"Long before that event my opinion of you was decided, when I heard of your dealings with Mr. Wickham," She challenged.

Darcy's eyes narrowed and the colour rose in his face. Closing the gap between them still further, Darcy now stood only a hand span from Elizabeth. Wickham! Once again that man's meddling in his life was causing him pain. He should have called him out last summer and finished it.

"You take an eager interest in that gentleman madam; I was unaware you were privy to all our dealings together," he said, looking calmer than he was feeling. The intense darkness of his eyes betrayed the anger that was brooding under the surface. This did not escape Elizabeth's notice, but she had come this far and so continued.

"He has suffered great misfortune and at your hands sir."

"His misfortunes," Darcy repeated softly, no longer trying to hide the contempt in his voice "yes, his misfortunes have been great indeed, but not at my hand madam, believe me. And so this is your opinion of me! I see Wickham's sentiments echoed in your words, and you believe my faults are heavy indeed. Perhaps you would have overlooked these offences had I been less honest. Had I concealed my struggles, flattered you maybe? But disguise of any kind is my abhorrence. Did you expect me to rejoice at the inferiority of your connections? To congratulate myself on an alliance with relations whose conditions in life is so decidedly below my own?"

Elizabeth's anger now rose to match Darcy's. To *think* such a thing was bad enough, but for him to avowal it to her in person was beyond contemptible. With their faces now only a whisper apart, she retorted,

"You are mistaken, Mr. Darcy. The mode of your declaration has spared me any concern which I might have felt in refusing you, had you behaved in a more gentleman-like manner."

She knew her arrow had hit its mark when she saw his body stiffen, and heard the sharp intake of breath as she questioned his honour. She had wanted to hurt him, for the pain he had caused her beloved Jane and then admitted with pride. As she boldly returned his stare she became aware of how close they had become, the heat from his body mingled with his scent seemed too washed over her.

His astonishment was obvious as he looked at her with an expression of both incredulity and mortification.

Deciding to make her point crystal clear she continued,

"Your arrogance, your conceit, and total disregard for the feelings of others appal me. Were you the last man in the world, even that inducement, would not be enough to prevail upon me to marry you."

Breathing heavily, she paused to catch her breath, but before she could resume her diatribe Darcy interjected.

"I think you have said quite enough now madam. I understand you find my proposal quite disgusting, although it was made with genuine affection. I now feel ashamed for expressing what my own feelings have been."

The silence between them was palpable. Darcy knew after receiving such a stinging assassination of his character he should retreat, yet he felt held by an invisible force. Examining her face, he saw her eyes were bright, and her cheeks were flushed from the exertion of their encounter, and the pleasant smell of lavender permeated his nostrils. The darkness in Darcy's eyes, which had moments ago been due to anger, was now replaced with desire. He liked that she did not cower from him, that she had stood her ground and made her case, even if some of it was erroneous. God she was beautiful, with her chin held defiantly high, and her bosom heaving. Darcy savoured the image. What a wife she would have been, passionate in all things he was sure. Remembering he had been soundly rejected, a notion formed in his head. If she would not have him and he was never to see her again, could he risk tasting those sweet lips, just once? They were alone, and he had nothing to lose; he would regard it as a farewell gesture. Besides they were unlikely to meet again after today. Slowly Darcy put his arm about her waist, and as he did so he lowered his head and gently brushed Elizabeth's lips with his own. They were soft and warm, and her breath was sweet, just as he had imagined. Drawing back he waited for her to scream or to feel the sting of a well-deserved slap, but nothing came. Darcy raised his right hand to tilt her chin, then gently brushing her cheek with the back of his hand as he tried to read her reaction to his bold advance.

Elizabeth knew when she felt Darcy's arm slip around her waist, that he would kiss her. She knew she should object, struggle or call for help. But she also knew she would not. As she had delivered the final words of her attack, she realised that her whole body was tingling with excitement. It was for this reason she had paused. Being so close to this man had been exciting, exhilarating and she had never felt so alive. Elizabeth realised she *wanted* his lips to deliver her first ever kiss, in fact, she had almost held her breath as she anticipated its arrival. Then it was over, the briefest of touches. A pleasant experience, but not quite as she had imagined it would be.

Without looking away Darcy claimed her lips for a second time, only now he lingered a little longer, and delivered the kiss with an increase of pressure. He felt Elizabeth's lips part slightly under his own, and a quiet sigh escaped her.

*This* is what she expected, she thought as the warmth of his mouth caressed her lips, as she began to savour the sensations it.

Darcy wondered if she was aware of the sound she made. He expected not, but he took the soft sigh as a sign of enjoyment, and was encouraged to continue.

He briefly chided himself, pull away now man before you scare her, or worse, you are discovered. But he knew that once he released her, he would never see her again. Amazed that the woman who filled his every waking minute, and haunted his dreams each night, was here in his arms, and it was sweeter than he could have ever imagined. Her warmth and softness, coupled with her spirit and wit was everything he knew it would be.

Encouraged by her shy response, Darcy knew he wanted more, so much more. He could have his pick of women, but he wanted Elizabeth, and he wanted her love. Slowly Darcy broke the kiss and pulled back to gaze at Elizabeth, her eyes were closed, and her lips slightly parted. He watched as she raised her lids with a sleepy slowness, and he savoured it. The anger that had made her eyes burn brightly before, was now replaced with the stirrings of desire. Unconsciously Elizabeth had brought her arms up, and they now rested gently on his chest. Dear God, Darcy thought, trying to keep a rein on his emotions, does she know what her touch is doing to me? It had been many months since he had visited the bordello, for once he had met Miss Elizabeth no other woman had fully satisfied his desire. The simple answer was no! She was oblivious to the effect she had on him, and it brought a wry smile to his lips. A woman who knows not her power over men, so refreshing from the women of the *Ton*, and another reason he loved her.

Through her lashes, Elizabeth noticed the change to his mouth, and thought how handsome he looked when his face was not covered with his usual indolent sneer. She smiled in return.

Darcy had no idea what had been the reason for this action, but he admired its effect on those fine eyes. He was totally lost, and he knew it. He claimed her lips again, and Elizabeth shyly slid her arms around his neck as if it was the most natural thing in the world. As she entwined her fingers in the dark curls that rested on his collar, Darcy moaned with pleasure. No other woman would feel as right in his arms as the second eldest Miss Bennet.

Holding her tighter, and deepening the kiss, he felt Elizabeth respond, both now lost in the pleasure of exploring, and savouring each other, oblivious to their surroundings. It was at this exact moment that they were rudely reminded of the real world, when they heard Mr. Collins almost scream,

"Elizabeth, you are undone!"

# CHAPTER 2

Elizabeth and Darcy broke apart, and then shared the briefest of glances. She tried to remove herself from his arms, but Elizabeth found Darcy's grip could not be broken. His hold on her waist tightened as she again tried to discreetly break free. Turning to face him, she hoped he would see her beseeching look and release her, but his glare never wavered from Mr. Collins. As Darcy began to address the parson, Elizabeth felt his outward appearance of calmness, was masking the incandescent rage he truly felt.

"The custom of knocking before one enters a room, where the occupants may be engaged in private conversation, is not observed in your house Mr. Collins?" Darcy asked as he raised a quizzical brow.

Although Mr. Collins felt certain of what he had witnessed, he did not wish to accuse the nephew of his esteemed patroness of any impropriety. Unfortunately, finding his cousin alone with a single gentleman left him no choice. Something must be said, and said now. As her only male relative to hand, it fell upon him to ask the uncomfortable question of what Mr. Darcy's intentions were. How very inconsiderate of Elizabeth to put him in this position. After all, had he not forgiven her for refusing his proposal, and then welcomed her into the very home that could have been hers. Mustering all his courage, and choosing his words with care, Mr. Collins began the greatest challenge of his life.

"I am, as always, your humble and obedient servant sir, but with all due deference and no offence intended Mr. Darcy, I respectfully remind you that this is my abode.

I was unaware of your presence, or that my cousin would not welcome my company after her recent spell of incapacity."

He paused, expecting Darcy to dismiss him out of hand, but when the gentleman said nothing, Mr. Collins grew bolder and continued,

"But from what I have observed, it appears that I am too late for such pleasantries, and I must ask, no demand, as Miss Elizabeth's only male relative present, that you explain yourself sir."

Mr. Collins inhaled and puffed himself up with all the righteous indignation he could muster, considering whom he was addressing. He sorely hoped Mr. Darcy would inform him that he was assisting Cousin Elizabeth with something in her eye, or some other plausible excuse, and he could then remove himself with all haste. What if Mr. Darcy took offence to being questioned? He might advise Lady Catherine to dismiss him, and him with a wife to support now. The agonising wait for Darcy to deliver his reply, saw Mr. Collins resolve falter, and he shuffled his feet nervously.

Elizabeth saw the indolent sneer had returned, and now masked Darcy's true thoughts and feelings. He turned to brush an invisible speck of fluff from his lapel, and then looked directly at Mr. Collins and met his gaze. Coolly he addressed his concerns.

"Come Mr. Collins, we are men of the world, are we not?" Darcy said, knowing Mr. Collins to be anything but, "Did you not seal your betrothal to Miss Lucas with a kiss?"

Turning back to Elizabeth, he bestowed a well-timed smile on her now clearly astonished face, whilst renewing his grip on her waist. He was pleased to see her give him a weak smile in acknowledgement of what he was doing. Facing Mr. Collins once more, Darcy asked the question he knew would silence the odious man once and for all.

"I hope you are not implying sir, that Miss Bennet is the sort of gentlewoman, who would bestow her favour on anyone but her future husband?"

Elizabeth knew by his choice of words, that he was conveying this was their only course of action, having been discovered in such a compromising situation. The irony was not lost on her though; he had won his suit after all. She would have to accept the engagement or face ruin. Turning to address Mr. Collins, who now stood open-mouthed at this question, Elizabeth added,

"Come Cousin; are you not happy for me?"

Seeing him waver she added an inducement she knew he could not resist,

"Just think, you will be cousin to Mr. Darcy, and connected to *all* his relations too."

He hesitated a moment as the importance of her statement filtered through to his brain. It was enough.

"I.... I am indeed most happy for you my dear cousin, and would be honoured if you would accept my sincere felicitations on your affiance." he stuttered, feeling awkward as he stood in his own parlour.

Their confident words and happy demeanour, made him think he might have misjudged the situation on his arrival. Were they merely sealing their engagement in the accepted method of the day? No matter, he had done his duty by Elizabeth, and was satisfied as well as relieved. Though he was certain that Lady Catherine, and her daughter Anne, would not share their joy. Their betrothal while Elizabeth was under his roof meant he would have to write and inform Mr. Bennet. He turned to remind them of this,

"I will make haste and write to your father with the good news dear cousin, that he might bestow his consent with all speed."

"No need Mr. Collins, it is but an easy fifty miles, and I will ride out at first light. I prefer to speak with Mr Bennet in person as propriety dictates."

Darcy said dismissively, making certain that Mr. Collins understood he would broach no interference in this personal matter. Besides, he certainly did not want Collins recounting the events of how he had discovered them, or impugning what he had told him. He already had some reservations about seeking an interview with Mr. Bennet. It seemed all of Hertfordshire knew of his slight to Elizabeth at the Meryton assembly, and with Elizabeth being Mr. Bennet's favourite child, well it was not a good start. Darcy accepted that his actions had instigated this situation, and although it had brought about the outcome he desired, it certainly was not the way he wanted Elizabeth to come to him. He returned his gaze to Mr. Collins, who knew better than to argue with his peers, and now loitered as an errant schoolboy awaiting instruction. Darcy sighed.

"Will you wait outside sir, that I may say my farewell to Miss Elizabeth in private?"

Both men knew that it was a rhetorical question. As Mr. Collins withdrew, Darcy turned back to Elizabeth and quickly brought his finger to rest gently on her lips. Quietly he said,

"Shh, I know you have much to say and berate me for, but now is not the time. Especially as I am sure the parson's ear is pressing against the other side of the door. I will ride to Longbourn tomorrow to seek your father's consent, but I would ask that you meet me at the edge of the park before breakfast. There is much to say before I leave. Will you do that for me Elizabeth?"

Mildly annoyed that he had taken to using her given name, she nodded. As he slowly took his hand from her lips, she wondered if he would kiss her again. Blushing furiously at her wanton thought, she hoped it had not been communicated to Darcy. Clearly he had been thinking along the same lines, and he lowered his head to brush Elizabeth's lips with his own. Without saying another word, he turned and opened the door, whereupon Mr Collins stumbled and nearly fell to his knees, so intent was he on listening at the keyhole.

Both Elizabeth and Mr. Collins watched from the parlour window as Nelson, Darcy's horse, and its rider disappeared from view. Mr. Collins turned to Elizabeth, fully intent on scolding her, but before he could speak she said,

"Let me thank you again for your kind words of felicitation on my betrothal cousin. I wonder, might you ask Charlotte to join me for a moment? As my oldest and dearest friend, I would like to share my good news with her also?"

Bowing in his toady like fashion, he left to find his wife, and returned a few minutes later. Charlotte was a little annoyed at being told to make haste and confer with their guest. Considering they had only just arrived home from taking tea with her ladyship, and she still had to instruct the cook about dinner, she could see no urgency for speaking to Elizabeth.

"What is it my dear Lizzie that cannot wait for me to catch my breath?"

Charlotte said casting her husband a puzzled look as he closed the door. Elizabeth stood silent, unsure of how to break the new. Charlotte enquired again,

"Lizzie, what is it?"

"Come Charlotte, I have exciting news."

Elizabeth finally said as she drew her friend deeper into the room. Once they were seated in front of the fire, Elizabeth took her friend by the hand.

"Charlotte, on your return did you see Mr. Darcy leaving?" Charlotte nodded.

"He came to make me an offer of marriage, and I have accepted him."

She knew the false happiness did not reach her eyes, but hoped her friend would not notice. When Charlotte remained silent Elizabeth became worried.  Did she suspect something was amiss?

"Are you not happy for me? I admit I have not always liked him as well as I do now, but I think we shall be quite content together."

"Yes of course I am happy for you," Charlotte finally responded, "It is just quite sudden is it not? I knew he was partial to you Lizzie, even though he tried to hide it. But to declare his feelings when you are away from home is somewhat unusual. When will he speak to your father?"

"He will leave early tomorrow morning, and I will return to Longbourn the next day. There is no cause for concern Charlotte, papa will recognise what a good match Mr Darcy is for me, and I cannot envisage mama letting him refuse his consent to such an influential suitor."

"Well Lizzie, I am truly happy for you then. It is just the match your mother had hoped to secure for Jane with Mr. Bingley. It will be a great advantage for your sisters too, helping them meet eligible suitors of similar standing."

Both women knew to which conversation she was referring, and they exchanged a conspiratorial smile. They rose and shared an embraced of genuine friendship, and then Elizabeth went to start preparing for her departure.

# CHAPTER 3

The next morning Elizabeth dressed quietly, arranging her hair in a simple style, then snatched up her bonnet and gloves and crept downstairs. She slipped into the kitchen unnoticed, and popped an apple into her pocket, before exited the back door to keep her rendezvous with Mr. Darcy. As she neared the designated meeting place, she spied him standing there, unaware of her approach. Elizabeth acknowledged he was an exceedingly handsome man. He cut such a dashing figure in his fashionable clothes; He could have, and was expected to, select his bride from the very best families that society had to offer. Instead, he had chosen her, the daughter of a simple country gentleman. She lingered to admire his physique, and then blushed furiously when Darcy spun round to greet her. Well aware that she had been caught, Elizabeth lowered her eyes as he strode towards her; he paused and gave her a curt bow.

"Good morning Miss Elizabeth, I am pleased to see you," he started, "I thought you might resist my entreaty to meet."

Returning his greeting with a slight curtsy she replied;

"Good Morning Mr. Darcy. I said I would come and as you can see, I am here."

Elizabeth noticed how he constantly fed the rim of his hat through his fingers, betraying his state of nervousness. Finally, he clasped his hands behind his back and began to address her.

"Miss Bennet, I must offer you my profound apologies for my behaviour yesterday, it was unforgivable.

I fear as a result of my actions, I have put you in an untenable position. I know and understand your sentiments in regard to my offer; indeed you made your feeling perfectly clear yesterday. But I feel under the circumstances, and with Mr. Collins untimely intrusion, there is no recourse left open to us but to marry."

Darcy searched her face to gauge the impact of his words. He expected her to raise any number of objections, or to berate him most severely at the very least, but instead she was smiling.

"Are you laughing at me Madam?" he said stiffly.

Elizabeth raised her eyes to meet his, and let her smile linger a little longer before saying,

"Why Mr. Darcy, what an eloquent speech, have you been rehearsing while you waited for me?" she asked playfully.

The truth was Elizabeth had been awake most of the night herself, turning the events over in her mind, and she too had come to the same conclusion. There was no point in fighting the inevitable, so she had decided to go forward with a positive frame of mind. Still, she could not help but tease him a little.

"It appears your days as an eligible bachelor are numbered Mr Darcy."

"Then we are agreed?" He asked, unable to hide the surprise in his voice, "The engagement stands?"

Elizabeth now treated Darcy to a full smile, then continued along the path, only to glanced back over her shoulder and add,

"The engagement stands."

Elizabeth was not party to the expression of great relief on his face, or the sagging of his shoulders as the tension left his body. He was sure that she would protest his actions, his intolerable high handedness; instead she was in full agreement. Also she was right in her surmise; he had been rehearsing his address to her. He had been so utterly wrong in his previous proposal; he could not risk alienating her again. But what had caught him off guard and made his heart skip a beat was her smile. That radiant full of life smile, it had been just for him. He ran to catch up with her and blocked the path. Elizabeth gave an inward sign. She had hoped to escape further discussion on the subject, but clearly Mr. Darcy had other ideas.

"Miss Elizabeth Bennet," he said using her full name "you never cease to surprise me. Do you know how much pleasure it brings me being in your company?" he asked with a smile of his own.

Momentarily taken aback by his sudden declaration of emotion, Elizabeth could not help herself. Raising her eyebrows she retorted slyly,

"After the occurrence of yesterday afternoon, I think you leave me in little doubt as to how much you savour my company sir," and she walked on.

Darcy threw back his head and gave a raucous laugh. He knew their life together would never be dull; her quick wit was just another reason he loved her. Yes, Elizabeth Bennet was the perfect woman for him, and he could not fault his taste. Taking the few strides needed to catch up with her he took her hand and gently kissed it. She tried to withdraw it, but he would not oblige. Instead, he caressed her fingers with his thumb as they continued along the path. Elizabeth was no longer aware of her surroundings; her mind was completely focused on the sensations Darcy's attention to her hand was creating. She was amazed at the effects such a small caress could have on her body. Her heart began to race as a tingling warmth radiate from the area Darcy touched. Giving herself a mental scold she became aware that they had stopped walking. Darcy was looking at her, his head slightly tilted as he studied her face. She lowered her gaze, fearful he would see the effect his closeness was having on her. Softly he spoke her name,

"Elizabeth, we have walked far enough. I must make haste to Longbourn and set things right. Before I leave, would you permit me to kiss you goodbye?"

Elizabeth knew she should be shocked at this blatant disregard for propriety. Instead she coyly gave her reply,

"I feel that on this occasion, it is acceptable for us to affirm our agreed betrothal in the manner you request Mr. Darcy," and she coyly waited for him to claim her lips.

In a gentle whisper Darcy said,

"Elizabeth, look at me Elizabeth."

Suddenly feeling shy, she was reluctant to meet his gaze. Sensing this reluctance, he ran a finger lightly down her cheek, and tilted her chin up. The smouldering desire he felt was unmistakably visible in his eyes, and suddenly she felt quite breathless. He bent his head and let his lips gently caress hers. The sensation his brief caress evoked, seemed to spark through her entire body. She raised her face a little more, and Darcy was encouraged to deepen the kiss, savouring her timid response. Her lips were delicious beyond belief, and he wanted to prolong the experience for as long as he dare. He craved to awaken the passion and desire still dormant in her, but he knew she did not love him, and that was the one thing he desired above all else. With reluctance Darcy pulled away, mindful of Elizabeth's innocence. He was pleased she had permitted such an intimate embrace before they were married. As she tried to catch her breath, and to restore a modicum of composure, Elizabeth realized she would need to be on her guard when in close proximity to Darcy. She enjoyed his kisses far too much!

"You are a hard man to resist Mr. Darcy," she said breathlessly.

"And I find you irresistible Miss Bennet," he replied.

This time Elizabeth did not shy away as he took her hand, and together they made their way back to the parsonage.

# CHAPTER 4

On the day of her departure Elizabeth had risen early, and enjoyed a last walk in the grounds around Rosings. She was not looking forward to the journey home. She was sure her mind would be full of images of a certain gentleman. A gentle knock on the door brought Elizabeth back from her reflections, and knowing it must be Charlotte she bade her enter.

"Good morning Lizzie, tis early I know, but I guessed you would be up and dressed. Have you been for a last walk in the grove? I thought we might breakfast together in my private parlour before you leave," she said.

"Aye, you know me so well dear Charlotte, and although I am not inclined to eat, I will take a dish of tea with you."

"Come Lizzie; you must eat something before your journey. I could not in all good conscience, send you off on an empty stomach."

Observing her friends countenance, Charlotte could see she was in low spirits, and must conclude it was because of her betrothal. She gently asked,

"Elizabeth, you are happy to be marrying Mr. Darcy, are you not?"

Her concerned enquiry was all the encouragement Elizabeth needed. She wanted to share her vexation with someone, and knew Charlotte to be completely trustworthy.

"Oh Charlotte, if only you knew. I am resigned to my fate and even share some of the blame," Elizabeth sighed "Had I not let my temper run away with me, this situation would never have come about. And I would not be going home to prepare for my wedding to a man who thinks my station is so decidedly below his," She expelled.

Charlotte stared at Elizabeth in disbelief.

"When you told me of your betrothal you were full of joy and happiness, surely you cannot mean that Mr. Darcy imparted such sentiments. His offer of marriage seems to belie such a remark."

"Oh yes, he said that and much more," replied Elizabeth.

Charlotte felt the sting of tears prick the back of her eye at this grave and hurtful revelation. Taking hold of her dear friend's hands, Charlotte asked,

"Lizzie, do you want to talk about it? I do not know the particulars, just what you imparted yesterday. If you are disinclined to wed Mr. Darcy, why did you accept him? I have long thought he held you in tender regard, and I am truly not surprised by his offer."

Charlotte was puzzled. How could things have changed so much in such a short space of time? For the past few weeks she had observed a thaw in the relationship between Elizabeth and Darcy, even if the other guests at Rosings had not. Elizabeth had seemed at ease in his company, and on several occasions teased him, bringing a smile to both their lips. And when he thought no one was observing him, Darcy let his eyes follow her every move, her every smile. When this was not possible, he resorted to watching her reflection in the window glass. Oh yes, Charlotte was certain Mr. Darcy loved her friend most ardently, yet his word seemed quite unkind, if he did indeed say them.

"Yes, we must marry Charlotte. I vowed I would not marry unless it was a deep, all-consuming love, not because I had been compromised!" Elizabeth snorted.

"Oh Lizzie, I did not know. Did he hurt you, are you well? I thought Mr. Darcy a gentleman, and find it hard to believe he would act so disrespectfully."

Charlotte was shocked at this confession. Mr. Darcy did not seem the kind of man who would need to force his attention on an unsuspecting female.

"Yes of course he is a gentleman Charlotte, but compromised I am and wed I must be."

She could see Charlotte's mind was begging for her unasked questions to be answered, however, Elizabeth needed time to gather her thoughts. Apart from Jane, Charlotte was the only other person whom she would trust with the true version of her betrothal.

"Come, I will reveal all over breakfast," Elizabeth said as they walked to the door.

Once seated in Charlotte's parlour, Elizabeth busied her hands in the hope she would be able to retell the events, without her face revealing how her body had betrayed her. She sipped a little tea and broke off a piece of hot cake to nibble on. Realising she could no longer forestall, put her cup back on its saucer and met Charlotte's gaze.

"Will you let me tell all before you speak, or pass judgement on me Charlotte?" Elizabeth asked.

"Of course Lizzie, but I doubt I'll judge you ill, for I know you to be beyond reproach in all that you do," Charlotte replied reassuringly.

Elizabeth gave a weak smile. First she remembered how much she was enjoying her stay, especially the first few weeks. It was nice to spend time with Charlotte again, even if it meant she also had to endure the company of Mr. Collins, who had once proposed to her. Most days she rose early, and enjoyed a morning walk before breakfast. Once she was clear from view of both the parsonage and Rosings, either Col. Fitzwilliam or Mr. Darcy would join her. No doubt to avoid Lady Catherine knowing their direction. She also wondered whether they were genuinely out for a morning constitutional as they claimed, or if they were waiting for her. Elizabeth laughed, either way she enjoyed their company. Though if they had spied her before she reached the bluff where they usually met, they would surely be very shocked indeed. With only a cursory glance to check she was unobserved, she would run along the leafy, woodland path with her bonnet off and her hair breaking free from its ribbons and pins. But by the time she had been joined by her companion of the day, she was a model of decorum. Once at the peak, they would sit on the rocks or a fallen tree and converse for a while, before falling silent to drink in the beauty and splendour of God's creation.

"Dear Charlotte, it was on just such a day, before the Colonel returned to London, that the conversation turned to Mr. Bingley."

She recalled their conversation and the effect it had on her.

"How long do you plan to stay in Kent," Elizabeth asked the Colonel.

"As long as my cousin requires me, I am completely at his disposal," he replied.

"As everyone seems to be," Elizabeth murmured.

"From what I heard on our journey here, Darcy recently came to the rescue of one of his friends, Mr. Bingley. Are you familiar with the gentleman?"

"Oh! Yes," said Elizabeth drily, "Mr. Darcy is uncommonly kind to Mr. Bingley. I understand he takes care of him prodigiously."

"Care of him, yes I believe he does."

"May I ask in what way did Mr. Darcy rescue Mr. Bingley?"

"It is a circumstance that Darcy would not wish to be generally known. If it was to be circulated and word got back to the lady's family, it could be most unpleasant. I understand Darcy saved him from an imprudent marriage."

"And did he give voice to his reasons for this interference?"

"I understand there were some strong objections to the lady."

"These objections Colonel, was it due to her lack of fortune maybe?" Elizabeth enquired.

"Her family I believe," replied Colonel Fitzwilliam, unaware it was to *her* family he referred.

Elizabeth made no answer but walked on, her chest swelling with indignation. So it was Darcy's interference that convinced Mr. Bingley to leave Netherfield, and cause poor Jane's heart to break. Elizabeth did not want the Colonel to feel he had betrayed a trust, so she abruptly changed the conversation. Then pleading a sudden headache she asked to return to the parsonage, and so they took a sedate walk back. She then bade him a hasty good day and went inside. Once in her own room, Elizabeth let the tears fall.

"There were strong objections against the lady," Colonel Fitzwilliam's had said. These strong objections he spoke of were probably an Uncle who was a country attorney, and another who was in trade. She could guess his thoughts on their residing in Cheapside. Elizabeth was annoyed that she had let her feelings soften towards him, that she had even occasionally imagined him making an offer for her. How could he share her company, knowing what he had done to his friend, and her dear, sweet sister?

"To Jane herself there could be no objection, she is all kindness and goodness. Mary and Kitty are quite inoffensive, though my mother and Lydia are not so easy to excuse," Elizabeth reasoned aloud.

Her tears turned to sobs, and she threw herself on the bed. Sometimes the injustices of life were too harsh to deal with when far from home. The tears had compounded her headache, and Elizabeth decided she could not be in the company of Mr. Darcy, and trust herself not to speak ill to him. She would not give him further reason to scorn her family.

Elizabeth paused in her narration and looked at Charlotte, who had remained silent as asked,

"I know you were party to some of the events that I have recounted Charlotte; have you no observation or questions at this point?"

"Dear Lizzie" said Charlotte "though I now understand the reason you did not come to Rosings with us, I've heard nothing that indicates you have been compromised. If this is all, I see no reason for a hasty marriage."

"Oh Charlotte, if only that was all."

Drawing a deep breath, Elizabeth continued her telling of the events that led to Mr. Collins entering the parlour, and finding her in Mr. Darcy's embrace.

Having revealed all, and nursing a fierce blush, Elizabeth asked,

"Please say you do not think ill of me dear friend?"

Charlotte squeezed Lizzie's hands and smiled a knowing smile.

"Oh Lizzie, I am neither shocked nor surprised. I have always known that you possessed a passionate nature. I have also suspected for several months that Mr. Darcy had feelings for you. Indeed, he watches you most prodigiously; especially when he thinks no-one else is looking. Did you know he timed his arrival at Rosings to coincide with your visit? No, I thought not. So you see, I already suspected he was considering making you an offer. It is unfortunate that you do not yet return his sentiment, but I am sure that will come in time," Charlotte offered reassuringly.

Managing a weak smile, Elizabeth looked at the clock. Time had passed more swiftly than she had realized. Soon she would have to depart, but before she did so she must make an earnest request of her friend.

"Charlotte, I know not a word of this will pass your lips, but if Mr. Collins..." Her words faltered as Charlotte held up her hand to silence her.

"Fear not Lizzie, I will impress upon my husband the version of events that will be universally accepted as the truth."

Relieved, Elizabeth embraced her friend and kissed her cheek. Charlotte felt she could not let Elizabeth depart without first reminding her of Lady Catherine's presumed displeasure, and with all seriousness turned and said,

"Of course, you realize Lady Catherine will not accept your engagement. She has long harbored the belief that Mr. Darcy will marry Anne."

"I expect not Charlotte, but I understand from Mr. Darcy that it is only *her* wish. He has spoken to his cousin at length on the matter, and fortunately she is adamant she would not have him either. Apparently her affections are already engaged elsewhere."

She had been both relieved and surprised when Darcy had reassured her that he was the master of his own destiny, and free to marry at will. Anne de Burgh appeared a slight and sickly girl, only mediocre in looks and completely dominated by her mother. She would be quite unable to satisfy Miss Bingleys requirements to be considered an accomplished lady, only her wealth would compensate for anything thought lacking.

"Then there are no obstacles to you both enjoying a long, and happy marriage. Now come, say your farewells to Mr. Collins as the carriage is waiting. Write soon, and let me know when the wedding date is set, and I will ensure my attendance. Oh I am going to miss you Lizzie."

"And I you Charlotte."

# CHAPTER 5

**T**he journey home was uneventful. Elizabeth intended to read her book, but after going over the same page several times, she decided to forgo trying. She conversed a few times with Bessie, Charlotte's maid, but soon the young girl's eyes drooped as she struggled to stay awake against the rhythm of the carriage. Turning towards the window, Elizabeth closed her eyes and feigned sleep, hoping Bessie would feel free to do the same. Soon her traveling companion was enjoying her slumber, unfortunately that luxury evaded Elizabeth.

The events of the past three days swirled around her mind. Although she had some reservations about becoming Mr. Darcy's wife, Elizabeth knew the decision was irreversible, without begetting disgrace. She and Darcy must marry; she would fulfil her obligations and duties as wife. and mistress of Pemberley. It was regrettable she did not love him. but she did respect him. Indeed, if it had not been for his interference with Jane and Bindley's budding romance, who knows where her affections for him might be. Neither was she ignorant of the benefits it would bring to her family, especially her sisters. And she could not deny that when they were in each other's presence, he had a most unsettling physical effect on her. Besides, had Darcy not declared to love her most ardently, and with passion? Perhaps, in time, she regard would grow into love. Charlotte's sensible advice had given Elizabeth reason to hope for a happy future, or at least a content one. Indeed Charlotte seemed to be at peace with her lot, and was she not married to the most ridiculous of men? Eventually, the swaying of the carriage made her eyelids heavy, and Elizabeth happily let sleep take her too.

The carriage rounded the bend, and drew off the lane onto the gravel driveway of Longbourn, her family home. It was modest as manor houses go, but had more than enough space for their needs. On the lower level were all the usual rooms that genteel people considered a necessity, whilst the second floor consisted of eight bedrooms, Mrs. Bennet's dressing room and a nursery suite, now mainly used by the Gardiner children. The two attic rooms were for the serving girls under instruction from Mrs. Hill. The grounds included a large lawn area to the front and rear of the house, two glasshouses, and a stable block. To the side was a small walled orchard with seats to take one's ease. Lastly, there was the farm that was situated a half mile away and overseen by Mr. Hill. It provided the family with the majority of their fresh vegetables, meat and dairy products. Financially, the main income of the estate came from the tenant farms, yielding two thousand pounds a year.

As the carriage drew nearer to the house, and the familiar sights and sounds washed over her, Elizabeth thought how good it was to be home. As she alighted, her sisters came forward to welcome her home. Jane was full of questions, and Kitty and Lydia were running around screeching in their usual boisterous fashion. Only Mary stood quietly waiting by the door, hoping to be noticed. Jane stepped forward and gave her a warm embrace, and kissed her cheek.

"I am so glad you are home Lizzie, it had been excessively dull without you. Well until yesterday that is,"

Jane teased "When we had a most unexpected visit from a certain gentleman of our acquaintance."

"I have missed you too Jane, and you also Mary,"

Elizabeth replied, purposely ignoring Jane's comment as she turned and embraced Mary before entering the house.

"Where have Lydia and Kitty gone," She enquired.

"Mama has sent the girls into Meryton. They are to place a special order with the butcher for tonight's repast. Though I do not think we are expecting guests, and the cupboards are fully stocked, but mama insisted."

As Elizabeth placed her bonnet and gloves on the hall table, she thought she could guess the answer to Jane's question, but did not offer to share it with her. Just at that moment Mrs. Bennet came bustling down the hallway, and after giving Elizabeth a brief kiss on the cheek, took her by the hand and began to propel her back along the corridor towards her father's library.

"Welcome back Lizzie, I must say you certainly know how to cause a stir, even when you are away from home. It has made my nerves all of a flutter. That does not mean it is an unpleasant, or unwelcome surprise though, quite the opposite. Come, your father is waiting to speak with you most urgently; there is not a moment to lose, hurry child."

With a firm push, her mother propelled her through the door and closed it behind her. Elizabeth had little doubt what the interview was about, and her mother's broad smile and speed of deliverance confirmed what she suspected. Once ensconced in her father's book room, she realised how much she had missed the time they spent in here together. They alone shared a love of books and knowledge, while her mother and younger siblings looked upon it as a waste of time. It was just one example of why she was her father's favourite. Elizabeth assumed that Mr. Darcy had spoken to her father, and that the match had been approved, giving her mother great joy at the prospect of having at least one daughter married.

"Come here my child," he said "sit by me, there is much to discuss,"

Mr. Bennet indicating the chair adjacent to his own, and Elizabeth sat where he bade and waited for him to continue. Knowing they had in the past shared a joke at the expense of her intended, Elizabeth expected her father to question why she had accepted him.

"You are aware that Mr. Darcy called on me yesterday, to seek my consent for your marriage. He assured me that when we spoke, you would be in full agreement with him. That you have, in fact, already given him your reply in the affirmative."

He rose and began to pace the floor directly in front of her. Elizabeth knew he had not yet finished so offered no reply.

"Are you out of your senses to be accepting this man Lizzie, have you not always hated him?" her father pressed on, "Oh fear not, I have given my consent. He is the kind of man you would never refuse anything, but are you sure this is what you want Lizzie?" He sat down and took her hand "He is rich enough to be sure, and you will have fine clothes and carriages a-plenty, but will he make you happy?" Her father looked to her for an answer.

"You believe me indifferent to him father?" she asked tentatively.

"Not if you tell me it is not so, but we all know him to be a proud and unpleasant man. Do you know otherwise my dear?"

In truth, he knew his Lizzie would not marry for convenience only, yet he had seen no evidence of affection towards Mr. Darcy before, thus his visit and request were a great shock. Mrs. Bennet had been unbearable in her praise of Darcy since she heard the news. And poor Mr. Bingley had been quite forgotten, well almost. Every few days she would lament how ill Jane had been used by him, while encouraging her not give up hope. She could not be so beautiful for nothing.

"I do father, and I like him very much, now. Though I did not always find him so agreeable, of late I have seen a different side of him. While I was in Kent he came to stay with his aunt, and I saw him more at ease when surrounded by his own family. He is intelligent, well read and an astute businessman. I also observed a much kinder and more thoughtful man, one I could respect. Indeed his affection for his sister is as deep as yours is for me papa, and this must be a testament of a good man, do you not agree?" Elizabeth asked, purposefully wording her reply.

"Well then my dear I have no more to say. If this is the case, and you feel assured of your happiness, he deserves you."

He spoke these last words tenderly, and leaning forward to kiss his beloved child. Unaccustomed to sharing such loving moments with his children, he turned away, cleared his throat, and said dismissively,

"Run along now child, your mother will be pacing outside in anticipation of your emergence. I believe we shall have to endure talk of nothing but weddings and lace from now on."

Smiling, she left the study to find her mother waiting outside as expected. Before she could protest fatigue from the journey, Mrs. Bennet took hold of her hand and drew her into the parlour.

"Come Lizzie, do hurry up. We have so much to do and so little time to do it in. Why the very idea, how am I to do all that is needed in only six weeks. To start with Mr. Hill will need to fatten and slaughter at least two pigs for the wedding breakfast. Then I will need to order quails and oyster for goodness knows how many guests! New outfits must be made for us all, and of course there is your dress Lizzie, which must reflect your new station in life. First though we must send the invitations and book the church, and the choir, and the bell ringers. Oh heavens! How are we ever to be ready in time," lamented Mrs. Bennet.

Elizabeth had stopped listening at six weeks. Pulling back on her mother's arm to bring her to a halt, she enquired,

"Six weeks mama, what do you mean only six weeks?" Mrs. Bennet turned and looked at her daughter with incredulity.

"Why it was Mr. Darcy my dear, he has set the date of six weeks hence, and would not be challenged on the subject. When your father suggested a six month engagement with a spring wedding, he would not hear of it. In fact, he was most insistent. Why, if it had been possible I am sure he would have said a mere three weeks, just enough time for the banns to be read. Come along girl, we have so much to do and so little time to do it in," she said pulling Elizabeth along behind her.

Elizabeth pursed her lips together. How typically insufferable of the man, this was something they should have discussed, or at the very least, he should have mentioned his desire to have an engagement of so short a duration. Clearly he had no idea of all that was involved. And how would it look to be wed with such haste, as well as leaving her to find out in such a fashion, it was inexcusable! She hoped he might be dissuaded from such a course. And where was he? Perhaps he was seeking refuge at Netherfield, waiting for her to calm down before showing his face. No, she knew he was no coward. Maybe he had chosen to take lodgings in Meryton; it was closer to Longbourn after all? Elizabeth turned and asked her mother,

"Speaking of Mr. Darcy mama, did he say where he was staying at present?"

"I believe he will be staying at Netherfield for the intervening period. Though he did indicate that he had business in town today, but he assured me he would return to dine with us tonight."

So that was why her mother had sent Lydia and Kitty to Meryton, to provide a feast of the proverbial fatted calf. Elizabeth smiled to herself. Well, now he was to be part of the Bennet family, he would have to become accustomed to her mother's excessive fawning. Then it struck her; he would not be a Bennet, she would be a Darcy. Only six weeks with her family before leaving Longbourn to start her new life in Derbyshire. The familiar ring of Miss Elizabeth Bennet would be no more, replaced with Mrs. Fitzwilliam Darcy, Mistress of Pemberley. Elizabeth hoped she would do it justice.

The rest of the day went by in a whirl. Her mother had already chosen a selection of dress designs, made a guest list and selected a variety dishes for the wedding feast. All this in just a day, Elizabeth marvelled. She was exceedingly pleased when her mother finally insisted she retire for a nap before her betrothed arrived. Having caught a man like Darcy she must now ensure she kept him, her mother had said.  Elizabeth was too tired to argue. The journey home had fatigued her more than she'd realised, and so she gladly went to her room. Elizabeth removed her dress and placed it on a chair before climbing under the heavy blankets. She had so many questions she wanted to ask, and no Darcy to give her the answers. Why had Darcy insisted on being married in only six weeks, it seemed indecently hasty to her? Why had he gone to town, leaving her to face the inquisition of her parents alone? What did he expect of her as his wife? When would she meet his sister? Oh, it was most vexing of him to leave her with no indication of what he was thinking, or indeed planning for their future! She punched the pillow in frustration, until he returned there was no point in fretting.

The calling of her name roused her from her slumber. Elizabeth realised she must have slept longer than she had intended, because Jane was gently shaking her by the shoulder.

"Lizzie, Lizzie, it is time to rise and dress for dinner. Mama has sent me to help you, and she is most insistent on what you are to wear tonight. It is to be the white muslin with the yellow daisies, with matching ribbons in your hair."

The irony that her mother had chosen *that* particular dress was not lost on either Jane or Elizabeth. Daisies were a symbol of loyal love, faith and innocence; whether Darcy knew this, or would even care, she did not know. As Jane began to brush Elizabeth's hair, she whispered in her ear,

"Mr. Darcy is to dine with us, are you not excited Lizzie?"

Elizabeth smiled offering no reply, she merely continued to hand Jane the pins for her hair. Excitement was not what she felt; mild annoyance better described what she was feeling at present. Jane decided she must take this opportunity to ask her sister a vital question concerning her betrothed. She hesitated, then asked,

"Lizzie, I know we have little time now, but answer me one thing before we join the others, am I to be happy he will be my brother?"

Elizabeth could see no point in burdening Jane with how her wanton behaviour had resulted in her betrothal, and so replied,

"You may take pleasure in welcoming Mr. Darcy as your brother Jane. Now come, or we will start the evening with a scolding from mama."

# CHAPTER 6

When Jane and Elizabeth entered the sitting room, they were surprised to see the rest of the family already gathered there. Her mother was seated in her favourite chair, the one that afforded her the best view of the room. Lydia and Kitty sat together on the divan by the window, and Mary sat at the table with her book of sermons open. Even their father was present. He was standing in front of the hearth with his coat tails thrown over his arms, warming himself by the fire. It was not Mr. Bennet's normal practise to join the ladies before dinner. Usually one of the girls was hastily despatched to recover him from his study in time to say Grace. The fact that he was already in attendance, marked the austerity of the occasion. The chairs to either side of Mrs. Bennet had been left vacant, clearly for the two remaining sisters. Elizabeth gave an inward sigh; her mother had certainly gone to great lengths to impress their guest this evening. Who, she noticed as the mantel clock chimed eight, appeared to be running late. Knowing Darcy to be a stickler for punctuality, this was most out of character for him. Before she had time to expand on this thought, the unmistakable sound of a carriage on the gravel drive could be heard. Her mother indicated where they were to sit, leaving just enough time for her to give everyone a final glance of approval, before Hill knocked and announced their guest.

"Mr. Darcy sir," Hill said, then moved aside to allow him entry. The Bennet women stood and executed their curtsies in unison, while Mr. Bennet gave the curtest of nods in acknowledgement of his arrival.

"Mr. Bennet, Mrs. Bennet, and Miss Bennet's," Darcy said.

As he gained entrance to the sitting room, he paused to make a slight bow, instantly seeking out Elizabeth and holding her gaze for the briefest of moments. Elizabeth felt her heart begin to race and her breathing felt constricted. This was their first meeting since their betrothal had been approved, and he knew she would be anxious. His glance had silently offered her his support.

Both Elizabeth and Darcy were also conscious that Mr. Bennet would be observing how they interacted together. Along with the entire household, thought Elizabeth. Darcy straightened and gave no one, least of all Mrs. Bennet, the chance to speak before he began his apology.

"I beg you would forgive my tardy arrival Sir, Ma'am, but my business in town was of a most urgent nature, and could not be delayed. It took slightly longer than I anticipated," He said addressing Elizabeth's parents, "and I am afraid I must ask your indulgence in one other matter if I may. I have brought another guest to sit at your table tonight. With your permission Ma'am?" he asked the lady of the house.

Well! Mrs. Bennet thought, still as high and mighty as ever. Conscious of the good fortune Lizzie and Darcy's marriage would bring to the rest of her family, she tempered her reply.

"Why of course Mr. Darcy, bring as many friends as you like. We are a sociable family and would welcome any acquaintance of yours to our table," she fawned insincerely.

Elizabeth felt her cheeks flush at her mother's artificial pleasure, and she looked under her lashes at Darcy, in an effort to gauge his reaction. Surprisingly, a warm smile graced his lips, with no trace of the indolent sneer he usually wore, especially when in close proximity to her mother. He excused himself with the promise to return momentarily. As the door opened, and Darcy re-entered, they all strained to see past him, wondering who would follow. When his guest emerged from the portal, loud gasps of recognition and approval rippled around the room. Getting to her feet, Mrs. Bennet gushed.

"Why Mr. Bingley, how very good to see you, you are most welcome sir, most welcome indeed."

She had managed to drown out everyone else's salutation; her genuine pleasure at his arrival was clear to all. She decided, having returned Mr. Bingley to their midst, even Mr. Darcy's tardy arrival could be forgiven.

"And you too Mr. Darcy, you are most welcome," and she gave a deep curtsy.

"Bingley," was all Mr. Bennet bothered to say, for he knew he stood no chance of being heard while the women fawned over the young buck.

Elizabeth looked at Jane and saw a rose blush stain her cheeks, while a shy smile formed on her lips as she looked at their unexpected guest. Bingley only had eyes for Jane, and was clearly as much in love with her as ever. So, Elizabeth mused, Bingley was his urgent business in London. He must have travelled to town in order to make a clean breast of it to him. It appeared he had taken her reproofs to heart, and was trying to make amends. Elizabeth glanced at her mother. The look of anticipation on her face, at the possibility of another daughter becoming engaged, was evident. Judging by her sister's countenance, she was not wrong in her expectations. Jane loved Charles still. At that moment, Mrs. Hill entered and announced dinner.

The evening repast was a lively event, with the ladies chattering about wedding preparations, and the gentlemen attempting to steer the conversation to more masculine pursuits. They failed miserably. After dessert the ladies excused themselves, and went to the withdrawing room for coffee. The men remained in the dining room to enjoy some of Mr. Bennet's finest port. The atmosphere and conversation had an over formal air. All three men were on edge, though for very different reasons. Darcy was well aware that Elizabeth's father was not fond of him, and eyed him with open suspicion. Bingley could hardly contain himself, and wanted to ask Mr. Bennet for his consent to marry Jane immediately. But he had yet to propose to her, and so must be content with asking if he may call early tomorrow. Mr. Bennet surveyed the two men who had sat at his table, ate his food, and now want one of his daughters. Both were very rich to be sure, but that was where the similarity ended. He knew Bingley had a good heart, and displayed a cheerful disposition; and it was obvious that Jane loved him deeply. When he offered for her tomorrow, he would bestow the lad with a favourable answer. Darcy was another matter. Mr. Bennet considered himself to be a good judge of character. Until now he was content with his view of Darcy as a proud and unpleasant fellow, use to having his own way in all things. Yet Lizzie had assured him otherwise, and was he to doubt her word? Yes, he admitted, it vexed him greatly that he could not define Darcy's character better.

Presently, the men joined the women for coffee, and all were vastly relieved to do so. The stilted conversation on shooting and fishing, had dried up very quickly, and long, pregnant pauses had followed, along with much foot shuffling by Bingley. In the dining room Mr. Bennet again took up his position in front of the fire, while Darcy and Bingley joined their ladies. After such a disastrous half hour, Darcy decided to make a concerted effort to engage Mr. Bennet on a subject he knew he enjoyed, books. During a lull in the conversation, he turned to Elizabeth's father and asked,

"Mr. Bennet, Miss Elizabeth had imparted to me that you share my passion for literature. Might I enquire if you have purchased anything of interest of late, perhaps something you could recommend?"

Mr. Bennet looked him square on. He saw no deceit in his face, but a genuine interest, and decided to throw the lad a line. Elizabeth approved of him, so he would make an effort to understand him better.

"I have Mr. Darcy, one I have found to be well written and most amusing. The Miseries of Human Life by a Mr. James Beresford, no doubt we could all find something in its text to relate to, don't you think. I'd be interested to have your thoughts on it sir. Lizzie, take Mr. Darcy through to the library, you may wait while he reads a few pages. Then come back and give me your verdict sir."

Darcy masked his surprise better than Elizabeth, at this unexpected opportunity to enjoy a few moments alone. When her father registered the look of concern on her face, he interjected,

"Fear not Lizzie, Mr. Darcy is a gentleman. Run along and don't keep the fellow on tender hooks. I would know what he thinks before the night is over."

Elizabeth picked up a candlestick and led the way to Mr. Bennet's book room. Shutting the door behind them, Darcy let his body fall against it. Alone at last, he thought. Had it only been two days since he had held her in his arms, tasted those sweet lips? Would she favour him with such a reward tonight, he wondered?

Elizabeth set the candle down on her father's desk, and walked to the long wall that was filled with bookshelves. Tracing her finger along the spines, she pretended to search for the required text. Aware that Darcy was watching, her she decided to give no credence to his observance. If she turned, he would surely notice how shallow her breathing had become, and the blush that stain her cheeks. This excitement she felt when in his presence was new and un-nerving, and she seemed unable to control it.

While Darcy waited for her to attend him, he wondered, has she missed me too? Growing impatient, he opened and closed the door again, but still she showed no sign of acknowledging him. Would that she paid such attention to me as those blasted books, he thought. Had he not rode to town and fessed all to Bingley to put right his interference, and then suffered a severe tongue lashing for his trouble. He had then rode hard back to

Longbourn with Charles in tow, so he could keep his dinner engagement with her family? Though she had been right about many of his faults, could she not acknowledge that he was trying his best to address them? Enough he decided, their time together was short, and all too soon they would be obliged to return.

"Miss Bennet," he called, his voice a little stiffer than he intended.

Elizabeth, all too aware of the effect his presence was having on her, briefly glanced over her shoulder at him, and then turned back to pull Mr. Beresford's book from the shelf. She let it fall open at a random page, and feigned reading it.

That single glance was all the invitation Darcy needed, and he crossed the room in three strides. Now so close, she could feel his warm breath on the nape of her neck; it was almost a caress in itself.

"Elizabeth," he whispered.

Taking the book from her hands, he dropped it on the desk, and then gently turned her to face him. She was unable to meet his scrutiny for fear of betraying her anticipation of his next action. Darcy tilted her chin up, and waited for her to meet his gaze. When her eyes remained downcast, he again whispered,

"Elizabeth,"

Slowly raising her lashes, she saw the smouldering desire that burnt in his eyes. Her innocent glance fuelled his desire, and finally he could wait no more. Drawing her into his arms, he kissed her with a passion that left Elizabeth in no doubt, as to how much he had missed her. He had meant the kiss to be chaste, to remind her of his love, but her welcoming response had inflamed him. Surprised by the intensity of her own longing, shivers of pleasure seeped through her every fibre, as they explored the delights of each other's mouth. Darcy withdrew and began to trace a line of kisses along her jaw, then dipped down to the small hollow, where her neck merged with her shoulder.

Lost in the emotions he aroused, Elizabeth unconsciously pulled him closer, enjoying the firmness of his strong arms as they enfolded her. Willingly, she tilted her head to one side that he might access her sensitive skin more easily, revelling in the delicious sensations it brought forth. He'd never experienced such desire, such longing, for any woman. Everything about her was intoxicating to him, and though a strong man, he had never felt more helpless in his life.

"Oh dear, sweet, Elizabeth how I have missed you."

His mouth sought hers again, plundering its depths until she totally surrendered, and a soft moan escaped her. Encouraged by her willingness, Darcy let his hand slide down to lightly caress her back through the muslin of her gown, and her soft, slender form perfectly moulded to his. He raised a hand to cup her cheek, and as he did so Elizabeth turned to place a kiss on his palm. As she bathed in his ministrations, her body flooded with a yearning, for what she knew not, but the pleasure his touch brought forth was devastating. Elizabeth felt adrift at each touch he bestowed, and she tried to savour every sensation his hands produced. He continued to caress her, his thumb circling her hip bone delivering a pulsing in the pit off her stomach, and just when she thought she must surely swoon, his muscular arms tightened around her. As she tilted her head back and moistened her lips a single word escaped her.

"Fitzwilliam,"

This simple utterance drove his desire to near breaking point, and he took possession of her mouth with a hunger he could not hide. As she tried to match his ardour, she naively probed his mouth with her tongue. For a few seconds Darcy revelled in the sensation her touch brought forth, before tearing his mouth away to hoarsely plead.

"For mercy's sake Elizabeth, tell me to stop."

But Elizabeth did not want him to stop; the sensations that were traveling through her veins as he kissed and caressed her, felt like her blood was on fire. The warmth it created was essential to her being, and should not be denied. Somewhere in the recesses of her mind, she heard his desperate plea. So before her resolve weakened, and she was once more immersed in the pleasure of his touch, she gently pushed his body from hers, and turned back to the book-case. They stood in silence for a few moments as both tried to compose themselves. Darcy rested his hands on the books either side of Elizabeth's shoulders, and as he hung his head, she could again feel his warm breath on the nape of her neck. At length, he straightened and spoke.

"Forgive me Elizabeth, I never meant for it to go that far," he paused, and when she remained silent he added "I am usually master of my emotions, but where you are concerned I have no self-control, just being alone with you…" his words trail off.

More composed now, Elizabeth realising she too was at fault, and she could not be angry with him. Once Darcy had taken her in his arms, she had longed for his touch, his kiss. Truthfully she enjoyed the hunger she saw in his face whenever he looked at her, his dark eyes smouldering with desire, his breath coming in ragged bursts. To know that someone found her so desirable, they could hardly contain themselves was quite satisfying, in its own way. She wondered if her countenance had taken on a similar hue, and she blushed anew. Knowing they must return shortly, and Darcy had yet to read some of the book, she turned to face him and said.

"Well Mr. Darcy, tis a good thing we are soon to be wed, is it not."

Elizabeth realised they must return to join the others, so to lighten the mood she smiled brightly, and spoke in a playful tone,

"Now, you have to at least read a few pages of Mr. Beresford's book for papa. I believe he observes humour in everyday disappointments," and she picking up the volume from where it had fallen.

"I can think of a few that will not be in here Miss Elizabeth."

He said, referring to the misery of unfulfilled yearnings. Grateful that they were content with each other, he perched on the edge of the desk, opened the book, and began to read.

# CHAPTER 7

**D**arcy had been awake for some time. He wanted to go for an early morning ride, before Charles came down, for he would then be obliged to join him for breakfast. In truth, Darcy was quietly enjoying recalling the events of last evening. The look of surprise on the faces of the Bennet family, when he had walked in with Bingley in tow, was a picture. The sudden change of attitude towards him by the mistress of the house, he found especially amusing. One minute professing to 'hate the very sight of him,' and the next he was 'so charming, so handsome, so tall...' At least she had shown enough restraint to withhold from saying what she really thought, which was 'so rich'. But foremost in his mind was the time he had spent in Mr. Bennet's book room with Elizabeth. Dearest Elizabeth, to think he once refused to dance with her, citing her as not handsome enough to tempt him. Last evening, when he held her in his arms, her face all aglow with passion and promise, he regretted he had ever uttered such a slight. He had not meant it even then, he had actually thought she was very pretty, but Charles had irritated him with his constant badgering to join in the dancing. Again his thoughts returned to their encounter, and he felt the stirring of his memories in a more material form. Deciding he was mooning about like a love-sick schoolboy, he tried to divert his thoughts. Instead, he recalled his confrontation and subsequent confession with Bingley. He had been shocked at his friend's reaction, but what had he said that was not deserved.

As usual Charles was pleased that his distinguished friend had come to call, and welcomed him with enthusiasm.

"Darcy, how good to see you. Are you well? When did you get back from Kent? I hope you found your aunt in good health," he said with a bow.

"I am in excellent health thank you Charles, as is my aunt. I arrived last night," and Darcy returned his salute.

"And you came straight to see me. Highly unusual Darcy, is all truly well?" Bingley asked with genuine concern.

"Well, yes and no to be honest Charles. I need to talk to you privately, are your sisters still abed, or abroad?" he enquired.

"Neither, well what I mean is that Caroline has spent the last weeks staying with Louisa and Hurst. She said I was not fit company to be around. I concede I have been in the doldrums of late, but I can find nothing to divert my attention in town. Then to top it all you went off to Kent," Bingley said reproachfully.

"Well, maybe I can help there. Charles I need to confess something to you."

Darcy looked at his young friend and indicated for him to take a seat, which he duly did. Bingley's brow furrowed with curiosity, as his eyes followed Darcy's wandering frame. Finally, coming to stand a few feet from his friend, Darcy stopped, took up his usual stance and said,

"Last spring I advised you to sever all ties in Hertfordshire, both in property and romantically. My impression was that Miss Bennet did not return your affection. Mistakenly, I assumed she was merely enjoying the attention of a wealthy young man."

"I say Darcy, that's a bit mercenary, I do not think Jane…" Bingley started, but Darcy cut him short with a raise of his hand.

"Charles, please, let me finish, tis difficult enough. I thought her countenance too serene, and she smiled too much. Indeed, the smile she bestowed on you was freely given to all; therefore, I concluded she did not return your sentiment. I have since learnt that she does, in fact, hold you in the utmost regard, and would have responded positively, had you made her an offer. Also," Seeing Bingley about to speak, Darcy continued quickly "I have to confess one other thing. After we returned to town, Miss Bennet also journeyed to London, where she stayed with her family in Cheapside. I believe she was there for some three months. A few days after her arrival, she paid a call on your sisters. I regret to say, on my advice, they discouraged her interest in you, and then severed the acquaintance."

As he spoke, Darcy realised how bad his confession sounded; indeed, he felt disgust at his own actions. Expelling a hearty sigh, he continued,

"If you are of a mind to end our friendship after what you have heard, I could not blame you. My interference in your affairs may have stripped you of a chance of happiness, and with a woman you care deeply for. I have maligned Miss Bennet's character most unjustly. I am deeply ashamed, and profoundly sorry for my actions. Though in my defence, you must remember Charles, I thought I was acting in your best interest."

Bingleys face had turned a dark shade of red; and his jaw and lips were clenched tight, making him look like he was about to explode. And that was just what he did. Getting to his feet, he glared at Darcy and roared,

"How dare you Darcy. I have a mind to throw you out on your ear. Do you know what your meddling has cost me, DO YOU?" he reiterated in a louder voice. "Not only have you condemned me to months of misery, and desolation, but you have also consigned Miss Bennet to the same. She will have been open to the derision of society, for disappointed hopes after my marked attention did not bring forth an offer, an offer that you talked me out of making. You implied Miss Bennet to be a fortune hunter. Well, I don't give a damn; I have more than enough money for both of us. If society wants to think I brought her regard, we will live without society. I would rather that, than live without Jane. And you say Caroline and Louisa were part of this subterfuge?" he asked sharply.

"They were," Darcy replied quietly.

"Well fear not, they will also know the full extent of my displeasure. And I will thank *you* to mind your own business in future."

Bingley rose and went to leave, but as he neared the door he stopped, a thought had struck him. Without turning he curtly asked of Darcy,

"How do you know she would have accepted my offer?"

Taking a deep breath, Darcy knew he must reveal that Elizabeth was his source.

"I have it on the best authority Charles, her sister Elizabeth told me. In fact, she gave me much the same tongue lashing as you have."

"When Darcy, when did she tell you this?" Bingley asked with unmasked irritation as he turned to glare at Darcy.

"In Kent, while she was staying with Mrs. Collins. Charles I know you are incensed at my actions, but if you come and sit down I will tell you everything. You may even take pity on me, when you hear the irony of my story."

Seeing the indecision on his friend's face, Darcy entreated,

"Please Charles."

Reluctantly, Charles came and sat down again, but remained upright and rigid, while glaring expectantly at his former mentor. Darcy took the seat beside him, and began his narration.

On hearing of Elizabeth's brutal refusal, Bingley could not stay mad at Darcy. Especially once he knew the particulars. Also, knowing that he had ridden to London, with the express purpose of reuniting him with his beloved Jane, softened his rage. He was still angry, but knowing for sure that Jane returned his love, was the potion he needed to restore his zest for life. And Darcy was pleased to see his friend's good humour return.

Bingley had hardly slept all night. As the dawn rays peaked over the horizon, and danced on the window panes at Netherfield, he decided to get up. After completing his ablutions, he selected his attire with care. After all, he had two very important addresses to make this morning. On finding himself quite alone in the breakfast room, he began to rehearse the speech he had devised while unable to sleep. He wanted it to convey the depth of his feelings, but with eloquence, and sincerity. He knew that on occasion, the words ran from his mouth in a jumble, making no sense at all, but this was one time he must be articulate. Aware that Darcy was also an early riser, he hoped he would soon join him, and offer an opinion.

"Miss Bennet, Jane. Since our first meeting at the Meryton Assembly, you cannot have failed to notice, my particular attention in seeking you out,"

He paused to repeat this opening line in his head, and then continued aloud,

"During these few months apart, my regard for you has not wavered, and I have come to believe you return my sentiment still. I have long realised that my future happiness lies with you. Simply put my dearest Jane, I love you most fervently, and would beg that you put a forlorn bachelor out of his misery, and consent to be my wife."

He spun round as he heard the sound of slow applause, coming from the door behind him. There he found Darcy, lolling against the door frame, eyeing him with amusement.

"Really Darcy, tis not polite to creep up on a fellow like that," he reprimanded.

"Besides, I only intend to do this once, so it had best be perfect, don't you agree?" he asked, now seeking his approval.

"Do not fret so Charles, it was a perfectly pretty speech and I have no doubt that Miss Bennet will be most happy to receive it,"

Darcy said trying to alleviate some of his friend's fears. Knowing he would now have to forego his morning ride, Darcy entered the breakfast room and joined Charles.

"You think she will still accept me then?"

He asked, unable to keep the hope, from shining through in his voice.

"Remember, I have it on the most reliable authority, the lady is as enamoured with you, as you are with her."

"Really Darcy," Charles exclaimed.

Darcy had hoped to leave it there, but clearly his friend was in need of further reassurance. He had hoped to put all this behind them, and move on. Every time he recalled the pain he had caused his friend and Elizabeth's sister, he was once more filled with remorse. And so, he would indulge Charles yet again.

"Yes, do you not recall my words of yesterday? You have no fears in that regard, for it was Miss Elizabeth who told me, of the depth of Miss Bennet's feelings for you. I am convinced I will be wishing you happy before the first course is finished. Though goodness knows what she sees in a flame haired, young buck like you," He said playfully with a glint in his eye.

Bingley ignored Darcy's unflattering characterisation, and continued,

"So, my address is decided; Now how to deliver it? Should I take her hand, and make my offer standing up, face to face, or do you think she would prefer if I go down on one knee. I believe the ladies' like that sort of thing, do they not?" he asked.

Darcy was in no mood to discuss the mechanics of a proposal. It reminded him of how woefully inadequate his own had been. He decided a speedy conclusion to the conversation was necessary, and replied impatiently,

"Dashed if I know man; take stock of the situation on your arrival, and then deliver it appropriately. If she is seated, tis best not to tower over her, don't you think?"

"Yes, quite so, I had not thought of that."

Charles knew his friend was becoming irate, but still he pressed on.

"I value your advice and insight Darcy; you are better versed than I. Why, twas less than a week past that you offered for Miss Elizabeth, was it not?"

Beware Bingley, Darcy thought, that is one route we will not be traveling, today or any day. If you but knew what a wretched occurrence that was, you would not be seeking guidance from me. I, who succeeded in pointing out all the reasons why we were *not* a good match, yet still I expected Elizabeth to accept me. As he recalled his words, he shuddered; Elizabeth had every right to feel insulted, and affronted by his address. He had not used sweet words of endearment to entice her. No, he had bluntly informed her, in deciding to make her an offer, he had chosen below his station, in both his, and society's eyes. With swagger, he had told her that he had managed to overcome his aversion to her appalling family, could disregard her lack of fortune and connections, solely in the pursuit of his own happiness. Dear God, what an arrogant ass he had been. He had assumed that any female he declared an interest in, would be so honoured by his attentions, that she would accept him without hesitation, to be grateful even. Shamed by his own words, he felt the colour rise to his cheeks.

"I said what do you think Darcy?"

He realising that Bingley was asking his advice; wearily he rubbed his brow, and turned his attention back to his friend.

"Sorry Charles, I was wool gathering. What was your question?"

"My attire man, is it suitable for the occasion? I say Darcy, are you quite well? You've gone the most peculiar colour?"

"Quite well thank you Charles, merely feeling a little harangued from all your fussing," Darcy replied, not wishing his friend to delve further.

Now truly looking at Bingley, who was soon to depart for possibly the most important meeting of his life, Darcy shuddered. Surveying him from top to toe, Darcy was appalled. Starting with the brown trousers, he travelled up to the orange waistcoat, and finished with the peacock green jacket. Only the white linen shirt and neckcloth passed Darcy's approval. Bingley had clearly been letting Caroline order his clothes again, and it could not have been more evident than now.

"Good Lord Bingley did your man lay out those clothes or did you select them yourself? They are a total miss match. Come, we have to rectify this mess before we leave for Longbourn."

Snatching up a warm roll, and cup of coffee, they retired to Bingley's room to redress him appropriately.

# CHAPTER 8

Elizabeth enjoyed an early breakfast, and then went straight to Jane's room. She wanted to help her prepare for Mr. Bingley's visit. He'd whispered to her last evening, while Darcy and Elizabeth were in the library, that he needed to speak with her most urgently on the morrow, and would it be, quite convenient, for him to pay an early call? Shyly, Jane had acquiesced. The gentlemen thanked Mrs. Bennet for a pleasant evening, then left to return to Netherfield. As the hour was late, everyone retired, except for Mrs. Bennet. She had slipped into Jane's room, and began instructing her on what actions and expressions she should make, to encourage a proposal from Mr. Bingley. It had been a most uncomfortable few minutes, leaving poor Jane quite upset; indeed she had fretted until she fell asleep. The next morning she was still upset, and Elizabeth was annoyed, at how thoughtless her mama had been. Seeking to offer her sister some reassurance, she told her.

"Jane, Mr. Bingley fell in love with you when you were just being yourself. Continue in this vein and he will not be disappointed, I assure you. Mama will not be present, and so will have no knowledge if you choose to ignore her directions. Come, wear the dress she indicated and she will be certain that you are adhering to her council."

Jane wished she had as much common sense and foresight as Elizabeth. She donned the pale blue dress, with small, white flowers as instructed by her mother. Elizabeth and Cissy finished dressing Jane's hair, and at last they were ready to go down and await the arrival of their guests. They had barely seated themselves in the parlour, before Mrs. Bennet joined them and began fussing.

"Now Jane, I have told the other girls to stay in their rooms until I send for them. I am sure we can do without their giggling for one morning. Sit up straight girl, and remember all I have said. Goodness you look excessively pale," and she walked over and pinched Jane's cheeks sharply. "Bite your lip's child, it helps them look plump and inviting," she continued.

"Mama, please!" Jane said casting Elizabeth a pleading look.

"Come mama; let us not be caught unprepared. Shall we take our seats now, and not have idle hands when Mr. Bingley arrives?" Elizabeth said, and gently guided her to her favourite armchair.

"You are right Lizzie. We must not look contrived, and I would have you at your ease Jane. Just think, two daughters wed. One with five thousand pounds a year and the other with ten thousand, I am so distracted I can scarcely contain myself," She effused "I cannot wait to tell your aunt Phillips, she will rejoice in our good fortune I know. And as for Charlotte Lucas who is very plain indeed, she is welcome to Mr. Collins. They are well suited."

"Mama, Charlotte is our friend and undeserving of such censure. She is a good match for Mr. Collins. Surely you would prefer someone we know to inherit Longbourn, rather than a total stranger," Elizabeth said defending her friend.

Thankfully, the sound of footsteps on the gravel path, alerted them to the arrival of their callers, and so

Mrs. Bennet ceased her rant. Hill announced their visitors, and the women stood and performed the required curtsies. Before either gentleman could respond, or enquire after the ladies wellbeing, their hostess began to effervesce.

"Why Mr. Bingley, Mr. Darcy, how very good to see you, and so soon after your last visit. You are both very welcome. You are well I hope? Tis a lovely day is it not, to be out and about so early?"

Mrs. Bennet indicated for the men to be seated, but both declined her offer, and elected to remain standing.

"It is indeed a fine day, is it not Darcy," Bingley replied nervously.

He turned to his friend and gave a barely discernible nod. At this pre-arranged signal, Darcy stepped forward and asked,

"Very fine Charles. Ladies, as it is such a pleasant morning, I wonder might you be persuaded to take a turn in the garden. I fear such outdoor pursuits will soon be limited."

Darcy opened the door to the garden and stood aside. It was clear to all the reason behind the suggested excursion. Mrs. Bennet and Elizabeth rose to oblige, leaving Bingley and Jane alone.

Darcy offered his arm to each woman, and they made their way around the garden. When Mrs. Bennet and Darcy began to converse, Elizabeth listened with amusement. Her mother had commented on whether a bee selected a flower to collect pollen from, by its colour or scent. It was quite a ridiculous notion, but he attended her query with all seriousness. Elizabeth was only too aware of how silly, and distracted her mother could be, something her two younger sisters had inherited. Yet Darcy was being quite charming, and amiable; indeed, she could detect no sneer or mock in his countenance. How things had changed. Only a few months ago her mama was professing how much she disliked him. And seeing Darcy go to such pains to be civil and solicitous, to a woman she knew he thought rude and mercenary, made her appreciate his efforts. And now Bingley was here too, hopefully proposing to Jane at this very moment. He was clearly going to great lengths to prove he was capable, and willing to change for her, which for a man like Darcy, was quite prodigious. These observations made her realise, there had been a considerable softening of her heart towards him, and she was not unhappy at the prospect.

On their return to the house, they caught a glimpse of Mr. Bingley entering Mr. Bennet's library. Seizing the opportunity, Mrs. Bennet disentangled herself from Darcy's, and rushed into the parlour. Elizabeth gave Darcy a rueful smile, and then followed her mother. Jane's countenance told her all she needed to know, and Mrs. Bennet seized her in a firm embrace.

"Oh, Jane how rich you will be, such fine things you will have and servants aplenty. I knew you were beautiful for a reason. Just think, two daughters wed; we are most fortunate, are we not?  Now the moment Mr. Bingley takes his leave, I must make haste and visit your aunt Phillips."

As her mother bustled out, and headed towards the stairs, Elizabeth could still hear her extolling the family's good fortune. Elizabeth quietly closed the door, and turned to face her sister.

"Well Jane?" she asked.

"Oh Lizzie, I shall surely die of happiness, is it possible do you think? He loves me Lizzie, as dearly as I love him. To think of all those wasted months apart, but I will not dwell on that, for we have a lifetime of happiness to look forward too."

"Oh Jane, it lifts my heart to see you so delirious, you do not deserve anything less. I take it he has already gone to speak to papa?" Elizabeth enquired.

"Yes, he could not wait until noon, and father was happy to oblige in seeing him early. He will ride to town this very afternoon, and share the news with his sisters. He will return the day after. Oh Lizzie, are we not both blessed with good fortune, to marry for love?" Jane asked. "I must go and let my sister's know, that they may share my joy too." Embracing Elizabeth once more, Jane went to seek out the others.

Elizabeth looked down at her hands. Soon a wedding band would be resting on her third finger too. Walking to the window, she looked out over the immaculate lawns of Longbourn. Several trees still clung to a few autumn coloured leaves, and they danced and waved in the breeze. Jane's words rang in her head, "Blessed with good fortune to marry for love." Had she been so convincing in her portrayal of loving Darcy, that even Jane had been deceived? Before her visit to Kent, she was secure in her opinion of him, and had no reason to doubt its source, namely Wickham. Yet on closer acquaintance, she had been exposed to a very different mode of man, one she had actually come to like. And he certainly did not fit in with the tales of woe that Wickham had recited. She must conclude he had taken her reproofs to heart, as he appeared to be making a concerted effort to remedy these faults. Jane and Charles were now celebrating their engagement, because of his mediation. His forbearance towards certain members of her family had shown a marked improvement. He even tolerated, if only for short durations, the company of her younger sisters. And with Jane and hers marriages, the family's future was secure, again by his hand. There was only one thing that still troubled her, his dealings with Wickham. Elizabeth recalled what Wickham had confided to her. He and Darcy were like brothers from early childhood, even though their social standing was worlds apart. Aware of his son's loneliness as an only child, old Mr. Darcy had encouraged their friendship. In later life, and to ensure Wickham's future, Darcy's father had promised him a living from one of the Pemberley parish's, namely the village of Kympton. It was here that she could not match what he had imparted, and what she had observed. Wickham has said Darcy would not honour his father's wishes, and had robbed him of that living. To act so would be abhorrent to Darcy. Honour to a man such as he, was everything. And there lie the puzzle.  She must also consider two other facts. Firstly, all these events between the two gentlemen, happened before she knew either of them, and secondly, she had only heard one side, namely that of George Wickham. It puzzled her why Darcy did not defend himself against these accusations when she confronted him? He had on two separate occasions, the opportunity to rectify her conception, on the night of the Ball at Netherfield, and again at the parsonage in Kent. Elizabeth realised, like it or not, she would have to broach the subject with him, if she were to gain any clarity on the situation. That was one encounter she was not going to relish, but the animosity between them, was evident to all. As for Wickham, could he now be content? He seemed settled in the militia, was well liked by the locals, and appeared to have many friends. Was this not a respectable life for the son of a squire?

Elizabeth was brought back from her reflections by the sound of Lydia and Kitty, who were obviously accosting Mr. Bingley in the hallway. They were offering their felicitations on his betrothal to Jane, in a very vocal way. She opened the door and waited for a lull in the fray, before also extending her congratulations. Charles then bade everyone a warm farewell, and joined Darcy on the front steps.

As Darcy had stood outside, waiting for Bingley to conclude his business with Mr. Bennet, he had been observing Elizabeth. As she gazed out of the window, it was clear she was deep in thought, and unaware he was watching her. Her brow revealed some inkling of the emotions she was experiencing; sometimes raised, sometimes drawn together in a frown. He could only wonder at what the cause was. As Bingley emerged, Darcy took Charles's hand and shook it firmly, while offering him his congratulations. He was pleased there would be at least one ally for him in the Bennet household.

Elizabeth assumed Darcy would accompany his friend to town, where he would offer his support when Bingley imparted the news to Miss Bingley and Mrs. Hurst. Her question to him regarding Wickham would have to wait.

That evening at dinner, Mr. Bennet, being the only male at the table, was again subjected to a barrage of wedding talk. Eager to escape, he quickly excused himself and disappeared to his library. He was not surprised to hear a gentle knock only a few minutes later, and his dear Lizzie seeking admittance.

"Well, well my dear, this is all we shall have for the next few months, are you not eager to contribute? I fear all will be decided without you otherwise?" He mused as he sat in his favourite fireside chair.

"I confess I am happy to leave the arrangements to mama and my sisters," Elizabeth replied sitting on the footstool beside him.

"Very wise my child. Your mother has been planning a wedding for these last one and twenty years, and I dare say it would have mattered little to her, which one of you walking down the aisle first."

Her father picking up the poker and began prodding at the embers in the hearth, before selected two small logs to place in the flames.

"So what do you think of young Bingley Lizzie, a different kettle of fish to your young man, ay?"

"I like him. I think Jane and Mr. Bingley are very much in love, and will be quite content together," Elizabeth replied, purposely making no reference to Darcy, "and your opinion of him sir?"

"There are few men I can tolerate well in this world, but I think he might be one of them. They are well suited and of a similar temperament. Both so complying that nothing will ever be resolved, so easy their servants will cheat them blind, and with the help of your mother, they will exceed their income every year."

He paused and looked at Lizzie with a smile. How he would miss evenings like this, he loved her as much as any father could.

"I have invited him and your Mr. Darcy to come and shoot with me next week. It will give your mother another excuse to spend a fortune on supplies we do not need."

They both smiled at the accuracy of his remark. For the next half hour, before Mrs. Bennet demanded Lizzie's attention, Elizabeth and her father enjoyed quiet companionship, surrounded by a cocoon of books.

# CHAPTER 9

**D**arcy and Bingley left for London directly after lunch, ensuring their arrival in town before dusk. They went straight to Airwhile house, Darcy's London residence, to freshen up. Miller, Darcy's butler who had also served his father before him, was one of his most trusted servants, and he greeted them in a formal but warm manner.

"Welcome home sir, I trust it was a good journey?"

"Thank you Miller, it was uneventful. Mr. Bingley will be staying here tonight, could you ask Jennings to assist him please?"

Darcy's suites of rooms, as well as a number of guest rooms, were kept in a state of constant readiness. Advising Miller there was to be an overnight guest at such short notice, would cause no inconvenience to the staff.

"Come Charles, you can bathe and change before we continue to Oak Lodge. I will meet you in the library in one hour," Darcy said, and the two men made their way upstairs.

On opening the library door, Bingley saw Darcy was already within, and just about to pour himself a drink. Turning to Bingley, he raised the bottle.

"Brandy Charles?" he offered "I thought a little fortification might be in order before we divulge the good news to your sisters," and he poured another glass.

Darcy and Bingley had first met at Cambridge; He saw how the younger man struggled to make friends, no doubt because his father's fortune came from trade, but he was a congenial fellow and Darcy liked him. Although Bingley had inherited enough money to ensure that most of polite society would accept him, there were still a few that would not. He needed a powerful friend, a sponsor, someone from the highest echelons. That is where Darcy came in. With his fortune, pedigree and connections, he was invited to every event society had to offer. If he actually attended one, which was rare, then the hostess's credibility increased tenfold. Even the Prince Regent turned his ear to Darcy for advice, favouring him over his now infamous confidant, Beau Brummel. Befriending Charles had not enhanced Darcy's fortune, or his social standing; indeed there were some who would say it had bruised it. But Darcy was rich enough, and powerful enough to ignore such slights. In truth, there were very few people who would risk his wrath, purely to cut Bingley. Besides, Darcy realised he needed a friend like Charles, even though he came with the baggage of an acid tongued sister. Their personalities complimented each other perfectly. Darcy was responsible and studious, while Bingley was affable and enthusiastic. It was for this reason he had agreed to Bingley's request, to be present when he revealed his betrothal to his sisters.

"Yes, thank you. I think I might need it" Charles said apprehensively. The slight quiver in his voice revealed how nervous he was. "I appreciate your support Darcy. Caroline and Louisa made it quite clear, they did not approve of my attachment to Miss Bennet. They made several derogatory remarks about Jane's family on our journey back from Netherfield, quite unabashed."

Darcy decided this would be an ideal opportunity for Bingley to try flexing his muscles of authority. After all, Caroline and the Hurst's enjoyed the lifestyle they did, only by the good grace of Charles. He supported them all, even Louisa and her husband, who had almost depleted Louisa's dowry. And Caroline would only receive her twenty thousand pounds dowry when she married. Their gratitude was to treat their brother with ridicule and contempt. Too long Bingley had let them ride roughshod over him; it was high time he took command of his own household and life.

"So Charles, have you considered how you will impart your news," Darcy asked.

"I have," He replied, "I am resolved to be firm, and tell them the truth. I am in love with Miss Bennet still, and she returns my affection, and has done me the great honour of accepting my hand in marriage. We will be wed six weeks after you and Miss Elizabeth, in early February; tis all agreed with her father," he finished with a satisfactory flourish.

"And if they should object or find fault. How will you deal with their rebuke?" Darcy quizzed.

"I" he paused "I will not stand for it?" he hesitantly asked rather than told.

"You most certainly will not stand for it," Darcy interjected, "you will use a firm tone, maintain eye contact and stand tall. Good God man they live on your benevolence, and will toe the line if they wish to continue doing so. Do you *want* to marry Miss Bennet, or do you want to live a life of regret with your sisters and Hurst?" Darcy demanded.

He knew he sounded harsh and intolerant, but this was one time he could not intercede for his friend. Caroline and Louisa continually coerced, and took advantage of their brother's good nature. It was time they acknowledged their good fortune rested with Charles, and to be aware that he could withdraw it at any time.

"By God Darcy you are right. And I have just the inducement that will make them accept my choice," Bingley replied.

Fortified by his friend's words and the brandy he foolishly gulped down the remaining portion, and then promptly choked when it caught in his throat. As a coughing fit ensued, and he gasped for air, he finally managed to splutter,

"We ride now Darcy!"

It seemed love was finally giving Charles the courage to be the man, Darcy knew he was capable of being. Darcy smiled, whilst trying to suppress the laugh that threatened to break his countenance. Giving Charles several hearty slaps on the back, he advised him thus,

"We ride, once you have composed yourself my eager young friend. If we arrive with you on your knees, and spluttering like an adolescent, any advantage will be lost, don't you think?"

Unable to speak and still gasp for air, Charles merely nodded.

"Engaged, to be married?"

Caroline Bingley quizzed as she looked up at Charles, and then scoffed in a dismissive tone.

"Surely you jest dear brother. Had we not already decided on the unsuitability of the lady some months ago?"

"No Caroline, *you* decided she was unsuitable, and I let myself be persuaded. My affection for Miss Bennet has never wavered, and I consider myself damn lucky she will still have me, after I abandoned her so. You will be happy for me Caroline or so help me," he left the threat to hang in the air.

"Or what Charles; Do not be tiresome and make me point out her lack of fortune, or her ghastly family. I ask you Louisa, that mother, can you imagine."

She turned to share a conspiratorial look with her sister, and they both sniggered openly. Enraged at her dismissive tone and unkind words, Charles took a deep breath and squared his shoulders. Remembering Darcy's advice, he decided to play his two trump cards together. He stepped forward to stand between his sisters, then held Caroline's gaze as he delivered his ultimatum.

"Or I can purchase a small cottage for you in Scarborough, close to Nanny Maud, where you may live quietly, with a nominal allowance until you marry. Assuming you can find someone immune to your corrosive tongue. The choice is yours Caroline, what is it to be?"

A sharp intake of breath from both Caroline, and Louisa reverberated around the otherwise silent room. Darcy, who had stationed himself at the window overlooking the street, was glad his face was obscured from view. He did not think the two women would appreciate the wry smile that was firmly placed on his lips. Bravo Charles, he thought, an ace card. The ladies exchanged worried looks at the mention of their former strict, and unbending governess. Her constant criticism, and fault finding in the two sisters, had been relentless. She had tried for years to change their acid personalities, into caring and acceptable ones, clearly with little success. Simultaneously they rose from their seats, rushed to his side, and began to gush at his good fortune. "How wonderful that dear Jane returned his feelings. How rewarding, that he had secured such a pliable and gentle bred girl," they said. They went on to enthuse that, under their tutelage, and with some time away from her mother, Jane would blossom from a country miss, into a respectable lady of society. Bingley glanced over his shoulder as Caroline again embraced him, and he cast his friend a beseeching look. Darcy took pity on him and once again, came to his rescue.

"As your sisters are in such a solicitous frame of mind Charles, may I have your permission to also share my good news?" Bingley hastily nodded "Very well ladies. It is with a full heart that I tell you I too am to be wed, to Miss Elizabeth Bennet. The ceremony will take place in Meryton, in a little over a month. You will attend I hope?" Darcy revealed with a smile.

Caroline drew in a sharp breath. She had spent the last few years with her cap firmly set on marrying Darcy herself. She thought in time he would recognise her qualities, and make her an offer. Now to hear this news! Unguarded and with venom, she said,

"Goodness, are we to be overrun with young ladies from a certain Hertfordshire estate; are there no farmers they could take to their beds?"

"Caroline!" interjected Bingley, "you will apologise to our guest at once!"

"Charles, do not fuss so my friend. I know my news must have come as a shock, and so quickly on the heels of your glad tiding. But Caroline and Louisa will soon be rejoicing at the prospect of having not two, but five new sisters," Darcy said slyly "I know beyond a shadow of a doubt, that they will welcome my bride as they will yours Charles, with affection and all sincerity."

Darcy's speech, though delivered under the guise of happy cordiality, was actually a thinly veiled threat. His stance and tone left no doubt in either woman's mind. He would broach no interference, or incivility to any of the Bennet sisters. One word from Darcy could see them ostracised from society, with no prospect of return unless at his particular invitation. Caroline decided gracious acceptance, was better that a cottage in Scarborough, while Louisa was tired of playing second fiddle to her sister's malice. They each joined in renewing their felicitations to both men, commenting on their wise choice of bride, and how sweet it would be to call them sister. Thankfully for all, Bingley's butler rescued them when he came in and announced that dinner was served. Edward Hurst, who had watched the entire encounter from a corner divan, had an amused smile on his lips. It had been a pleasure watching Bingley stand up to his sisters, finally. But the best entertainment had been Darcy's calm, yet deadly serious set down. As he led the ladies into the dining room, he complimented them lavishly, soothing their battered egos, all the while, quietly looking forward to their next meeting with Mrs. Bennet. Darcy and Bingley followed a few paces behind. Darcy put his hand on Charles's shoulder and said,

"Tis done, we are all set then."

Bingley returned the brotherly embrace, and as they followed the others into the dining room, their faces bore a smile of smug satisfaction.

# CHAPTER 10

Darcy decided not to linger after dining at Bingley's house, but returned home and went directly to the library. With so much happening in such a short space of time, he knew, he had been remiss in writing to his sister. He must rectify that with all haste, before she heard about his engagement from another source. Georgiana was more than ten years his junior, and from the time of their father's death, five years previous, he had been both parent and brother to her. Although the responsibility was great, he bore it with fortitude, for he loved his sister dearly. Georgiana was a shy, yet bright girl, naive in the ways of the world. Because of this she looked to her brother for guidance in all that she did. Too often his business or social obligations took him from her side, sometimes for weeks at a time. To ease her loneliness, he had hired a widow to be her companion, one Mrs. Annesley. He had discreetly made it known he was looking to employ his sister a companion and his aunt Abigail, the Countess of Matlock, had put forward the lady's name. Darcy had made vigorous enquiries and followed up all her references with a personal visit. Her late husband was a clergyman, who had died from consumption when only one and forty, leaving her alone, and childless at thirty-two. Darcy thought this an agreeable age for Georgiana's companion. Not so old as to be set in her ways, or indifferent to things that would interest a young girl, yet not too young to be of a silly, or troublesome nature. She was well read, musical and spoke several languages, as well as being accomplished in all the usual pursuits that occupied a ladies time. He had invited her to spend a weekend at Pemberley with Georgiana, under the watchful eye of both himself, and Mrs. Reynolds. After her departure, Georgiana declared she liked her very well. Stating she had found her to be almost as knowledgeable as he was; finally, when Darcy was happy with her credentials, and that she was of good character, he offered her the position, with a three-month probationary period. If either party felt dissatisfied during this time, they could terminate the contract with ease. The arrangement had worked well, and she had been in his employment for just over a year now.

It was unthinkable for Darcy to tell his sister about Elizabeth in a letter, and so he merely wrote her a short note.

Airwhile House,
London
Friday November 8th 1811

*My Dearest Georgiana,*
*I hope my missive finds you enjoying good health, and taking care of yourself now winter is upon us.*
*I write to let you know that I will be journeying north on the morrow, and hope to join you within two days of your receipt of this note.*
*I would like to introduce you to Miss Elizabeth Bennet. If you are in agreement, we will return directly, and then spend a few weeks at Charles Bingley's residence in Hertfordshire. I believe Charles would be most*

*appreciative, if you would act as his hostess while his sisters are in town.*

*Assuming the affirmative, I will join you anon.*


*Your affectionate brother,*
*Fitzwilliam Darcy*


He folded the letter and stamped his seal on it. Miller would despatch it first thing in the morning. Wearily, he rubbed his brow and decided to retire. Tomorrow he would make an early start back to Longbourn. He had yet to inform Elizabeth he would be journeying north for a few days, possibly a week. He must explain it was to bring Georgiana back to attend their wedding. He had shared only a few snippets of information with Georgiana in reference to Elizabeth. She always loved to hear him talk of his travels, and the sparkling events he attended when in town; however, he had not revealed the depth of his regards for Elizabeth. He had merely divulged that he had met a most engaging young lady, who, unlike the majority of single females of marriageable age, along with their mamas, did not give a jot about his wealth or social position. He found her refreshingly honest. Georgiana had asked but one question of him that day.

"Is she fair of face brother?"

"Miss Elizabeth Bennet is one of the most handsome women of my acquaintance," he replied, and then in a soft, almost wistful tone, he murmured, "yes Georgie, she is quite beautiful."

Climbing the stairs, Darcy expected his slumber would be full of dreams about Elizabeth, as was every night. He longed for the comfort of it, yet dreaded waking to the realization that it was indeed, another fantasy.

Finally, Darcy thought. For the better part of the journey back to Longbourn, Bingley had constantly effervesced about the virtues of his intended, almost to the point where he was repeating himself. But at last he had succumbed to the rhythm of the carriage and fallen asleep. Darcy had never seen such a love-sick pup in all his days, and the condition seemed to have addled his brain. It had been his sole topic of conversation for the entire journey. Darcy feared his poor ears could not take much more, before he would have to berate his friend into silence. Thankfully the carriage had done the job for him. Darcy embraced the quiet. He had much to occupy his thoughts before he set off for Pemberley tomorrow, and now Charles was silent, he could turn his thoughts to the task at hand. Also, he needed to speak to Elizabeth's father on several matters before he left for Derbyshire. One subject in particular he did not relish bringing up, and was steeling himself for a frosty reception, but it must be done. It would require tact, and firmness, attributes he thought he was well versed in, only never with one's future father-in-law before. It was imperative he did not offend Mr. Bennet, and then be forced to endure the consequences he could put in their path regarding their wedding, namely a long engagement.

Bingley roused about five miles from Netherfield, and ran his fingers through his tousled red hair; though it still looked wild he seemed to feel better for it.

"Well," Bingley asked.

"Well what Charles!" Darcy replies in a low tone "and do not extol any more of Miss Bennet's virtues to me, for I know them as well as any man, who is not her husband, should."

He gave his now reticent friend a scowl, and turned his attention back to the passing scenery. Bingley, having observed Darcy end conversations in this manner before, knew it was best to intrude no further. The remainder of the journey passed in silence, and both men were relieved when the carriage drew up at the steps of Netherfield House.

Within the hour, the two friends were refreshed, mounted and on their way to Longbourn. It was a sober ride, but Darcy allowed himself a sly chuckle. It was one of the first times he had known Charles to be ready on time! Miss Bennet must be commended for achieving something he had been unable to instil in his friend for years, punctuality.

Mrs. Hill showed them into the sitting room, and advised them the mistress would be down directly. Only it was not Mrs. Bennet who joined them, but Jane and Elizabeth. Darcy and Bingley bowed, and then Darcy made a polite enquiry as to their wellbeing.

"It is good to see you again Miss Bennet, Miss Elizabeth, I trust you are in good health?"

Jane smiled warmly, and gave a small nod though her eyes never left her betrothed. Undeterred Darcy continued,

"If agreeable," he now looking to Elizabeth "I thought Miss Elizabeth and I might enjoy a turn in the garden, you are both welcome to join us, if you so wish."

Bingley and Jane exchanged glances, and then shook their heads simultaneously, which made them smile even broader. Elizabeth quickly went and put on a pelisse, then took Darcy' arm. She was not surprised when he covered her hand with his own, and guided her out into the garden. The warmth from his touch was like an electric shock that radiated up her arm. Although distracted by this sensation, she managed to hold her composure as they walked away from the house. After a few minutes of silence, Darcy turned to glance at her.

"You and your sister seem in good health Miss Elizabeth, I trust it is so?"

Elizabeth smiled, and was tempted to answer his enquiry in earnest, but the unexpected pleasure she felt at seeing him, brought a smile to her lips, and she teased,

"Yes, I thank you sir, we are both in excellent health. Now maybe we can discuss the mildness of these early winter days, and then say our polite conversation is concluded, that we may walk in silence?"

"You are most astute Miss Elizabeth, and quite right. I do have a matter of business to discuss with your father, one that must be conducted in person," He stopped to face her, "However; I could not pass up the opportunity to spend some time in *your* company madam."

He bent low and kissed her hand, lingering a little longer than propriety allowed. His reward was a shy, but genuine smile of affection.

Elizabeth found their verbal sparring quite invigorating, and had to admit she looked forward to it, but today it was the touch of his warm lips on her gloved hand, that made her pulse race. She smiled her acceptance of his declaration, and they walked on.

"Miss Elizabeth, it seems unusually quiet at Longbourn today, your mother and sisters are they gone to Meryton?" he asked.

"You are only part correct sir; it is Brighton they are enjoying at present. Col. Forster and his wife invited them to accompany them, and Mama insisted they accept. Mary was reluctant at first, but the offer to experience sea bathing was enough to persuade her. I believe Kitty and Lydia were happy to accept the invitation without the promise of sea bathing. Knowing the regiment was in residence was all the inducement they needed. Mama will also have the advantage of being able to purchase material newly shipped from the continent, for Jane and mine trousseau's. I believe she has already engaged several ladies in the port to make our gowns."

"I see," Darcy said sombrely, as a deep frown creased his brow.

"And do I assume Mr. Wickham has also gone to Brighton with the regiment?"

Elizabeth wondered if he realised the pressure of his grip on her hands, had also increased since the mention of Wickham. It was now quite painful.

"Yes, I believe the regiment in its entirety has removed to Brighton."

As he had raised the subject of Wickham, she wondered if now would be a good time to ask him about their association? Tentatively she broached the subject.

"Mr Darcy, you once told me that your good opinion once lost, was lost forever, are you still of that mind?"

"I am madam," he replied curtly, apprehensive of where this was leading.

"And this is the case with Mr. Wickham, is it not?"

"It is madam, why do you ask?" Darcy had visibly stiffened, and she could see the muscles of his jaw tighten.

"Forgive me, but if we are to deal at all well together, we must navigate a conversation on the subject of that very gentleman. You cannot deny that the mere mention of his name, distresses you greatly."

Darcy stopped, turned, and glared at Elizabeth. She saw a thundercloud of anger cross his face at her suggestion, and he withdrew his hand from hers. In an icy tone, he informed her,

"My quarrel with that man, for he is no gentleman, is of a private nature madam. Should I be inclined to enlighten you, or to share my experiences at some future date, you will be the first to know," taking a step back he continued, "I must speak with your father now, Good day madam." and with the briefest of nods he returned the way they had come.

Elizabeth stood in shock for a moment. Such a cutting set down was not what she had expected. Clearly the animosity between the two men ran deep. Curiously, both Charles and Caroline Bingley had intimated that George Wickham was a scoundrel, though neither of them knew any particulars. Frustrated by his silence, she wondered if he would ever trust her enough to confide in her. It was all most vexing. A sudden gust of cold air made her shiver, and she thought about returning to the house, but she suspected Jane and Charles would be engaged in more enjoyable pursuits than she had endured. Another five minutes she thought.

*********

"Come."

Mr. Bennet called when he heard a rap on his study door, hoping it might be Jane or Lizzie, come to keep him company. Mr. Darcy was the last person he expected to cross the threshold. Rising from his chair, he extended his hand.

"Why Mr. Darcy, what brings you to Longbourn, as if I did not know. Are you chaperoning young Bingley with my Jane? And who will keep an eye on you and the fair Elizabeth, I wonder?" and he chuckled "Sit yourself down lad, shall I ring for tea or would you like something a little stronger?"

"Good Day sir," Darcy replied while shaking Mr. Bennet's hand.

He sat in the chair offered and was then momentarily distracted. His seat afforded him a view of the garden, and he could see Elizabeth walking between the rose bushes. Her thin jacket would afford her little protection from the cold wind he thought, as he watched the wind tug at her hair ribbons. A wave of remorse swept over him, and her words of reproach came back to haunt him, "If you had behaved in a more gentlemanlike manner." She was right. He had abandoned her in the garden because he found her comments irksome.

Mr. Bennet, who had had his fill of tea over the last few days, hoped Darcy would opt for something a bit stronger.

"A small brandy would be most warming, thank you sir," Darcy replied absently.

"So lad, what can I do for you?" asked Mr. Bennet as he passed a glass to Darcy.

"Mr. Bennet, I must first extend my apologies to you. I am unable to attend tomorrow's shoot. I am to travel to my estate in Derbyshire, and escort my sister back to Netherfield. Charles has kindly bid her stay there until after the wedding."

"There will be other times of that I am sure. But come lad, that look tells me there is more on your mind than the shooting of a few cubbies."

Darcy emptied his glass in one gulp, and as he felt the smooth liquid heat his throat, he evoked his rehearsed speech.

"Mr. Bennet, with the upcoming nuptials between Elizabeth and myself, I understand there is a great deal to be done, and purchased. I am also aware that, at my insistence, time is short. To ensure everything is done to an acceptable standard, and in the allotted time," he paused briefly, "well it may become quite expensive."

If Mr. Bennet knew where Darcy was going with this conversation, he showed no sign of it. Feeling mildly uncomfortable, Darcy squirmed in his chair.

"Because of my position in society, and the relations I must invite, the expense is probably going to escalate quite considerably," He flustered.

He must know where this is leading, Darcy thought. He was unaccustomed to being the one made to feel awkward; it was usually the other way round! Mr. Bennet's countenance remained unchanged, and so Darcy blustered on.

"And so, I have opened a line of credit with my bank for you to draw on, to meet those extended costs. Elizabeth's trousseau must reflect her new station in life, as my wife and mistress of Pemberley. As should her mother, her sisters," and feeling a touch more embarrassed, he added "and her father."

Mr. Bennet held up his hand to silence Darcy, he then rose, walked to the door and opened it.

"Hill, another bottle of brandy if you please," He shouted.

The two men looked at each other, Darcy with nervous apprehension, and Mr. Bennet with a bemused smile.

"I think this could well be a two bottle discussion. Well lad, that was the most eloquent of speeches, but I must confess the best bit was watching you squirm. Having just paid to send four of my ladies to Brighton, all garbed in the latest fashion, I confess it has put a strain on my purse. And I confess, it is a while since I visited the outfitters, so, I accept your offer with thanks. There now, we are in accord are we not, and no one need be the wiser. Agreed?" he chuckled and offered Darcy his hand.

Darcy, relieved that he had survived the uncomfortable interview unscathed, drained his glass, and then stood to shake his future father-in-laws hand.

"Agreed," he said.

# CHAPTER 11

Darcy was in no mood to seek Elizabeth out before he returned to Netherfield. Now sitting at the desk in his chamber, Darcy recalled their parting words. Damn Wickham! Once more he had come between Elizabeth and him. He could not blame Elizabeth for seeing no fault in Wickham; she had heard only his honeyed words on their dealings together. He ruefully admitted that only his pride, and silence on the matter, had let Wickham divide them. If he had taken the opportunity to enlighten Elizabeth as to Wickham's true character, she would understand why there was no place in his heart for forgiveness. This error on his part must be rectified, and before his departure for Pemberley. He could not bear for Elizabeth to think ill of him, or worse, that he was angry with her. Opening the desk drawer, he retrieved paper, ink and a quill. He would put down on paper what he could not bring himself to speak. Choosing his word with care, he began to write Elizabeth a letter, detailing his dealings with George Wickham.

*Netherfield*
*Hertfordshire*
*Saturday 9th November 1811*

*My Dearest Elizabeth,*

*This morning, after we had parted, I reflected on what had transpired between us, and I must conclude that I have done you a great injustice. I have expected you to be understanding, in a matter of which I have given you no details. Because of this, you have only the word of George Wickham, to testify as to his dealings with me, and my family. Therefore, I have decided to share my confidence with you.*

*It is true that Wickham is the son of a very respectable man, my father's late steward, who managed Pemberley for many years. My father was proud to be his godfather, and treated him as a son. He paid for his education, and sending him to Cambridge with me. There I observed his behaviour to be both licentious, and unrestrained, but said nothing to either my father or his. One day, he declared to my father he would like to take holy orders, so when my own excellent father died five years ago, he recommended in his will, that a living be made available to him, along with a one thousand pound legacy. His own father did not survive past half a year after mine. It was at this time, Wickham informed me he had decided against joining the church, and he hoped to study law instead. He asked me to recompense him for the living promised, which I duly did, to the sum of three thousand pounds. I wished, rather than believed him sincere. All connections between our two families now seemed dissolved. He went to live in town, and lead a life of idleness and dissipation. That is where our connection should have ended. Two years ago, he heard that the living that could have been his was now free, and he again petitioned me for it, which I denied. Not only had he already been handsomely compensated for it, but I had interviewed, and offered the position, to a more suitable young curate. At my refusal to acquiesce, his verbal abuse toward me was most violent, which only confirmed my resolve. He then disappeared and again, all ties were severed.*

Darcy briefly broke off from his writing; he must phrase the next sentences with care, so as not to cause Elizabeth offence, or to besmirch his sister's character. It pained him greatly to recall these events, but they must be told. He continued writing.

*I know I can trust on your discretion, for what I am about to impart is of the most delicate nature. As you know, I have one sister, Georgiana, who is more than ten years, my junior. Her guardianship was entrusted to me and my cousin, Colonel Richard Fitzwilliam. A little over one year ago, when her official schooling came to an end, I set up an establishment for her by the sea. I then hired a lady to oversee it, one Mrs Younge. A woman who's character I was greatly deceived about. Last summer they journeyed to Ramsgate, to take the air for a few weeks. It was whilst here, they met up with none other than George Wickham, prearranged between the two accomplices. Over the next few weeks, they convince Georgiana she was in love with him, and regrettably, she agreed to an elopement. She was then but fifteen. Fortunately, I decided to join her three days earlier than arranged, and thus stumbled across their plan. Georgiana, not wanting to hurt, or distress a much-loved brother, confessed all. I have no doubt his object was twofold, Georgiana's thirty thousand pound fortune, and to seek revenge on me. Had his plan come to fruition, his revenge would have been complete indeed. Upon me making it quite clear he would not see one penny of her money, he left. I had not seen him since, until my arrival in Meryton.*

*This is a faithful narrative of all my dealings with George Wickham, but should you require further confirmation of the events I have described, you may contact Col. Fitzwilliam, who can bear witness to all I have said.*

*So you see, my dearest Elizabeth, why the mere mention of George Wickham gives me cause for concern. If he has set the poisonous seed of doubt in your mind in regards to me, can I ever, fully remove it?*

*Yours affectionately,*
*Fitzwilliam Darcy.*

He sealed the letter and called for Fletcher, his valet. It had grown dark whilst he had been writing, but he must see Elizabeth tonight, and place it safely in her hands. He quickly changed his clothes, and then set off to see Elizabeth for the second time that day.

Although Longbourn was only three miles from Netherfield, the distance could not be crossed fast enough for Darcy. The winter moon lit his path, and he urged his horse on. Having arrived at his destination, Darcy silently guided his horse across the immaculate lawns. At the edge of the gravel path he dismounted, and let the reins fall to the ground. Standing back from the house, in the shadow of a tree, he took stock of the situation. Candlelight was visible in two of the bedroom windows, and one downstairs window. He assumed due to the lateness of the hour, that the women had retired, and that it was Mr Bennet who was still abroad the house. He knew Elizabeth's room was to the front of the house, but which one was it. If he got Jane's room in error, would she give him away, or be compliant and procure Elizabeth for him?

Time for action he thought, and picked up a few small pebbles from the path. Gently he tossed them against the window of the first bedroom, before taking a step nearer the building, to hide in the shadows. As he waited to see who came to the window, he shook his head, and mentally chided himself. 'Good grief man, if your friends and peers could see you now, skulking about in the shrubbery like a love-sick school boy, why you'd be the laughing-stock of polite society.' Still, he couldn't help but smile at his predicament. After a few minutes, he saw Elizabeth's face appear at the window, and he moved out of the shadows to catch her attention. The look of shock at seeing *him* there was evident on her face, but she quickly masked it and put her finger to her lips, in silent entreaty. She signalled she would come down, and then disappeared from view. He had almost given up hope, when she suddenly appeared from around the side of the house. She motioned for him to follow her, and then turned and retraced her steps. Making haste to catch up with her, he instinctively offered her his arm. She ignored his gesture, and walked on at an even faster pace.

Arriving at the door of a large glasshouse, Elizabeth entered, and after a quick glance over his shoulder, Darcy followed.

The not unpleasant odour of damp earth, and ripened vegetables, swept over them as they moved deeper into the building. When Elizabeth was sure the foliage was tall enough to conceal them, she rounded on him with fire in her eyes.

"Mr. Darcy! Firstly we are not in a ballroom or polite company now. Offering me your arm while we furtively wander about the garden, after a time when most respectable country folk are abed, is not necessary. And secondly, what can you be thinking? My reputation, should we have been observed, will be in tatters. *And* I have yet to return to the house undetected," she scolded.

Darcy's face, illuminated by the moonlight, wore a broad smile. Before she could reiterate the seriousness of their situation, he took her hand and said,

"Dearest Elizabeth, I hope you will scold me often when we are wed, for the fire it brings to your eyes, could warm a man's heart," and he raised her hand to place a lingering kiss on it.

Well! Thought Elizabeth; now severely annoyed. Not only had he summonsed her in the most furtive manner imaginable, but he seemed openly happy at their predicament.

Darcy placed a further clutch of kisses on her wrist, and when she felt the familiar tingle of excitement, where his lips caressed her naked skin, her anger evaporated. Her body had a habit of betraying her whenever it was near to Mr. Darcy, and already the effect of such a simple act, had ignited a heat in her cheeks that was evident to him. Darcy drank in the sight of his beloved, and every fibre of his being ached for her. His desire had only increased over the months, and with her dark locks falling down past her shoulders, and the red bow of her lips invitingly parted, it was all he could do not to pull her into his arms. The memory of why he had instigated this meeting, gave his reason to rein in his desire. He retrieved the letter he'd taken such pains to write, and offered it to her. Elizabeth looked down at the missive, and listened as Darcy made his apology.

"My behaviour this morning was unforgivable, and by way of explanation, I have drafted this letter to answer your questions. I realise protocol dictates you refuse it, and if I could confer its contents to you in any other way, I would, but I find the subject matter hard to talk of. Would you do me the honour of reading it while I am away?" he asked.

"Away sir, you are taking a journey?" she enquired, absently taking the letter, and tucking it into her dressing gown pocket.

"I leave at first light for Pemberley. I must have my sister by my side when we marry, and I prefer to escort her myself. That is why I had to see you tonight. I could not leave without offering you an explanation. Besides, this way I can tell her all about you," he said with a playful twinkle in his eye, "You will like Georgiana, I am sure of it."

"I am sure I will. How long will you be gone?" She enquired, trying to mask her disappointment at him leaving again so soon.

"Five days, certainly no more than a week."

Hopefully the lesser, he thought. I have little enough time to win your heart, dearest Elizabeth, I cannot afford to be absent for too long.

"I understand she is about Lydia's age, would you liken her to one of my younger sisters, or maybe Charlotte Collins?" she asked.

Elizabeth needed a few minutes to absorb that he would be gone for a full week. Realising she would actually miss him, was something of a shock to her.

"Heavens no!" he said before apologising for his outburst,

"I beg your pardon. If I had to encapsulate her character, I would say she is a younger version of, Jane," he answered triumphantly.

"Then I am sure I will like her very well." Elizabeth smiled.

They stood awkwardly in silence for a minute or two, Elizabeth looking around at the colourless vegetation, purposely avoiding his gaze, while Darcy stared at her unabashedly. As the silence stretched on, she risked a glance in his direction, the realised her mistake instantly. Darcy wore his desire like a beacon, and it was a look she had come to recognise. Hastily she said,

"It is quite late Mr. Darcy, and if I should be discovered here, alone, with you in my night attire, we will be forced to marry on the morrow. Let us say farewell, and therein I wish you a safe and speedy journey sir."

"*I would not care if we were discovered; in fact I would welcome it. To be wed tomorrow, to quench this fire that rages in my veins, to possess the thing I most desire. No, I would not object to being discovered my love,*" he said tenderly.

As he spoke, he traced a finger up her arm, stopping only to brush a wayward curl from her shoulder. The soft, milky flesh it had been hiding was now exposed. Mesmerised, Elizabeth watched as Darcy lowered his head, and gently caressed the curve of her neck, with a soft kiss. His touch was like a drug, exquisite and intoxicating, while making her yearn for more. She tilted her head to the side, allowing him access to roam further, whilst absently clutching his sides to steady herself. She savoured the heat of his breath her skin, just before the touch of his lips made it burn with pleasure. Encouraged, Darcy moved to taste her mouth, and he claimed her lips while guiding her arms around his neck. Folding her in his embrace he instinctively let his hands dip down to pull her closer, stopping only when their bodies connected. He explored the warmth of her mouth with his tongue, and delighted in her welcoming response.

Daringly, he stroked the hollow of her back, and then boldly explored further, over the curve of her buttocks. Shocked, but driven by desire, she arched herself against him. Yearning for more, Elizabeth pulled his head down and returned his demanding kiss, with a fervent all of her own. Happy to oblige, and lost to his needs, he raised a hand and through the soft cotton fabric, he gently cupped her breast. Elizabeth's body throbbed with a longing she had never experienced before, a craving for his attention to those secret places, no man had ever touched, yet she would have willingly surrendered them to him tonight. Darcy had long suspected Elizabeth would be a willing pupil, and a passionate lover, and tonight her response had confirmed this. She let out a moan of approval, as he drew her tighter to him, all the while whispering her name,

"Elizabeth, Elizabeth."

Darcy knew he must stop; for soon he would be at the point of no return. Yes, he could bring them both untold pleasure tonight, but in the morning, she would hate him, and rightly so. To take advantage of Elizabeth's naivety was abhorrent to him. Mustering all his resolution, he slowly broke their kiss, and rested his forehead on hers. Reluctantly he removed her arms from about his neck, and held them to his breast. In a ragged voice he murmured,

"Tempt me no more, my love, for I am only flesh and blood."

The void her absent body left was like a chasm, and he could not bear to be parted from her. Unrepentantly, he cradled her in his arms once more, placing soft kisses on her brow. until they were once more composed.

Elizabeth was grateful to him for putting an end to their encounter. She was unaware that such a burning passion, and desire, could be felt by a woman. All sense of decorum, and propriety had fled, as she had enjoyed his caresses. The longing that afflicted her entire body, pulsed through her veins, and yet it was not enough. When he had touched her breast, the exquisite sensation that radiated along every fibre in her body, had made her dizzy with pleasure. If he could arouse such feelings in her with a few brief kisses and caresses, how would their wedding night unfold? Elizabeth, mortified that she could so easily lose her senses while in Darcy's arms, then let such thoughts enter her head, blushed crimson. It was past time they concluded this encounter, and humour seemed the best method of escape.

"Mr. Darcy," she said still breathless, "I trust our farewell will keep you fortified while you are away."

He knew she was teasing, and in an amused tone he replied,

"Miss. Bennet, be assured, my thirst for you will never, be quenched."

They shared one last chaste kiss before parting. Darcy waited for her to signal from her window, that her absence had gone undiscovered, and then he walked Nelson to the gate before mounting him. Their encounter had been beyond enjoyable, but foolish. His excuse that he was a red blooded male, with needs and desires, was not a good enough excuse. His resolve to be more circumspect when in Elizabeth's company seem to evaporate into thin air whenever he was alone with her. As he led Nelson along the track, he berated himself for being weak in both mind and body, a condition that was alien to him. He must stop taking these liberties, and behave as a gentleman should. He had only to be master of his own resolve for another month, and then…..yes then life would be as sweet as it could be.

# CHAPTER 12

Elizabeth watched the large black horse carry its master out of sight, before pulling his letter from its hiding place. She wondered what it could contain for him to risk so much. She twisted her chair closer to the candlelight and tucking her feet up to keep them warm. Turning the letter over in her hands, Elizabeth detected the aroma of sandalwood and pepper radiating from it. Gently she ran her fingers over the Darcy seal; soon it would grace her correspondence too. Carefully, she broke the wax fastening and unfolded the letter, noting the bold, yet well-designed script in neatly conformed lines. It read,

*My Dearest Elizabeth,*
*This morning after we had parted I reflected on what...*

Elizabeth was shocked at the letters contents. As she read it for a second time, a myriad of emotions coursed through her. She was angry and disgusted that Georgiana had been subjected to such a plan, to be used as a pawn by Wickham to exact his revenge on Darcy, and for a wrong that did not exist! That his accomplice was a woman, one of her own sex, was a double betrayal. No wonder Darcy had not apprised others of the details of their estrangement, his sisters good name, her reputation, would have been in tatters before she was even 'out.' It was now clear to Elizabeth, that from the onset of their acquaintance, George Wickham had knowingly lied to her, and her family, drawing *them* into *his* web of deceit. The thought that she once imagined herself in love with him, now disgusted her. But was she not guilty of complacency in forming her opinion of Darcy? Indeed, she had relished the tales Wickham fed her, confirming her ill opinion of Darcy. Verily, if she had not felt slighted by Darcy's refusal to dance with her that first night in Meryton, would she have been so ready to believe those lies? She had welcomed, and compounded Wickham's false testimony, to justify her own form of revenge on Darcy, by maligning his character to her sister Jane. Although in her defence, she had not known they were lies until now.

It was abundantly clear to her, that the only person to have acted with decorum, and honour, was Darcy. When she thought of how she had refused his proposal, citing his ill-treatment of Wickham as part of the reason, she was mortified. And now, at her insistence, he'd had to recall and recount the deeds that pained him the most. She was aware that Darcy was an intensely private man, who guarded his family with a fierce, and impenetrable protectiveness at all times. How could she to face him again, after the revelations he had been compelled to share with her tonight? If only she had not pressed him so relentlessly on the matter.

Elizabeth woke early the next morning. She wrapped a shawl around her shoulders, and crept barefooted along the corridor to her sister's bedroom. Tapping gently on the door, she listened for a reply.

When none was forthcoming, she quietly called to her,

"Jane, are you awake, tis Lizzie?"

"Lizzie?" her sister asked sleepily, "Come in, have I slept over?"

Elizabeth opened the door and softly padded to her sister's bedside. After putting the candle on the side, she pulled back the covers and slipped neatly in beside her. It was warm and inviting, where Jane had been under the covers, trying to ward off the morning chill. She tucked the blanket around her cold feet, then turning to answer to Jane's question.

"No Jane, 'tis a little after six," Elizabeth assured her, "but I must speak with you before we go down this morning. I have a letter I want you to read, but must ask that you do not divulge the contents to a living soul."

Immediately Jane sat up, a worried frown on her brow.

"Lizzie, what is it, you have me most concerned now, is it bad news? Is it from mama or.... oh no, is it from Mr. Bingley...?"

"Jane!"

Elizabeth cried, cutting her sister off mid-sentence.

"It is a private correspondence from Mr. Darcy to me; I would have you read it and advise me. I find myself in a quandary as to what action to take."

Jane took the letter and gave her sister a bewildered look. Twisting to let the candlelight illuminated the paper, she began to read. Elizabeth watched as Jane scanned the pages. On reaching the end, she opened her eyes wide in shock.

"Oh Lizzie, how we have been deceived; is it true? But it must be true, for I cannot believe Mr. Darcy would slander his own sister. How regrettable that Mr. Wickham used his friendship with Mr. Darcy's sister, to cause hurt and resentment. He always seemed so very pleasant and affable."

Elizabeth looked at her sister. Jane had not seen past the contents of the letter as she had, reluctantly she would have to point it out to her.

"You are quite right Jane," Elizabeth said patiently, "while Mr. Wickham appears to be all goodness and Mr. Darcy does not, it is quite the opposite. No dearest, what we now have to be concerned with is, do we tell papa? Might he want to warn mama and our sister's to avoid Mr. Wickham's company, or maybe even bid them return home? They are due to stay there another seven nights yet. Do you not see Jane; we must be concerned for Lydia and Kitty now. Papa is right, they are two very silly girls, and I fear insincere compliments may easily turn their heads. Do you think they are safe in the society of Col. Forster and his wife, while Wickham is near?"

Jane briefly glanced back at the letter, and after a few moments contemplation, she said,

"I am sure after observing Mr. Wickham these past months, he must have seen the error of his ways, and has decided to conform. In his dealing with you Lizzie, he has acted within the boundaries set by society, has he not? No, the girls have both mama, and Col.

Forster to watch over them. I do not think papa would have given his consent, if he thought anything improper might occur. What do you think dearest?"

"Yes, Mr. Wickham has acted the perfect gentleman whenever we have shared each other's company. I only hope Mama will be watchful, and hopefully curtail Lydia's enthusiasm a little. Besides, they have no fortune and very few contacts, which seem paramount to Wickham in his quest for matrimony. So we are agreed to say nothing to papa then?" Jane nodded.

Kissing her sister on the cheek, Elizabeth slipped from Jane's warm bed, and went back to her own room.

With so many tasks to be completed before the wedding, Elizabeth was grateful for the arrangements her mother had completed, before leaving for Brighton. Reverend Muir had been consulted, and the church booked. The hymns were chosen, and the bell ringers retained. Due to the growing number of guests, Mr. Bingley had offered the use of Netherfield house and grounds, which Mrs. Bennet had gratefully accepted. She had then proceeded to thank him profusely saying, 'to have the use of such a property with a separate ballroom, will mean our guests can dine at their leisure while the dancing continues.' Elizabeth agreed it was a generous offer indeed.

The cooks at Netherfield had been preparing a variety of dishes for Jane and Elizabeth to sample, much to the amusement of Mr. Bennet. They had even brought some samples home for him to try, much to the chagrin of Mrs. Hill. Everything was coming together perfectly, and if Elizabeth was honest, she felt a little bored. With Darcy away and only her father and Jane in residence, time was passing too slowly. Could she be missing Darcy?

Later that day a courier arrived from Brighton, with a number of packages from her mother. Jane and Elizabeth opened them excitedly; they were delighted to find a number of gowns, hats, and several reticules for each of them, while another contained fans, gloves and undergarments. Mrs. Bennet had even included extra material for the cobbler to make matching footwear. Finally in the last parcel they found a letter from Mrs. Bennet.


*Dear Jane and Lizzie,*

*I have no time to waste writing letters really, yet feel I must give you instructions, even though it is from afar. You must make haste and try on all these garments. Check that they fit and look well, comfort is secondary. If they are in need of alteration, I have arranged for the Roberts sisters to be at your disposal. You may discard only the turbans if you feel so inclined; truthfully I detest them, for they remind me of Caroline Bingley, all plumes and vinegar.*

*Is it not fortunate that your Aunt and Uncle Gardiner are here? They came to escort the shipment of the new fabrics, for their warehouse in Cheapside? It is from their stock I have selected the materials for your gowns. I hope you are as delighted as I am, in the selection I have made, and at a discount too. Mr. Gardiner has agreed to keep the material back until after your nuptials, that way, everyone will be looking to you with envy. Although my dear Jane, they would have to go very far, to find a girl as pretty as you.*

*Now, I trust you are both doing all you can, to encourage the affections of your betrothed, especially you Lizzie.*

*Pass on my regards and affections to Mr Bennet, (Though I doubt he has poked his nose out of his study to notice I am gone.)*

*Your sister's send their love; though they are far too busy enjoying themselves to write.*

*Your affectionate mother,*
*Mrs Fanny Bennet.*

Elizabeth read the note aloud, and smiled when Jane rolled her eyes at the mention of their fiancés. Both expected, and ignored the reproof aimed at Elizabeth in regards to Mr. Darcy. Happy to have something more to occupy their time, they both rushed upstairs, with Hill and Cissy following close behind.

# CHAPTER 13

Darcy's journey to his Derbyshire estate, had taken only two days. He had elected to ride through the night, much to the irritation of Fletcher. If he tarried too long it would add another day to his journey, and another day away from Elizabeth. Truthfully, he was eager to see his sister, and spend some time at Pemberley, but at the moment, Hertfordshire held a jewel far more appealing. Glancing over at Fletcher, an easy smile creased his face. Fletcher's head was rolling from side to side, mimicking the rhythm of the carriage. Every so often, he would struggle to open his eyes, but the lack of a comfortable bed and a good night's sleep, meant fatigue had won the day. Darcy was less fortunate, and had managed to sleep only a little. He had so many questions and concerns, that his mind would not be still long enough for slumber. What would Georgiana's reaction be to his news? Would she be happy for him? Would she like Elizabeth? Had Elizabeth read his letter, and if so, had it been enough to banish Wickham's lies? Maybe it would soften her heart in his favour, even a little? Looking over at the sleeping Fletcher, Darcy envied him his simple life. His only duty was to cater for Darcy's needs, and to ensure his comfort. In return, Fletcher enjoyed a comfortable home, a generous wage, and three meals a day, although he might disagree with that statement today. Darcy was aware Fletcher enjoyed a certain status below stairs, but he was well liked by the other servants too. It was a shame he had no son to follow in his footsteps, but he did not seem unhappy with his bachelor status.

They had been on Pemberley ground for more than an hour before nearing the house, and Darcy looked out of the window expectantly. They emerged from the forest that had been planted by his great-grandfather, and Pemberley came into view. A wave of happiness washed over him, as he looked down on his ancestral home. An impressively large stone building, that was situated on high ground amidst a natural valley. To the rear of the house were the formal gardens and a pretty meadow area. This then led to a large wooded area that was home to a well-established deer herd. While to the front, it boasted an impressive expanse of lawns and a lake. Slowly they descended the hill, and then crossed the bridge that traversed the lake. The driver pulled the horses to a stop, and a footman jumped down to open the door for his master. Mr. and Mrs. Reynolds stepped forward to greet Mr. Darcy.

"Welcome home sir, we were not expecting you until tomorrow," said Mr. Reynolds with a bow.

"Thank you, it is good to be home," he said acknowledging their welcome "we travelled through the night. All is well Mrs. Reynolds? Where is my sister?"

"All is as it should be sir. Miss Georgiana is waiting for you in the sitting room," she said with a small curtsy and a big smile.

"Tell her I will take tea with her in thirty minutes. Oh and Reynolds," he said, as he walked up the front steps, "Rouse Fletcher will you. When he has regained his wits, send him to me directly, thank you."

Darcy almost made it across the atrium and to the foot of the stairs, before he heard, rather than saw, the approaching dog. He spun round just in time to be greeted by two large paws, which came to rest on his chest. Trafalgar attempted to smother his face with a very long, and very wet tongue.

"So, monster, you have found me. Have you been behaving yourself?" Darcy said in a stern, yet playful voice. Then he bent down and whisper close to his ear. "Have you been watching over all that is dear to us, my trusted friend?"

Eventually he pushed the animal down, and scratched behind his ears. Trafalgar showed his appreciation by the thunderous wagging of his tail. After several minutes, Darcy straightened and began to make his way up the stairs. With a single click of his fingers, Trafalgar fell into step beside him. Normally Darcy would have gone directly to see Georgiana, but after wearing the same clothes for two days, he was in no fit state to be received. He would bathe fully before dinner, but for now a quick wash and change of clothes would suffice. Trafalgar sat before the fire enjoying its warmth, trailing his master with adoring eyes. Darcy tried to struggle out of his tail coat, and cursed the latest fashion for wearing them so snug. Suddenly he felt the expert hands of Fletcher tugging at the cuffs, and miraculously the accursed article then slipped off with ease. Turning so Fletcher could unbutton his waistcoat, Darcy noticed his bloodshot eyes. Fletcher was a good man, but no longer a young man Darcy realised. Although nothing, or at least very little, stopped him from voicing his opinion. Thankfully Darcy knew when such a moment was coming, for he preluded it with, "Well begging your pardon sir," or "I am sure I know my place....but," Darcy smiled. He knew one day he would have to find a replacement, but hopefully not for many years yet.

"I see the hound wasted no time in seeking you out sir."

Fletcher gave the now sleeping dog a scowl. It was not that Fletcher disliked the dog, but through necessity they had come to an understanding. As long as Trafalgar did not steal, or chew up the master's boots, Fletcher would not chase him out of Darcy's rooms. They had struck an accord.

"Yes, monster came upon me before I had even climbed the first step," Darcy confirmed, "I will take a bath before dinner Fletcher, and then wear my easy jacket and black trousers to dine. I will not need you after that."

He hoped Fletcher would use the opportunity to catch up on his rest.

"Thank you sir," Fletcher replied, his weariness evident in his voice.

Darcy's long strides made short work of the reception area, and after turning the ornate handle, he entered the sitting room. It was lofty in height, but a well-proportioned room suitably furnished to the fortune of its owner, nothing gaudy, but decorated with tasteful elegance in lemon and cream. His eyes went straight to the young woman sitting on the blue and yellow divan. He called her name,

"Georgiana,"

Forgetting that she intended to show him how much she had matured since he had last seen her, Georgiana rushed into his outstretched arms and held him tightly.

"Oh William, it is good to see you, I have missed you so much," she cried.

"I have missed you to dearest. Are you well?"

"Oh yes, I am very well thank you brother. We did not expect you until the morning, but I am so glad you have come home early."

She lifted her face to look at him. Unshed tears glistened in her eyes, and Darcy wished he had not left her alone for so long. Placing a kiss upon her forehead, he resolved to be more attentive in the future.

"If this is the welcome I can expect, then I must go away more often," he teased, "Shall we have some tea, I have news to share."

Sitting on an easy chair next to Georgiana, he waited while she poured them a dish of tea, and then accepted his one. She looked expectantly at him, and it made him feel awkward and self-conscious. Unable to hold her gaze, he toyed with his spoon a moment.

"My dear, do you recall when I stayed with Bingley at his house in the shires, I mentioned that I had met the daughter of the local squire?"

"Why yes William, Miss Elizabeth Bennet was it not?" she returned softly.

"Err yes, Miss Bennet," he confirmed with a cough.

"Well, when I went to Kent to check Aunt Catherine's estate, I was able to renew our acquaintance. Her friend had recently married Aunt Catherine's parson and Eliz...." He started to say her name before quickly correcting himself.

"Miss Bennet happened to be paying her an extended visit."

He paused, looking up to gauge her reaction. Had she noticed his slip? Georgiana's countenance seemed unchanged, although he thought he detected the hint of a smile about her mouth.

"During my free time, I decided to reacquaint myself with some of the walks I enjoyed as a boy. While exploring these paths I bumped into Miss Bennet, several times actually, and we then decided to explore them together. The parsonage party also enjoyed several excursions to Rosings, for tea or to dine and play cards in the evening. During this time, Miss Bennet and I found that we had much in common," he paused, wanting to choose his words with care,

"I confess Georgiana, the time we spent together made my visit to Rosings considerably more bearable. You know how condescending Lady Catherine can be, and her continued nonsense about Anne and I being betrothed."

He paused again. Why was he finding it so difficult to tell her, she was his sister after all? Just get to the point for goodness sake, he scolded himself.

"Well, the point I am trying to get to dearest, is that I found Miss Bennet's reception to my company most welcoming, and after much consideration, I asked her to be my wife. She has accepted me and we are engaged."

A wave of relief washed over him, and he looked to Georgiana for her reaction. He was not disappointed. Georgiana wore a hearty smile on her face. Putting down her cup, she rose and threw her arms about him in an exuberant hug.

"I am so happy for you William; it will be wonderful to have a sister, and how fortunate that you chose *that* particular time to visit Aunt Catherine," she said innocently.

Darcy was not sure if there was an undertone to her comment. She could not possibly know he had purposely changed his plans, having found out about Elizabeth's intended visit... could she?

"You not surprised by my declaration Georgiana?"

"Oh no brother, I hoped this was the news you wanted to share with me, I am delighted for you both. When will I meet her, and will you be wed here in the Pemberley chapel?" she asked gaily.

"Explain if you please," he said raising a quizzical eyebrow.

"It was obvious William; whenever you spoke of Miss Bennet your voice became, well wistful. Then in one of your letters you told me she was beautiful. I knew then that this was someone special. The fact that Miss Bennet accepted you does not surprise me at all, for you are the very best of men, dear brother."

If he had been so transparent, so unguarded that even Georgiana had correctly interpreted the signs, who else had arrived at the same conclusion, he wondered? Not wanting to dwell on this thought, he decided to respond to her earlier questions.

"To answer your questions Georgiana, we are to be married in the church at Meryton, three weeks hence; that is why I have come home, I could not get married without my Georgie at my side, now could I?" he said, confirming the place she held in his heart.

"We will leave directly after breakfast tomorrow. I have arranged lodgings along the way, and we should be in Hertfordshire in three days. I trust you received my note, and all the preparations are complete," He asked.

"The wedding is in only three weeks, but why so soon William? I will not have time to arrange a visit to town, or have a new dress made."

"I see no point in a long engagement, and Miss Bennet agrees with me. Besides, I am eager to spend Christmas at Pemberley; we can enjoy a pre-honeymoon, honeymoon." And he smiled at the prospect of Elizabeth's first Christmas in her new home.

"I see," she said quietly, "Well, all is ready for our visit to Mr Bingley's, and I will try to select something suitable to wear from my wardrobe. Though I should have liked something not previously seen by Miss Bingley, she can be so very cutting with her remarks."

Darcy detected a slight tremor in her voice, and quickly spoke to reassure her,

"Do not fret Georgiana, I anticipated your needs, and have already arranged for Mrs. Simmons, and her assistant to travel from town and await your instruction. I hope this is acceptable?"

Darcy's reward was to see her countenance instantly brighten, along with a kiss on the cheek, and another tight embrace. He smiled as he watched her return to her seat. She refreshed his cup and passed it back to him, before refilling her own. He looked at her, perched on the edge of her seat looking every inch a lady of quality. How she had grown, clearly no longer a child, but a young woman.

Once tea was finished, Darcy left Georgiana to practice her music. Noting there was a quite some time before dinner, he decided to address some of the neglected correspondence. McFayden, his advisor, always put items that needed his direct attention, on his desk. Non urgent business was put into one of the many labelled folders on a side table. These he could deal with at a more sedate pace. Now though, with quill in hand and ink ready, the waiting paper remained blank. Something kept pulling his mind back to the conversation he'd just had with Georgiana. Recalling all they had discussed, he still felt something was amiss, something concerning Elizabeth.

He was accustomed to having an orderly life and mind, and it was most vexing that something was eluding him. Deciding his head was not attuned to letter writing, he rose and went to the window. He looked out at the garden, now barely visible in the fading light, and admired the diligence of the groundsmen. It was their hard work kept Pemberley looking so magnificent, and the envy of many people. All had been made ready for the expected harsh winter, with bushes pruned, perennials lifted, and hedges trimmed. Further afield, the young saplings that were planter in the spring to replace any felled trees would now be coddled. And finally the vast lawns would have been raked and cleared of moss, all ready for spring re-seeding. Yes, all was ready for winter, *and* a new mistress he thought. Realising he must inform the Reynolds of his impending nuptials, he summonsed them to his library, although he suspected Fletcher had probably regale all below stairs with the details by now. Darcy merely advised them that he was to be married, and after the wedding they would return to Pemberley for Christmas and the New Year. He told Mrs Reynolds which suite of rooms to prepare, namely the ones adjoining his. Then would she kindly make a list of capable applicants from the female staff, wishing to become Elizabeth's personal maid. Then gratefully and with thanks, he accepted their happy felicitations, before they returned to their duties.

He sighed, if he intended to be away for nigh on another month, he must make a start on this paperwork. He sat at his desk and again took up his quill.

With only Darcy and Georgiana in residence, dinner was an intimate affair. Afterwards, they retired to the music room, where Georgiana played the pianoforte for Darcy. As the soothing music washed over him, Darcy felt the effects of his hasty journey north and lack of sleep, and he welcomed it when the clock chimed nine. He reminded Georgiana of their early start, and then bade her sleep well.

Remembering he had dismissed Fletcher for the evening, he shrugged out of his jacket and laid it over a chair arm. During dinner he had spoken to Georgiana, about giving Elizabeth their mother's betrothal ring, which she had bequeathed to him. Most of her personal jewellery was to go to Georgiana, but all the family heirlooms had come to Darcy, to keep, or to dispose of, at his will. Happily she had agreed, and thought it a wonderful idea. He would retrieve it from the safe in the morning. He half-filled an exquisitely cut glass with brandy, and then pulled his chair nearer the fire. Taking a sip, he felt the amber liquid trail a path of warmth down his throat; soon, the feeling of tiredness washed over him again as the alcohol, a full stomach and the warmth from the fire acted together. He may be younger, but he realised he needed his rest as just as much as Fletcher. Putting the glass down, he untied his neck cloth and tossed it towards the chair. It fell short and drop to the floor in a snowy heap. Not wishing to incur Fletcher's tut, tutting at his disregard for fine cloth, he leaned forward to retrieve the errant item. As he twisted out of his chair and onto one knee, it hit him. *THAT* was it. What a fool he was! When they were at the parsonage, and the odious Mr. Collins had discovered them, locked in their amorous embrace,

Darcy had informed him that Elizabeth had accepted his proposal. But that was just it, she had *never* actually said *yes*!

## CHAPTER 14

Darcy leant forward and put his head in his hands. How could he have been so stupid? He was trying to change, to be the kind of man whom Elizabeth would want to marry, be proud to marry. Yet in his arrogance and conceit, he had assumed she would acquiesce to his offer of protection, and even be glad. Oh, she had agreed with his version of events, but only through necessity, nothing else. Having instigated the encounter, he should have dealt with the subsequent outcome better. The truth was, he had been taught good principles as a child, only to be left to follow them with pride and conceit. It was never more evident, than now.

"Gods teeth!" he bellowed, rising from his chair.

He paced the room with agitated steps. What was he to do? Obviously he must rectify it as quickly as possible, for unless Elizabeth confirmed her willingness to be his wife, how their engagement came about would forever taint their relationship. Running his fingers through his hair, Darcy caught sight of his reflection; he stared back at the man in the mirror. His hair was in disarray, and he had dark circles under his eyes from lack of sleep, both a visible reminder of how exhausted he was. He sighed deeply; in essence the solution was simple. He must ask Elizabeth again. This time he would not insult her, or recite the obstacles he had overcome, and he most certainly would not refer to the difference in their social standing. The emotional and mental struggle had been his alone. He knew society was fickle, and though the *Ton* might censure them initially, it would only last until the next scandal came along. If Elizabeth would have him, then he *would* have Elizabeth. He would lay bare his heart, and pray she would accept it. The possibility that she might refuse him was acknowledged, but their recent encounters gave him reason to hope. Another wave of tiredness engulfed him, and he knew he must rest. Naked, he wearily climbed between the soft sheets, and let sleep claimed him.

*Elizabeth shut the door behind her, and started to close the space between them, the fragrant scent of lavender preceding her. Darcy drank in the vision of loveliness before him. Her hair, now free of all constraints, cascaded over her shoulders in soft tendrils. From his fireside chair, he could make out the desire in her eyes, and seductive smile on her cherry lips. Kneeling before him, she stretched up to caress his face, before reaching for his loosened cravat, which she cast aside with gusto. Placing her hands on his chest, she let them slowly travel over the contours of his firm torso, ensuring her fingers lingered over his nipples, before continuing down to his navel. Her touch wreaked havoc with his self-control. Unable to remain passive any longer, he pushed the chair back, and knelt on the floor before her. He was brutally aware that it was not the heat from the library fire that warmed him, but his desire to possess her, that seared through his veins. As she continued to slowly unbutton his shirt, he entwined his fingers through her mass of luminous curls. He gave it a gentle pull, forcing her to tilt her chin up, bringing their gaze level. How beautiful she was. She searched his face for a second, and then slowly teased his shirt apart. She boldly placed kisses and nibbled on his exposed skin, making his breath catch in his throat. The trail of fire ignited by her lips heightened his desire. Pulling her to closer him, he savoured the feeling as their bodies moulded together. He tugged her head back again, and with a desperate hunger took possession of her mouth, welcoming her attempt to match his urgency. Letting his hands wander over the soft curves of her hips and buttocks, he felt her tremble with anticipation. Lifting his eyes, he wanted to savour the innocent passion on her face; instead he found one of wanton invitation. In one effortless move, he twisted them around until they sank down onto the soft rug before the flames. Looking down at her welcoming smile, and outstretched arms, he murmured her name.*

*"Elizabeth."*

*She pulled him even closer and asked seductively,*

*"Have you waited long for me William?"*

*His need to possess her was now all-consuming, but not before he huskily replied,*

*"All my life Elizabeth, all my life."*

"Oh, I beg your pardon Mr Darcy, when I heard you talking I thought you were about sir."

Fletcher said apologetically as he entered his master's bedchamber.

"Shall I come back sir?" Darcy shook his head.

"No Fletcher, wait in the dressing room and I will come through momentarily, just give me a moment to come to my senses."

Fletcher gave a small nod, and then disappeared into the adjoining room to lay out Darcy's shaving articles.

Another dream, Darcy thought woefully, so vivid he found himself still aroused. Recalling every detail, he suffered the unfulfilled longing yet again. The effect this woman had on him was both frightening, and marvellous. Having regained control over his body, he summoned Fletcher back to his side.

"Are we all secure for a nine o'clock departure, the trunks are loaded? And my sister, has she been roused? I want no delay to our journey."

"Yes sir, every detail has been attended to."

Fletcher sniffed haughtily, as if Mr. Darcy had to tell him his job! Yes, the sooner his master and the lovely Miss Bennet were married the better. He had observed his masters moods change drastically, when not within an easy distance of her, and not for the better either. Fletcher heartily approved, of Mr. Darcy's engagement to the captivating Miss Bennet. Though to ease his own mind, he had made discreet enquiries of the servants at Longbourn, Netherfield and Hunsford. He had seen many a fortune hunting mama, throw their daughter in the path of Mr. Darcy. As a good and loyal gentleman's gentleman, he considered it his duty to check for skeletons in their past. He could warn his master if need be. So, with a softer edge to his voice, Fletcher asked,

"Are you ready for your shave *now* sir?"

Darcy nodded his assent and followed him back into the dressing room. When Fletcher had finished both shaving, and dressing him, Darcy joined Georgiana for breakfast. Having ensured she was ready to leave promptly, he made his way to the library to retrieve the ring he wanted to present to Elizabeth. Carefully, he lifted it out of the rosewood box his mother had placed it in all those years ago. Slipping it from its velvet pouch he wondered, would *she* have approved of his choice?

Anne Darcy and her only son had enjoyed a close relationship. Normally, after the birth, a mother was expected to hand over their child to nannies and tutors; however, Anne disapproved of this practice and was involved in all aspects of her child's upbringing. She had an infectious vivacity for life, coupled with a lively wit, and a love of laughter. They spent many hours together, conversing and debating on a variety of subjects, or playing games such as backgammon or Loo. She was a compassionate and thoughtful woman, always thinking of others, and even when she knew the end was inevitable, she refused to succumb to self-pity. When she died, the life and love at Pemberley, seemed to die with her. Darcy thought Elizabeth had many of these qualities, and hoped she would restore the harmony at Pemberley once more. Yes; he thought, as he popped the pouch into his waistcoat pocket, Mama would have liked Elizabeth very well.

They left Pemberley on the strike of nine, with Darcy and Georgiana in the first carriage and Fletcher, Mrs. Annesley and Georgiana's maid in the second. Their trunks had already gone on ahead. Darcy had decided, other servants needed while in the country, would be sourced from the local villages. He hoped to impress Mrs. Bennet's by using her recommendations. The return journey would be at a more sedate pace for the ladies' comfort, even so, the next three days would seem an eternity to him, until he was once more at Elizabeth's side.

Georgiana had brought a book, and her sewing to help pass the time, when not employed with either of these, she would ask Darcy for news from London. Often, they would both lapse into silence and admire the passing scenery. Darcy was grateful his sister was not obsessing about Elizabeth, unfortunately for him she had never been far from his thoughts.

Now only a few miles from Netherfield, he was still at a loss as to what to say to her. He had composed a dozen scenarios over the last three days, then decided none would suit. As the carriage came to a halt at the steps of Netherfield, Charles stepped forward to greet them.

"Darcy, Miss Darcy, it is so good to have you at Netherfield," cried Bingley with a smile of genuine pleasure.

"Miss Darcy it has been too long, I hope you are well," he continued, giving her a welcoming bow.

"Thank you Mr Bingley, I am quite well."

Georgiana curtsied, and proffered her hand to accept his salute. Darcy was pleased to see she still felt at ease in Bingleys presence, and also moved forward to greet him.

"It's good to see you Charles, and how is the fair Miss Bennet?" he asked, half serious half teasing.

"Wonderful Darcy, just wonderful," he replied, as a flush of pink crept over his collar. "But you will see for yourself tonight. I have invited Jane and Miss Elizabeth to dine with us. An intimate gathering to introduce Miss Darcy to our intended, I hope you both approve?" he asked, turning to giving Georgiana a slight nod in acceptance of her smile of gratitude.

"An excellent idea Charles, most considerate of you," Darcy acknowledged on behalf of them both, and they made their way into the warm interior.

# CHAPTER 15

Jane and Elizabeth were grateful Mr. Darcy had sent his carriage for them. The air had become chilled with the first frosts of winter, and it was altogether a superior ride compared to their own carriage. With plush, well sprung seat it was far more comfortable, more spacious, and a lot warmer too. Once safely inside Netherfield, and divulged of their outer garments by the footmen, they quickly checked each other's appearance. Satisfied they were unruffled by the journey, they signalled their readiness to enter the drawing room. As they walked in Darcy and Bingleys stood, their eyes going to their respected partners. After the customary salutes were executed, they all turned their attention to the young woman seated by the fire. Darcy stepped forward to make the introductions.

"Miss Bennet, Miss Elizabeth, please allow me to present my sister, Miss Georgiana Darcy."

The sisters curtsied, and Georgiana stood and shyly returned their greeting.

"I hope the journey from Derbyshire was a pleasant one Miss Darcy, and you are not too fatigued," Jane enquired softly.

"It was Miss Bennet, I thank you. My brother is always most attentive to my comfort," Georgiana replied in a quiet voice.

Elizabeth touched Jane's hand and smiled, whereupon she excused herself, and went to sit next to Mr. Bingley. They exchanged shy smiles, and were soon lost in quiet conversation. Elizabeth took the seat next to the young woman, and observed she was twisting her handkerchief between her fingers. Remembering all that Darcy had said about her, and in light of his recent disclosure, Elizabeth realised she was but a shy young girl. Her perfectly dressed golden hair reflected the firelight, giving her an ethereal look. Coupled with her delicate features, and unblemished complexion, she truly did look angelic. Elizabeth understood why Darcy protected her so fiercely; indeed, her countenance and fortune would make her a target for genuine suitors and fortune hunters alike. But with two years to go before she could be presented at court, there was still time to bring her out of her shell. As for genuine admirers and suitors, Elizabeth knew Darcy would vet all-comers most diligently.

"Miss Darcy, your brother tells me you enjoy music, the pianoforte in particular," Elizabeth said.

She had decided to open the conversation with a topic she hoped, Miss Darcy would feel comfortable with.

"I do so love to play, and William has just purchased a beautiful new instrument for me, and it was delivered only last week. He said you played very well too, Miss Elizabeth," She said enthusiastically, then stopped abruptly.

She turned to look at her brother, afraid she had been unladylike in her eagerness, but he smiled, and gently touched her shoulder in reassurance. Elizabeth could see she was as shy as Darcy had said, and set about putting her at her ease; after all, they were to be sisters.

"Oh, I am afraid he has grossly misled you, for I play very little, and very ill," Elizabeth replied playfully as she glanced at Darcy.

"No, I said you played quite well. I have heard many ladies play a lot worse than you, Miss Elizabeth, many indeed," and Darcy returned her smile.

"Then I am satisfied. If you like, perhaps we can play a duet after dinner Miss Darcy?" Elizabeth asked.

Georgiana smiled and nodded. Watching the easy banter between her brother and his fiancé pleased her. And although she was only sixteen, Georgiana could recognise the sparks of sexual chemistry between them. Miss Elizabeth Bennet would certainly keep William on his toes, she mused.

They continued to discuss the latest trends in fashion and hair, before switching to the theatre and opera, so Darcy might join in. Georgiana gradually began to participate more, even opening a few of the discussions herself. After a pleasant half hour of easy conversation, dinner was announced. Jane took Bingley's arm, while Darcy escorted both Elizabeth, and Georgiana.

Before their guests arrived, the two men had enjoyed a pre-dinner drink in the library. Darcy had contrived the opportunity, in order to advise Bingley that he had a gift for Elizabeth, and would be obliged if he could entertain the other ladies while they slipped away, thus giving him the chance to present her with it in private. He had not imparted any further details, but Charles had consented to entertain Jane and Georgiana for a few minutes.

All evening Darcy had been watching Elizabeth, noting how she had slowly coaxed Georgiana out of herself, with gentle enquiries and attentive listening. He had been right to confide in Elizabeth the events of last year, and the profound effect it had had on his sister. Seeing Elizabeth's budding and genuine affection for Georgiana, made Darcy's heart swelled with pride. Her kind and sensitive nature had helped Georgiana overcome her shy demeanour, and enjoy the evening. How he had missed her these last few days.

After dinner, the gentlemen decided to forgo the usual separation to indulge in brandy and cigars; instead they joined the women for coffee. Georgiana, acting as hostess, waited until they had all been served before announcing she was, after all, feeling a little fatigued from the journey, and would retire directly. She bade them all goodnight, and then accepted Darcy's arm, letting him escort her into the hall. He took the opportunity to ensure it was nothing more than tiredness that ailed her, and was relieved when she gave him her assurance that it was so. Darcy then kissed her on the cheek, and bid her sleep well. There would be ample opportunity to ask how she liked Elizabeth tomorrow. He returned to the drawing-room and circled passed Charles and Jane, catching his friend's eye in a pre-arranged signal, then continued on to Elizabeth.

"Miss Elizabeth, I wonder if I might elicit your opinion on a recent purchase Mr. Bingley has acquired for his library?" he smiled and held out his hand.

Elizabeth looked over to Jane and Bingley. They were ensconced together on the settee with eyes for only one another, and so she accepted Darcy's offer. On taking his hand, she felt a surge of heat transfer from him as their naked hands touched. It was electrifying. She gave him a sidelong glance to see if he too had felt it, but what was evident on his face was a look of worry. Then as he guided her through the library door, she felt his hand touch the small of her back. Such a pleasant sensation, and it radiated from the point of contact, and coursed through her entire body. He could not fail to notice the effect his touch was having on her now, she thought, conscious that both her heart rate and breathing has increased. But Darcy appeared oblivious to Elizabeth's heightened state, and merely guided her to a chair by the fire. Once seated, she expectantly waited for him to bring forth the promised book. Instead, he paced back and forth in front of her, his hands clasped firmly behind his back. Occasionally, he stopped to study her face, only to resume his pacing once again. Having seen Darcy act in this manner once before, she knew he was building up to something. Finally, he stopped before her and said in an exasperated voice,

"Miss Bennet, we are to be wed in two weeks, are we not?"

His formal address worried her. When they were alone he usually called her by her given name, or even Miss Elizabeth, but never Miss Bennet. Couple this with his reference to their wedding, well, she found it quite disturbing. She folded her hands in her lap before calmly replying,

"That is my belief, sir."

He resumed his pacing. Damn, why will the words not come, he inwardly cursed? She must think me a tongue-tied fool. He stopped to gaze at her; she is quite exquisite, he mused. Like Charles, I am the luckiest of men to have found such a woman. Unlike Charles, I have not yet 'won' her. Instead, I lay claim to her by default. Thoughts flashed through his mind until finally, the clouds of confusion lifted. Keep it simple, tell her what you feel, offer her your heart and hope she is willing to accept it. He knew that if he did not give her the choice, he would forever suspect her reasons for marrying him. As much as he wanted her, he would not condemn her to a life of regret. Recalling his mother's advice when he once nursed a sick deer, 'if you love something enough, you have to set it free. If it comes back, it is yours forever. If it does not return, it was never yours in the first place,' Darcy knew what he must do. Drawing a deep breath he began,

"Miss Bennet, I know that you have taken our intended nuptials, as the only recourse open to you after the events at Hunsford, but in all good conscience, I must give you the choice to be free of me," he said heavily.

He gave her a few seconds to digest his words before continuing,

"I will, of course, take full responsibility for the breakdown of our engagement, should you decide on that course. You could announce that you found me lacking in the social niceties," he finished with a wry grimace.

Elizabeth raised her brows at the statement. 'To be free of me,' she repeated to herself. It was true, she had never expected to be engaged to Mr. Darcy; indeed their betrothal had sprung from her actually refusing him. But after the initial shock, she had grown accustomed to the idea of being his wife. The prospect of being Mrs. Fitzwilliam Darcy of Pemberley did not daunt her unduly, and came with considerable benefits. Darcy had proved himself to be quite capable of being amicable and civil, and after their recent encounters, she had no reason to believe them incompatible in the bedroom. The thought made her cheeks burn, but it was something she could neither ignore, nor deny. Breaking the engagement had not crossed her mind since that first day, but clearly it had Darcy's. Did he find the thought of being bound to her so repellent? If this was indeed the case, she must also give him the opportunity to be free of her. Thankfully, their engagement was not yet common knowledge, and could hopefully be dissolved with little inconvenience to either party. She felt quite strange at the prospect of him releasing her, bereft almost. Choosing her words with care, she replied,

"And is this your wish Mr. Darcy?" her tone even and unrevealing.

Darcy met her gaze and tried to read her face, but it was serene, if a little flushed. He was taken aback at her reply. He had not expected her to answer him with a question. He thought she would be eager to accept his offer, and to break their engagement readily.

"It is not," he said with vigour, "but I would not have you regret your decision at a later date madam. I am mindful of your reply to my original offer."

So, he did not want to sever their connection either. Elizabeth was puzzled, why ask now then? It had been more than three weeks since Hunsford, and on several occasions she had allowed him to take liberties that she only ever intended to share with her husband. Was that it? Did he think her wanton, and lacking in the proprieties? But she could not deny having feelings for Darcy; he had elicited responses, and stirred emotions in her she never knew existed. Examining how she felt on seeing him again after an absence of nearly a week, Elizabeth owned that her heart had beat a little faster, especially when his eyes held hers. She felt a warm glow of satisfaction that he looked at her so. She could think of nothing she had said or done, to indicate that she was reluctant to continue with the engagement. Therefore, she must conclude he was trying to do what he thought was right. Darcy watched as a myriad of emotions played across her face. Was she trying to find the words to accept his offer, to be rid of him? After what seemed an eternity, Elizabeth raised her eyes, and began her reply,

"I cannot pretend to understand you making this offer to me now Mr Darcy. You know me well enough to be assured, that if I did not want to wed you, nothing could have induced me to do so," she paused, "but, if it is your earnest desire to call off the wedding, I will not keep you to your obligation." She finished.

Darcy did not care that the relief that flooded his entire body, clearly showed on his face, and he gave her the broadest of smiles.

"Miss Bennet, Elizabeth," he said, "I am well aware that you are not afraid to speak your mind, and I would not have it any other way." Still beaming he continued "Will you indulge me with one more question before we re-join the others?"

He waited nervously for her to nod her assent. He had decided to speak from his heart as he had never done so before. Taking a step forward and dropped to one knee, he reaching for Elizabeth's hands. Gently, he folded them in his own, and looked lovingly into her soft, brown eyes.

"Dearest Elizabeth, I have misjudged you in the past, and I dare not ask your feelings at present, but I must tell you of my own. Too long I have laboured in the service of propriety, and I now realise that my life would be untenable without you in it. I had searched to find that special person, someone I could love and respect, someone to share my life with, but it was all in vain. And then I met you. You are the one, Elizabeth, the only woman I have ever had a desire to marry, to give my name. Thoughts of you fill my every waking minute. I long to please you Elizabeth, to bring you joy and happiness, in all that we do. To be worthy of your love and affection; dear, sweet, Elizabeth, my love for you is of the most ardent nature, and I offer you my heart, and my protection, unconditionally; will you do me the honour of consenting to be my wife?"

Blinking back the tears, Elizabeth drew in a ragged breath. His proposal was not only unexpected, but a complete reversal of the one he had made in Kent. He offered no insults or regrets, no excuses to justify why he loved her, or his inner struggle. He just loved her. It was perfect.

"I thank you for your offer sir, and would be honoured to accept," she said shyly.

Darcy bent his head and kissed both her hands, before pulling the ring from his waistcoat pocket. He carefully slipped it on her finger, and they were both happy to see it was perfect fit.

"Dear, sweet Elizabeth, my heart rejoices at our accord. You have my vow, that every day that I breathe God's good air, I will strive to make you happy, and to be worthy of your affection." Kissing her hands once again, he looked at her expectantly.

"Does it please you, my love, it was my mother's?" he asked.

"It is perfect Mr. Darcy, I will cherish it always."

Blinking back the unshed tears of happiness, she ventured to tease him a little,

"I see you anticipated my acceptance sir; so you have not forgone all your pride?"

Darcy threw back his head and laughed aloud. Was there ever a time she would not bait him? And yes, a little presumptuous maybe, but he would not admit it.

After the Bennet ladies had returned to Longbourn, and Bingley had long retired, Darcy sat by the library fire enjoying a quiet brandy. Thinking on the events of the day, he was content. Elizabeth and Georgiana seemed to be forming a warm friendship, and this pleased him enormously. Elizabeth's influence, and nurturing nature, would surely help Georgiana grow into a confident young woman. And in his heart, he knew he had done the right thing in offering Elizabeth her freedom. Knowing she came to him willingly, made him feel strangely warm inside. He could pretend it was the alcohol, or the warmth from the flames that gave him this glow of contentment, but he was too happy to deny his love.

So *this* is how Charles feels, he mused; he owned it was not an unpleasant sensation. His thoughts turned again to his mother, and how her words of wisdom had served him well. The three day journey back to Netherfield had seemed an eternity, mainly because he was fretting on the outcome of this interview with Elizabeth, but in just a few minutes, all his fears had been dispelled. Ruminating on the passage of time, he had long known if it was something unpleasant, time went slowly, yet when it was something pleasant, time went swiftly. As he swirled the last tot of amber liquid around the bowl of the glass, he resolved to savour the latter more.

# CHAPTER 16

Darcy was shocked, but not entirely surprised by what he was hearing. Having witnessed the behaviour of Lydia, and to a lesser extent Kitty, at the Netherfield ball, to now hear that Lydia Bennet had eloped with the scoundrel Wickham, did not come as a revelation at all. Considering the total absence of parental supervision, it was inevitable something like this would happen. In the past few years, George Wickham had reportedly convinced several young heiresses to elope with him, only to never reach Gretna Green as promised. He hoped to secure his fortune by blackmailing the unfortunate girl's family, thus funding his debauch lifestyle. In return they could be assured of his silence. This time though, Darcy knew it was another motive that goaded Wickham on, it was revenge, revenge for all their past dealings, real and imaginary. Now he was engaged to Elizabeth, he should have realised that one of the two youngest Bennet girls would be his next target, even though they had no fortune, and no connections. It was down to him to ensure an acceptable, and by that he meant wedded, conclusion to this matter. Make no mistake, he had no desire to be associated with Wickham in any way what-so-ever, but the blaggard had picked his target well. Wickham knew Darcy would have to intervene. If this scandal was to become public knowledge, he doubted if even his illustrious name and influence, could stop it from ruining the Bennet's. In effect, it would mean an end his engagement to Elizabeth. It would not do!

He suddenly became aware that Elizabeth's father was talking.

"I must leave for London at once and try to find them, but where to start, where to start?"

Mr. Bennet was clearly agitated, and the letter slipped from his hand, and fluttered down to land on his desk. He ran a hand through his grey hair, and began pacing the study floor. A wave of regret washed over him, why had he not paid more attention to his family, instead of choosing to immerse himself in his books and garden. This mess could have been avoided, if only he had not left the daily responsibilities of the house, and child rearing to his wife. Lizzie was right; a keener interest in the comings and goings of his children could have prevented this. If Lydia were not found, it would mean the ruination of his whole family. But having ventured to town rarely, he had no idea where to start looking for the runaways. And now his family were looking to *him* for a speedy solution.

It was an impertinence he knew, but Darcy recognised the dilemma of the elder man, and stepped forward to take charge of the situation.

"Mr. Bennet, I feel this is my fault entirely, and would prefer if you let me go to town in your stead. It might be possible for me to remedy the situation with alacrity. I have certain contacts, they will be able to infiltrate the more unsavoury locations that Wickham is apt to frequent," he offered.

Seeing the older man was now lost in his own thoughts, Darcy moved to stand in his path. Gently he placed a hand on Mr. Bennet's arm.

"Sir, I am better equipped, and resourced, to deal with this matter. I am the one at fault, for not making his true character known. I feel you must let me own this, my conscience demands it."

Seeing uncertainty written on the old man's face, Darcy offered him further reasons as to why he should remain home.

"Your wife and daughters will be arriving home tomorrow; they will be in need of your strength, support and guidance, until this matter is resolved. Elizabeth and Jane will also be at your side."

He paused to let his words sink in, unaware of his breach of propriety in using the ladies' given names. Removing his hand from Mr. Bennet's arm, Darcy straightened and continued in a firmer voice.

"We are wasting time; I will broach no further argument sir. I will keep you informed via Mr. Gardiner if that is acceptable?"

"Yes, yes most acceptable Mr. Darcy, for in truth, I am not a young man and would have no idea where to start looking."

Mr. Bennet dropped into his chair and picked up the letter again.

"I will write a note for you to give to Mr. Gardiner, informing him of all events, then when you call he will assist you, no need to leave your card beforehand lad..." and his voice trailed off.

With gentle encouragement, Mr. Bennet scribbled a few lines and handed it to Darcy. As he went to leave, Darcy turned back to offer Mr. Bennet words of reassurance, but already he was no longer aware of his presence. He was re-reading the letter from Col Forster, wondering how a child of fifteen could be so thoughtless. To jeopardise the family's future in such a cavalier way, was beyond him. Darcy quietly closed the door behind him.

Mr. Bennet stared at the note, the firm, bold script apt for a man used to being in command.

*Sir,*

*It is with the utmost regret, and at the behest of your lady wife, that I write to inform you of a dire situation that has arisen.*

*Early yesterday morning one of my officers, Mr. George Wickham, and your youngest daughter, Miss Lydia Bennet absconded from their respective lodgings. We know they are together as Miss Lydia left a note for my wife. It contained details of their planned journey to Gretna Green. It has since been confirmed that they have not travelled beyond London. It can only be surmised that she has been compromised. I have sent a small party of men to discreetly try to locate them, but do not hold out much hope of finding them in time to save the young ladies reputation. Wickham, being absent without leave, will be dealt with accordingly when he is found.*

*I have made arrangements for the rest of your party to return to Hertfordshire at their earliest convenience, and they should arrive one day after you receive this correspondence. I will of course keep you informed of any progress in their recovery. Please accept my sincere condolences.*

*Your obedient servant,*
*Colonel Forster.*

A gentle tapping at the door brought Mr. Bennet back to his senses, and he bid them enter. Elizabeth and Jane came in; their faces stained with tears from the news, and while Jane sat on the footstool, Elizabeth knelt at her father's feet.

"Oh papa," she lamented "If only I had shared the contents of Mr. Darcy's letter with you, this might have been prevented. As soon as I had been apprised of Wickham's true character, I should have informed you. You might have accompanied them to Brighton, or even withdrawn your permission for them to go. With mama and the girls already left for Brighton, and at the direct invitation of Col. Forster, I thought them safe." She turned her face away from his gaze and cried, "How poorly I have judged."

"Come, Lizzie, do not reproach yourself; I am not blameless in this affair, there had been rumours amongst my acquaintances in Meryton for weeks, of unpaid debts and drunken gambling by Wickham," he spat. "I have no doubt Lydia did not take much persuading either. Her head has been full of nothing but officers since the regiment arrived, and your mother encouraged her in her silliness."

He sighed. Looking at Jane and Elizabeth, he realized he was affording them little comfort by reproaching their mother.    Remembered Darcy's words he said,

"We must hope for a positive outcome, at present we can do nothing more. It comforts me to know I have at least two daughters I can be proud of. Dry those tears and run along now, make sure everything is ready for your mother's arrival tomorrow, and if you can spare the time, I would welcome some tea."

Jane and Elizabeth rose, and each placed a gentle kiss on his brow, before making their way to the kitchen. They did not speak as they mad his tea, or buttered his bread and cut him a slice of cake. Jane watched as her sister rearranged the tray, and then said in an optimistic voice.

"It was fortunate that Mr. Darcy was here when the letter arrived, was it not Lizzie?"

Elizabeth made reply.

"I think because he can claim a previous acquaintance with Mr. Wickham, he may know where to find him, so we may hope of a positive outcome, what do you think?"

Still Elizabeth remained silent, but heaved a heavy sigh. Then Jane called her name in question.

"Lizzie?"

"Oh Jane, can you not see what this means? If they do not marry, and marry quickly, it will not only be Lydia who is disgraced, but all of us," Elizabeth cried in an exasperated tone.

"Do you think Mr. Bingley and Mr. Darcy will continue their address once our disgrace is made public? No, Lydia has ruined us all, and at the call of Wickham."

Elizabeth could see Jane was shocked by her outburst, and instantly regretted it. She held out her arms, and Jane came to her side and accepted her embrace.

"Oh, Lizzie, I cannot lose Mr. Bingley for a second time. I am not strong enough to bear the shame of being deserted twice by the same man. Do you really think the outcome will be the ruination of us all?" Jane cried.

"Let us hope Mr. Darcy is successful in his endeavour dearest," was all the encouragement Elizabeth could offer.

Elizabeth loved her mother and all her sisters, but she was not naive enough to think her mother had not encouraged Lydia to enjoy herself to the fullest extent. She also knew Lydia to be a wilful and spoilt girl, and as the youngest their mother had indulged her to excess. But to run off in the middle of the night, with no thought to the consequences it would have on her family, was the epitome of selfishness. With only two weeks to her wedding, Elizabeth wondered if indeed she would be a bride. She hugged her sister once more, and then picking up the tray, and making her way back to the library.

They asked Hill to go to Meryton in their stead, as they did not want to be importuned by the neighbours, and she duly obliged. A few shop keepers did ask when the young ladies would return, but only because their profits had suffered since they went to Brighton. Therefore, all was ready by nightfall, and it was a sombre house that waited the return of its mistress.

The carriage came to a halt at the front of the house, and Elizabeth ran down the stairs to meet it, almost colliding with Jane. Together they opened the door, and went out to greet their mother and sisters. Elizabeth had resolved not to cry, there would surely be more than enough tears from her mother. She was proved correct in her assumption, for as soon as Mrs. Bennet alighted from the carriage she began to wail.

"Oh Lizzie, Jane, what are we to do, what is to become of us. That wicked girl will be the undoing of all of us. If your father finds them he will surely challenge Wickham to a duel and be killed, and then what will become of us. I'll tell you what, that odious man Collins will turn us out before the night falls, mark my words. Oh, my poor nerves, I have such a flutter in my stomach I cannot tell you. Hill, Hill, where is that woman, Hill."

"Come mama, we must remain hopeful until we know otherwise, and Papa has not gone to London, he is in the library. Tis Mr. Darcy who has journeyed to town in the hope of recovering Lydia," Jane said, trying to calm her distraught mother.

Mrs. Bennet leant heavily on Jane's arm for support, until Hill appeared to help her off with her coat and bonnet.

"Do not mention her name to me, and what is this you are saying? Mr. Bennet does not go to find his own daughter, but sends Mr. Darcy in his stead? I never heard such a thing, the nerve of that man. Oh it is all most vexing."

Mrs. Bennet seemed to have recovered her usual demeanour momentarily, and Elizabeth turned to Jane and asked quietly,

"The nerve of which man, Papa or Mr. Darcy?"

On entering the parlour, Jane sent Hill to bring her mother some tea, while Kitty and Mary, who had so far been silent, quietly greeted their sisters. Elizabeth took pity on them after having to bear witness to their mothers lamenting all the way from Brighton. Deciding they would welcome some time away from her, Elizabeth offered them an escape.

"Mary, Kitty you look tired and a little dusty from your journey. You should go and rest awhile, but join us for supper."

This would give them some time free, from the continuous grieving they all knew Mrs. Bennet would indulge in, until the matter was resolved. They gave her a silent 'thank you,' and quickly headed to their room.

"I must also take to my bed, for I feel a faint coming on, quick girl get my salts," said Mrs. Bennet to no-one in particular.

Jane and Lizzie both knew their mama's health to be robust, but she was apt to use this excuse as a way to escape her responsibilities.

"Then I will have a dish of tea sent up to you mama, and Jane will bring your salts," Elizabeth said as she guided her mother toward the stairs.

"And some of Hill's delicious fruitcake. Do not forget the fruitcake, for I am half-starved. The inn we stopped at served us very ill, very ill indeed," Mrs. Bennet lamented as she made her way up the stairs.

"Oh Jane, what a mess; I fear neither of our parents are going to be much help in resolving this matter."

"But what can we do Lizzie? We cannot go to town and search ourselves?" Jane said.

"No Jane, but if Mr. Darcy is unsuccessful, we must resign ourselves to retiring from society, to bear the disgrace the best we can. Let us hope he is effective."

This was all the reply Elizabeth could muster.

## CHAPTER 17

Darcy made good time and managed to get to town just after nightfall. He instructed Miller not to replace the knocker on the front door, thus not announcing he was in residence. Weary and covered in mud, he needed a bath and some food, but first he must write a letter. He instructed Miller to send a tray to his room and have a bath filled. Jennings could valet for him until Fletcher arrived tomorrow. Miller was one of his father's servants, but there had never been any thought of replacing him. His arrival at Airwhile House was a surprise, but Miller acted as if it was the most natural thing in the world.

Darcy sat behind the green, leather topped desk in his study, and began composing a letter Col. Fitzwilliam.

*Airwhile House*
*London*
*December 4th 1811*

*Richard,*
*Forgive the intrusion, but I am in need of your assistance with an urgent and sensitive matter. Time is of the essence and discretion vital. Come to Airwhile House tomorrow for breakfast, I will reveal all then. My future happiness depends on its outcome.*
*Your cousin,*
*FD*

He would offer him breakfast, and then explained the situation. They could then plan the next step together, although in truth Darcy had devised a plan on his journey. The grumbling of his stomach reminded him he had not eaten since breakfast at Netherfield. He rang for Miller and instructed him to send one of the stable lads to deliver the letter tonight. Wearily, he climbed the stairs to bed.

Sitting in his dressing gown, bathed and refreshed, he picked at the food on the tray before him. The cold meat, pickles and fresh crusty bread, were accompanied by a small selection of fruit, and a pot of hot tea. Normally an ideal supper, but he was not thinking of food tonight, he was thinking of Elizabeth. That morning he had decided to ride over early and visit with her, but they had barely had time to exchange pleasantries, before a messenger arrived with the express from Col. Forster. She had taken it directly to her father, and waited while he read it. The look on his face was enough to prompt her to take the missive from his hand, and read it aloud. Darcy had followed her to the doorway, and listened as she narrated its contents. He had witnessed first-hand the impact it had on the three people in the room. He felt their need justified him overstepping the boundaries of politeness, and he entered the room. Clearly they were all in shock, but only its timing had surprised him. Having been through such a thing at Wickham's hand before, Darcy knew better than anyone what needed to be done.

He had grown tired of cleaning up after Wickham, and although he owed him nothing, it seemed George's jealousy would never be sated. He could not rule out the possibility that Bingley would also be asked to pay.

Fatigue washed over him, and he pushed the tray away and went to his bed. Tomorrow he would put into motion the plan he had devised, to recover the foolish chit, but tonight he needed to rest.

Darcy told Miller that he was expecting an early caller, and that they would breakfast together, so when Col. Fitzwilliam arrived, he was shown directly into the breakfast room. Darcy was already waiting for him and said,.

"Richard, good of you to come on such short notice."

Darcy put his coffee down, and shook his cousin's hand in a firm shake.

"Come, let us talk over breakfast." He turned to the footmen and continued, "We will serve ourselves, thank you."

Once alone, and seated with a hearty breakfast in front of them, Richard turned to Darcy and questioned him.

"So Darcy, what's this cloak and dagger meeting about? Your note was enticing but uninformative," he said, whilst savouring the expensive blend of coffee Darcy preferred.

"As you know, I have recently become engaged to Miss Elizabeth Bennet. She has several younger sisters, and lately they have been visiting Brighton and enjoying the attention of the Militia. The youngest of these sisters, Miss Lydia Bennet, has been convinced to elope by one of the officers," He paused before saying the name of the man Richard despised almost, as much as he did.

"With George Wickham."

Richard glared at Darcy then replied,

"This is grave indeed Darcy. Is it certain they have not gone to Scotland?" Darcy nodded, and Richard continued,

"So Wickham has found another way to get to you dear cousin. I now see the urgency of the matter, how may I help. Do you know where they are holed up?"

"No, that is where I thought you might be able to assist me. Not that I am denigrating your men at all, but I understand they are apt to frequent the more unsavoury establishments, that Wickham's pocket will run to," Darcy replied as he refilled his cup.

"No offence taken," Richard said acceptingly, I will set four of my most trusted, yet dissolute men on discovering his whereabouts. What are your plans Fitz?"

"I will be following another line of enquiry. Do you remember Mrs. Younge? I imagine she will be involved in this somewhere, as with Georgiana. If I find her, I believe she may be easily persuaded to give up her accomplice, for a price of course. I have a purse of fifty guineas to take with me. We must move with all speed on this Richard; they have been gone three days already." Richard nodded as he took another mouthful of coffee before asking,

"How does the Bennet family fair after this news?"

"Mr. Bennet is somewhat ineffectual, and Mrs. Bennet and the two other daughters return to Longbourn today. I fear Elizabeth and Jane will bear the brunt of things, for they are the only ones with any wits about them. I wanted to stay and assist them, but I can be more effective here, and besides, even I cannot be in two places at once." Darcy sighed.

They finished their repast, and then Richard left to start the search for Wickham. Darcy meanwhile, went directly to the agent he had hired Mrs. Younge from.

Darcy exited the man's office with the last known address for Mrs. Younge in his pocket. He had not wanted to give it up without some form of monetary remuneration, but with a very angry Darcy towering over him, he saw the error of his ways. He quickly copied the address onto a scrap of paper, and nervously placed it in Darcy's waiting hand. Once outside he climbed back into the hackney carriage Miller had hailed for him. He recited the address to the driver, and the carriage lurched into motion. The lady in question had somehow secured enough funds to purchase a house in the city. It was in a rundown area, but apparently she earned an income by renting out the rooms. As they neared his destination, the driver slowed the horse to a walk, and then leant down to ask,

"Begging 'ur pardon governor, but are you sure you want me to take you to this address? It's not a place for the likes of you, sir."

He pulled at his cap in deference to Darcy's station. He was probably only in his thirties, but looked much older, and his clothes although clean, had definitely seen better days.

"Yes, quite sure, thank you. Stop a few doors before and wait for me, there will be a guinea in it for you."

He knew he was tipping the man more than he could earn in a month. But it was a small price to pay not to be stranded in this unsavoury neighbourhood.

"Right you are governor."

The driver's eyes lit up at the prospect of such a tip. He drew the horse to a stop about twenty yards from the house, and jumped down to open the door for Darcy, while pulling the cap from his head.

As he walked the few paces to the house, he took stock of his surroundings. The stench from the open sewers assaulted his nostrils, and women of easy virtue loitered in the shadows and doorways. The buildings were run-down, and the signs of overcrowding were all around. Rubbish and litter abounded, and street urchins were begging off anyone not dressed in rags. The house itself was solid in foundation, with the lower half being brick-built, but the upper floors were made of timber, and covered with flaking paint and grime from years of neglect. The windows were small, and the glass was filthy, yet there appeared to be some semblance of curtains hanging, probably to forestall prying eyes. Darcy stood as close to the door as he could without actually touching it, then rapped several times with his cane. Presently the door opened, and there before him stood Mrs. Younge. She tried to shut the door in his face, but Darcy was too quick. Putting his foot in the frame, he placed his gloved hand on the door, and then with little effort on his part, forced it open and entered.

"Madam I see your fortunes have changed since last we met?" He said in a sardonic drawl as he removed his hat. She was looking every inch her forty years he thought. Her dress appeared to be several seasons old, and was covered with a sallow, grey apron. Also, he noticed she had taken to, or maybe resumed, the wearing of rouge on her cheeks. It clogged into her wrinkled skin and pores, giving her a ghoulish burnt look.

"It is hard to find a position without references, as you well know Mr. Darcy," she said venomously.

Not wanting to linger any longer than need be, Darcy came straight to the point.

"Well, maybe we can find some financial remedy for any inconvenience you have suffered, imaginary or otherwise," he said quietly, as he reluctantly rested his hat on a dusty side table.

"I'm listening," she said.

As I suspected! Darcy thought; her loyalty *can* be brought, so much for honour amongst thieves.

"I am looking for a mutual acquaintance of ours Mrs. Younge. George Wickham, do you know where he is?"

He feigned indifference as he inspected the silver lion's head on his cane.

"I might," she replied.

His need meant there could be the possibility to make some easy money, she thought. It would serve him right, and recompense her for how he had dismissed her last year, with no reference and no wages.

"I will give you," he paused, and looked her up and down as if mulling her worth, "ten pounds to reveal his whereabouts, and to sooth any injuries your reputations may have suffered."

Knowing this was more money than she could earn in a year renting out rooms, he was still not surprised when she asked for more.

"Twenty and not a penny less; that is what it will cost you to loosen my tongue sir, and I prefer guineas," she said greedily.

"Very well guineas. I will give you half now, and the remainder when I have confirmed your information. But, and mark my words well, if you forewarn Wickham and he runs, not only will I not honour the second payment, but I will summons the police and have you brought before a magistrate, is that clear?"

His eyes narrowed as he waited her reply. She knew he would carry out his threat, and decided if she gave up Wickham she could keep the whole twenty guineas for herself. Besides, Wickham had become a liability; always drunk and ranting on about how Darcy had ruined his life, and plotting revenge. It had grown tiresome.

"Quite clear sir, Wickham is a liability, and a drunkard, I am done with him."

Darcy pulled out the purse he had filled before leaving Grosvenor Square. She held out her hand, but Darcy would not relinquish it until he had an address. Only then did he place the coins into her out-stretched palm.

The address safely in his possession he started to walk towards the waiting hackney carriage when he heard her shout,

"My regards to Miss. Darcy."

And as she slammed the door he could hear her laughing. Momentarily his steps faltered, and he gripped his cane till it left an impression in the leather of his glove. Keep walking, he told himself, just keep walking. Once inside the carriage he asked the driver to take him to Richard's headquarters, where he left a pre-scribed note and waited. A few moments later Richard bounded down the steps and joined him in the carriage.

"You have some intelligence, what have you discovered?" Richard asked.

"Mrs. Younge was most willing to give up Wickham's whereabouts for twenty guineas, and although it is not a fortune, it is worth every penny if correct. I am going there directly, but I need to request some assistance from you cousin."

"Name it and it shall be yours."

"Thank you. What I would ask is that you have this address discreetly watched, just in case Wickham tries to flee. You can appreciate with my wedding so close, I cannot waste time having to search for him a second time."

Darcy showed Richard the scrap of paper with the address on. The name and location of the tavern where the couple was hiding stood out. On seeing it Richard let out a low whistle.

"My God Darcy, he has taken a young gentlewoman to this place! It is vile, full of bad uns to be sure. I will have my men in place in thirty minutes; you must wait until then for I cannot in good conscience, let you go there until it is secure."

Darcy bowed to Richard's superior knowledge of the seedier side of London, and agreed to his request to wait.

Col. Fitzwilliam dashed back inside and quickly made the arrangements, while Darcy idled in the carriage. When all was prepared, Richard returned and climbed in next to him.

"I will broach no argument Darcy, I am coming with you. I will stay concealed if that is your wish, but I am coming," he said firmly.

Darcy knew there was no point in trying to convince him otherwise, and in truth he was pleased to have an ally by his side. Then he told the driver of their new destination.

"But guvnor, this is worse than the last place; I cannot take a gentleman like you to this cesspool!"

"I thank you for your concern driver, but this is where I must go, and now. With all haste, my good man," Darcy replied.

With a shake of his head and a heavy sigh, he cracked the reins and encouraged the horses to pick up the pace. Even he, a humble working man, would not frequent an establishment like this. Known for attracting the lowest forms of life from across the city, it was unchallenged in the depths of depravity concealed within. Every robber, con-man and trickster would know a welcome within its walls, and even highway men and murderer we left unquestioned and unchallenged. He wondered if he should ask for his guinea now.

# CHAPTER 18

Even before they reached the doorway of the designated hostelry, the smell and noise accosted their senses. Groups of men in various states of drunkenness littered the street; some were squatting down playing dice, while others dallied with women of easy virtue. The driver had reluctantly dropped them off at the corner of the street, and again Darcy secured the cabbie's services to wait for them. As they approached the entrance, a man fell backwards out of the door, and lay sprawled on the path before them, barely missing Darcy's feet. He had clearly been engaged in a brawl. Darcy looked at Richard, who had refused to wait in the cab, and then back to the prostrate man, who had now begun to crawl away on all fours. He was thankful that Richard, wearing his sword and with two pistols tucked in his belt, had ignored him and insisted he would be at Darcy's side throughout.

They ducked to navigate the low entrance, and slowly made their way to the bar. The floor was sticky and covered in grime, and the biting stench of stale beer and urine filled the air. Momentarily the din abated, as many eyes took in the new visitors. Once they were certain it was not the runners they became disinterested, and the noise rose once more. They made it to the counter without being further accosted, only to be eyed with suspicion by the man serving behind the bar. His shining bald head was white in comparison to his red, sweat covered face. He wiped the rough wooden surface with a small, stained rag, and then raised it to mop his brow. Darcy observed his large hands; they were filthy, and the knuckles were torn and scabbed from fighting. Not wishing to be here any longer than necessary, he spoke to the man.

"I am looking for a friend of mine, and have been informed he has taken lodgings within, Mr. George Wickham, is he here?"

Toffs! The owner inwardly scoffed, men like these never came into his establishment unless they wanted something, and desperately. Perhaps there was a chance to make some easy coinage, he surmised.

"Well well, friends of Georgie boy are you? I should have believed him when 'e said 'e 'ad friends in the high places. I *might* have information you would be interested in, but at a price. First you settle his bill," he replied menacingly, not wanting to miss the opportunity to recoup Wickham's unpaid board and lodgings.

Darcy placed five shillings on the beer stained bar, and looked at the man with a raised eyebrow. Grabbing the coins, he brought them to his mouth, biting hard on them.

"You ain't the first gents to come looking for Georgie boy this morning, though the others were not of a mind to be as sociable. Three others came about an hour ago. Very reluctant to go he was, and there was quite a scuffle." He laughed revealing the loss of several teeth.

Darcy looked at Richard and raised his brows. Richard stepped forward and took over the questioning.

"I understand part of being a good innkeeper, is to know all that goes on under one's roof?" Giving him no time to reply, Richard continued, "so if you can enlighten us further, I am sure that my friend here would be willing to match his already generous gift."

The innkeeper eyed Darcy expectantly, so he nodded his assent and pulled out a further five coins, but he held his palm out of the man's reach. He looked at the coins, and then back at Darcy who had again raised his brows, signalling for him to continue. He glared at Darcy and gave a feral scowl, but continues with his tale.

"I believe they were here in regard to Georgie Boys involvement with a young lady, more precisely the loss of her virtue. He tried to buy them off, insisting he could reimburse them if only they would wait, give him some time, but they were in no mood for talking. They were most insistent if you get my drift, and even through his protests, they dragged him out and into their carriage. I did catch mention of satisfaction being demanded."

He thrust out his hand and Darcy, distracted by his words, handed over his reward. Darcy and Richard looked at each other in disbelief. If Wickham had been 'called out,' there was only one place to go, and although time was of the essence, they must first locate Lydia. Richard turned back to the man with the rugged face.

"And his traveling companion, what of her?"

"Oh, you mean miss high and bloody mighty; well she is still in her room, and has been sending down her demands all morning. You're welcome to remove that baggage any day of the week."

Darcy made for the stairs with Richard on his heels.

"First on the right," the innkeeper called and went back to his business.

Now standing outside the door Darcy, looked to his cousin. Richard held his hands up and took a step back, intimating for Darcy to go in alone. He made a wry grimace, turned and tapped softly on the door.

Lydia ran to the door and opened it, hoping Wickham had returned, but her disappointed was evident when she saw Darcy standing there.

"Lord, what are you doing here, is George with you?" she said, and peered over his shoulder. Realising Wickham was not with them, she flounced back into her room. Darcy gave an inward sigh as he entered; as usual she speaks without thinking, he thought. He made sure the door was wedged open for propriety's sake, before removing his hat to give Lydia a curt bow.

"Miss Bennet," he said.

Lydia had walked back to the window, and was looked down at the street. She turned back to acknowledge his greeting with a slight curtsy, then said,

"I am at a loss as to why you are here Mr. Darcy; I cannot think George would be pleased to find you here, for he speaks of you very ill. Unless you have seen him, did he send you to fetch me?"

"No Miss Bennet, I have not seen Wickham," Darcy replied.

"Oh. Should I be concerned do you think, he has been gone an absolute age? Some very rude men came to speak to him this morning, and my dear Wickham was pressed into going with them. They were very rude and most insistent. They would not listen when he offered them reassurance that his finances were about to improve. Are you sure you have no word of him, he promised we could visit the shops today?"

She walked towards him twisting the ribbons on her dress, and Darcy noted the genuine concern on her face. I must tread with care he thought, if indeed her emotions are engaged. Though he knew her to be a wilful and spoilt child, if he was to get the desired outcome, it was imperative he did not agitate her. Using a soft, low tone, he said,

"Miss Bennet, I am aware of the circumstances of Mr. Wickham's departure, and I too am concerned for him. I feel it would be beneficial for all, if we located him as quickly as possible. I know it will be frowned upon for you to ride in the carriage with two single gentlemen, but in the absence of another female, I fear it is the only recourse open to us. Will you come?" he urged.

"I will Mr Darcy, but only so that I can be reunited with my dear Wickham," she replied petulantly.

She pulled on her bonnet, and let Darcy slip her thick winter cloak around her shoulders, then walked through the open door, leaving Darcy to follow. Richard fell into step as they made their way downstairs, then all three of them climbed into the waiting hackney carriage.

As they headed to Green Park, the driver cracked the whip to encourage the horse to travel at greater speed, making the journey swift but uncomfortable. Through necessity, they sat in silence, holding on as the carriage lurched from side to side. It took all the drivers skill to navigate the ruts, and holes in the road. Darcy knew a few of his more impulsive friends had been involved in duels, fortunately, all but one had survived, but he had a bad feeling about this. If, as Mrs. Younge had intimated, Wickham was more often than not in his cups, he would be no match against a sober opponent, even a poor marksman. Oh, Wickham was a fair shot, and comfortable handling firearms from his time at Pemberley, but any man's aim would be affected while under the influence of alcohol. As they entered the park, they found it almost deserted due to the inclement weather, and so made swift time to the clearing in the woods. It was a favourite place for men to settle their differences, secluded, and away from prying eyes. As they approached, Darcy could make out a form lying on the frost-bitten grass. He called to the driver to stop short. Fearing the worst, he turned to Richard, though his speech was intended for Lydia also,

"Richard, would you wait with Miss Lydia while I step out, I will be but a moment?"

The gravity in his tone told Col. Fitzwilliam it was serious. Turning to Lydia and leaning closer, he gently spoke.

"I would be honoured if Miss Bennet would permit me to wait with her."

Flattered that two distinguished gentlemen were being so attentive, she gave a childish giggle and nodded her assent. Darcy pulled his great-coat tighter, hoping to ward off the biting December wind. Reluctantly, he made his way towards the dark form on the frozen turf. As he drew near, he could see it was a man, and his feeling of dread intensified. The face was turned down towards the grass, and as Darcy knelt down, he reached out and touched the body. It was still warm. Gently, he pulled on the shoulder, until it rolled to face up. He saw the familiar features of his childhood friend, staring up at the grey winter sky, his eyes open, but now unseeing. The dark red stain on his white shirt, attested to a shot through the heart, thankfully death would have been instant. Beside him lay a pistol, the shot unfired, and a lady's handkerchief had been stuffed into his waistband. Pulling it out, Darcy saw it was embroidered in green and pink, the initials MK stark again the brilliant white lace. He slipped it into his own coat pocket, no point in risking more scandal or questions than need be. Then he saw Wickham's pocket watch, or to be more precise, Darcy's fathers pocket watch. As he retrieved it, he realised removing it from the corpse, was a sad way to reclaim what was rightfully his. Even with all the heartache, deceit, and dishonour Wickham had created, Darcy was still saddened to see such a promising life extinguished prematurely. He ran his hand over Wickham's eyelids, and closed his eyes for the last time. With leaden steps he walked back to the waiting carriage and opened the door.

"I am afraid I must make use of the blanket Miss Lydia," he said, retrieving the cover from around her knees.

He closed the door and called to the driver to alight.

"Make haste to fetch a constable." he said.

Seeing him hesitate, Darcy shouted at him,

"Jump to it man here, a sign of my goodwill and security on your property," and he thrust the promised guinea into his hand.

Darcy walked back and gently placed the blanket over Wickham's body. With a heavy heart he thought, how did it come to this George? Remembering the days of their youth when they would run to the lake, fishing rods in hand, to catch a trout for tea, or eating unripe apples from the orchard, until they were confined to bed with a belly ache. Where had it all gone wrong? Perhaps, allowing him to mix with his betters had created the festering jealousy that seemed to drive him to excess. Straightening up, he filled his lungs with the crisp morning air. He must now break the news to Lydia. Squaring his shoulders, Darcy trudged back to the carriage to begin the unpleasant task.

"Richard, I need to speak to Miss Bennet, would you mind if I had a moment alone?" and he raised his brows to signal for him to go.

Richard understood Darcy's reason, and alighted from the carriage. Taking a seat opposite the quiet young woman, Darcy realised she was just a frightened child who had been left to run wild. If her affections were truly engaged in regard to Wickham, then this would be a hard blow indeed. He leant forward, and gently took her gloved hands into his.

"Miss Bennet, there are times in life when we have to be very brave, and I fear this is just such a time. I wish I could spare you what I am about to impart, but I cannot."

He saw her eyes brim with tears, and decided it would be kinder to let Wickham remain a hero in her eyes.

"It seems George was defending your honour, and has been fatally wounded."

He watched as a tear silently trickle down her pale cheek.

"I am afraid he did not survive his injuries," Darcy concluded.

Knowing Lydia's character, he thought there might be histrionics, or even screaming at this news, but this quiet sobbing was not on his agenda.

"He loved me deeply do you think Mr. Darcy?" She asked in an almost inaudible voice.

"Oh yes Miss Lydia," he said softly, "to be willing to risk one's life for another, speaks of a love most profound," he replied, saying what he knew she needed to hear.

"Come; let me take you to your Aunt Gardiner's house for tonight. Tomorrow we will journey home to Longbourn together."

Lydia dabbed at her eyes, and nodded her agreement.

# CHAPTER 19

Darcy and Richard took Lydia directly to the Gardiner's house in Gracechurch Street. On their arrival, Darcy handed the letter from Mr. Bennet to the maid, and was then quickly ushered into the parlour. Mrs. Gardiner, having also read the letter, immediately took Lydia's hand and guided her upstairs.

"Goodness me girl, you must come and bathe and change out of those clothes immediately. You have the smell of a tavern about you and it is not pleasant!"

Lydia went to protest, but thought better of it when she saw the scowl on her aunt's face.

The two cousins followed Mr. Gardiner into his study, and then apprised him of recent events. He agreed that Lydia should return home with all alacrity, and he would provide a maid to travel with them. Some minutes later the maid entered with a message from Mrs. Gardiner. It appeared that Miss Bennet was concerned about her belongings, having left her newest bonnet at the inn. Darcy immediately volunteered Fitzwilliam and himself to collect them, broaching no argument from Mr. Gardiner, and they left directly.

"Why could we not send a couple of my men to collect the chit's baggage Darcy? It is not a place one should visit twice in a lifetime, never mind twice in a day!" Richard moaned.

Darcy looked at his cousin through drawn eyes and replied,

"I must ease something that is troubling my mind Richard, something the innkeeper said. When directing us to Miss Bennet he said, 'she is in her room,' not their room, but *her* room. If there is a chance her virtue is intact, I have to make certain before I speak to the Gardiners again."

Richard understood the importance of this, for the young woman's future prospects, and that of her sisters, hinged on this information, and could impact on Darcy's engagement to Elizabeth. So Richard held his tongue, all the while cursing Wickham under his breath. They travelled the last few streets in silence, until Darcy bade the driver pull up at the same spot as before. He knew it would cost him more coinage, but he must know the truth.

The innkeeper was only too willing to give Darcy the information he needed, and once rewarded, he was more than willing to oblige. Wickham had indeed taken two sets of rooms, and even requested that they were not adjoining. While in his cups, which was daily, he had made it clear to all who would listen that he could not stand the silly, giggling and often petulant chit. Often he loudly broadcast that he was biding his time, until a rich acquaintance paid him a handsome ransom for her. He had no doubt that with her charms, she could make a living in some way, and he laughed crudely. His implication was clear to all. It seemed elopement, blackmail, and desertion was

Wickham's preferred method of supplementing his income.

As Darcy listened, his mood darkened, until he was blind with rage, at both Wickham and himself. To have his worst fears about the blaggard confirmed was nearly his undoing, but at least Wickham was true to his character. Darcy berated himself. He called himself a gentleman, yet *his* silence had put Lydia where she was, *his* pride had caused Elizabeth and her family untold pain and anguish, and *his* arrogance had made him think he was impervious to anything Wickham could concoct. How wrong he had been. Wickham found the one thing Darcy cherished above all else, even Georgiana. His aim was to taint and defile Elizabeth by association, and he had almost succeeded. It was best he was dead, Darcy thought angrily, for only Lydia will mourn his passing.

Having collected Lydia's belongings and the few meagre possessions left in Wickham's room, he re-joined Fitzwilliam in the carriage. Richard recognised and understood Darcy's pain and anger, and shared his sentiment. The few times he had witnessed his cousin in such a rage, had taught him it was best to leave him be. In time he would talk through his anguish, and come out stronger for it.

They returned to Gracechurch Street where Darcy revealed his conversation with the innkeeper to the Gardiner's and Richard. As the subject was of the most delicate nature, it was agreed Mrs. Gardiner would try to ascertain the truth from Lydia. The three men took it in turns to sit or pace the room, until after almost an hour had elapsed, and Mrs. Gardiner rejoined them. Her face was flushed from having to discuss such an indelicate subject, but she had coaxed the girl into revealing all. Thankfully, Darcy's suspicions had been correct; Wickham had been either too drunk or disinclined to consummate their relationship. Lydia was still a maid. The relief in the room was palpable. Embarrassed, they moved on swiftly, arranging to collect Lydia and the maid the next morning. Meanwhile Mr. Gardiner would send an express to his brother-in-law, informing him of their imminent arrival. Satisfied they had done all they could for now, Darcy and Richard returned to Airwhile House.

After a hot bath and a change of clothes, they met in the salon for a pre-dinner drink. Darcy informed Richard of the brief conversation he had had with the constables at Green Park. They seemed to readily accept Darcy's conclusion that it was suicide, though the location of the wound would belie this. In truth, they were not inclined to follow-up another case of toff's duelling over honour. Leaving him to dispose of the body, they could then mark the case as solved with very little effort to them. Darcy had then arranged for his personal physician to contact the undertakers, who would then collect Wickham's body. Mindful of their past connection and once friendship, he felt he could do no less than give Wickham a decent burial. He would commission his London steward to accompany the body back to Pemberley, and there have George lay to rest with his parents. He could have made the journey himself, but he intended to escort Elizabeth to a pre wedding ball being given at Lucas Lodge. Richard offered to go in his stead, but Darcy declined, insisting he did not want Wickham to disrupt his life anymore, not even for this one last time. After dinner they returned to the library, and over several brandies discussed the events of the day. Both agreed Lydia was a very fortunate girl, and Wickham's early death had in many ways been inevitable. Jubilant in their success, they retired to bed.

The next morning Darcy was surprised to see Richard ready to travel with him, rather than returning to his regiment.

"Good morning Richard, do I take it you are to accompany us to the shires?"

"I am if it is agreeable with you Darcy, wouldn't want to leave you to the mercies of Miss Bennet don't you know," he replied jovially.

Raising a quizzical brow, Darcy eyed his cousin, but said nothing.

"Truthfully old man, who would pass up the opportunity to spend a few extra days in the company of the charming Miss Elizabeth, besides I admit to a certain amount of curiosity as to how Miss Lydia will fair once she's back home'"

"As you wish," Darcy replied stoically.

Directly after breakfast the men went to collect Lydia. Darcy waited at the carriage door for Lydia, who came out and kissed her aunt and uncle goodbye and then walked towards him. She accepted his hand

and gave him a brief glance from under her bonnet, then began giggling as she quickly averted her gaze. Oh Lord, he thought, this is going to be a long journey. Darcy thanked the Gardiners for all their help and bid them farewell.

Once on their way Col. Fitzwilliam quickly fell asleep, leaving Darcy to exchange acceptable pleasantries with both ladies. Darcy concluded that an inescapable carriage ride was the perfect location to try to illicit some explanation from Lydia for her actions.

"Miss Lydia, may I ask you about George and yourself?" he asked discreetly.

She turned and glanced at the young maid sitting next to her, who then acknowledged her unspoken request, and moved a little closer to the window, thus affording them a greater degree of privacy. Leaning forward, Lydia said,

"The pain is still acute Mr. Darcy, but talking of my dear Wickham may ease it. What is it you wish to know?"

"Miss Lydia, I take it Wickham did propose to you before you left Brighton?"

"Lord of course he did Mr. Darcy! I may be only fifteen, but I do have some understanding of the proprieties. George promised me I would be the first of my sisters to be married. They do pick on me dreadfully you know? I think it is because I am the prettiest, and they are all jealous of me. Anyway, dear George mentioned what a hoot it would be whilst still in Meryton. It was not until we journeyed to Brighton, that we had the opportunity to put our plan into action. He said *you* especially would find it amusing. I told him I thought you too stuffy to appreciate such a lark, but he said the irony would not be lost on you, whatever that means. Also, once you and Lizzie are married, you and I will be brother and sister in earnest. You of all people would find it most diverting, that he had at last managed to get one of your sisters to the altar," she giggled, but his meaning was lost on her.

She could not imagine the impact her words had on him. Still, Darcy thought, even now from beyond the grave Wickham taunts me. Closing his eyes, he took a calming breath and said,

"I am at a loss as to why you stopped in London then madam, why did you not journey directly to Gretna Green? Surely you knew the impropriety of such an action?"

"Well we would have journeyed straight to Scotland, and I confess I thought that was our direction, but George insisted we rest for a few days before going on to Gretna Green. He said he had to collect additional funds from an acquaintance in town, and then we might buy new clothes for the ceremony. But he did let me purchase this bonnet, do you not think it suits me. I confess it was quite ugly when I bought it, but I have added a few ribbons to match my gown, do you see? I thought I might as well have it as not."

She pulled her cloak aside to expose her dark blue traveling dress. Darcy nodded while his mind toiled. He had been correct; he *was* the intended blackmail target. Was she truly that naive to think Wickham was the lover he portrayed? Clearly so;

"We will be stopping for refreshments, will we not Mr. Darcy, for Lord I am famished. Are you not famished too?" she asked turning to the maid.

Yes, it was going to be a long journey, Darcy thought!

Not soon enough for Darcy they arrived in Hertfordshire. They dropped Col. Fitzwilliam off at Netherfield, and then Darcy's carriage went on to Longbourn. Lydia's incessant chattering had continued the whole distance, and Darcy was thankful when the groomsman jumped down and opened the carriage door. Mrs. Bennet ran out to greet Lydia as if she was merely returning from a day out.

"Lydia, dearest, you must be frozen, come inside and warm yourself by the fire. I am longing for you to tell me all about your adventure, and where is Mr. Wickham? I must greet my new son-in-law," she effused.

"Madam, it has been a trying journey and Miss Lydia is in need of the comfort of her room without delay," Darcy said sternly.

He caught Elizabeth's eye and tossed his head, indicating for her to remove Lydia from her mother's grasps. Understanding his direction, Elizabeth walked over to the women and spoke quietly to her sister.

"Come Lydia, you must be fatigued, let us see to your comfort. We can go to your room, and I will brush your hair while we wait for Hill to arrange you a bath. Then Jane can bring you some hot chocolate and warm muffins."

As Elizabeth steered her towards the stairs, Darcy caught part of Lydia's reply.

"It *has* been a particularly hard week Lizzie. I had no chance to go to the fashionable shops in town, even though Wickham promised me we would. And then I had to ride home with boring old Mr Darcy of all people."

The temerity of the girl, after all he had done for her!

Darcy took a deep breath in readiness to address Mrs. Bennet's questions, but he was saved by the appearance of her husband.

"Cease your prattling woman and listen hard. I have matters to discuss with Mr. Darcy and you will await my summons on the hall chair. Should you choose to disobey my directive, you will suffer the full extent of my displeasure. Do you understand?" he said in a cold, angry tone. Turning to Darcy he continued,

"Follow me lad, and you two girls go to the kitchen and assist Hill with something," he said addressing Mary and Kitty, who quickly scuttled off out of sight.

Once safely ensconced in the privacy of the library, Mr. Bennet turned to Darcy and said,

"Tell me all Sir, leave nothing out."

Darcy accepted the proffered chair and retold the events of his time in London, feeling acutely uncomfortable when imparting his final findings.

"It has been confirmed to Mrs Gardiner by Lydia herself, that relations between the runaways were not, accomplished shall we say."

Bitingly embarrassed to be discussing the girl's virtue with her father, Darcy hoped he had not been indelicate. He was then astounded by the directness of Mr. Bennet.

"Knowing Wickham as I do now, I am surprised she is still a maid, deflowering virgins seems to be his wont. I must find her a match, and quickly. Young Johnson from the neighbouring estate has had a hankering for her these last six months, but I thought her too young. Well, she has proved me wrong there. He is a good lad, pleasing to look at in a foppish sort of way and with fifteen hundred a year, that's more than enough to keep Lydia in bonnets and ribbons." Then addressing Darcy in an earnest tone he continued,

"I am indebted to you in many ways sir, and will probably never be able to repay you. Nevertheless you have my earnest thanks and gratitude for your assistance, and silence in this matter."

He rose and held out his hand. Darcy, who gauged the interview was over, shook his hand and went to leave, when he heard Mr. Bennet offer,

"You will do very well for my Lizzie, very well indeed."

Darcy knew these words were Mr. Bennet's seal of approval on their engagement, and he was satisfied. He felt they now shared a bond, and hopefully an ally in the Bennet household. As he closed the study, Darcy passed Mrs. Bennet, still seated in the hall. She was muttering about the way her husband had treated her in front of company. He gave her a brief nod then continued to the parlour to await Elizabeth's return.

"Madam, you will come in here, NOW," Mr. Bennet bellowed, finally re-establishing his position as head of the household. Darcy smiled, first Charles and now Mr. Bennet!

"Wickham is dead!" Elizabeth said as she took a seat next to Darcy. "I can scarce believe it. I admit to entertaining harsh thoughts of him these past weeks, but dead! And you think it was a duel?"

"I can only surmise that, going on what the inn keeper told me and the evidence when I arrived at Green Park. It is *the* fashionable place for duelling at the moment, and his watch and fob were intact, which would rule out robbery. The pistol by his hand had not been fired, and was still with the body."

He paused to show her the initialled handkerchief. The implication to Mary King was self-explanatory, and Elizabeth drew in a sharp breath.

"Your sister has been more fortunate than others. You say Lydia seems largely unaffected by events? I also determined that, which is good. I believe your father has formed an agreeable plan to secure her future. Hopefully all will be well."

Elizabeth lowered her eyes and spoke hesitantly.

"When I discovered whom she had eloped with, I thought we were all ruined. I feared that you might want to reconsider our engagement."

"You think my love for you could be so easily affected Elizabeth, what could the worst have been?" He raised her hand to his lips. "To be shunned by the Ton and forced to seek refuge at Pemberley until it had faded from memory?" He paused to place a few feather kisses along her wrist.

"Dearest Elizabeth, my heart would rejoice at having you all to myself," the delicate aroma of lavender that emanated from her skin invaded his senses, and he murmured. "How I have missed you."

"I missed you too," she returned shyly, a gentle blush coming to her cheeks.

Mortified that he had been unguarded enough to let the words slip from his lips, he froze,. Yet Elizabeth had professed to have missed him also? This was progress of the most positive and encouraging kind. He held her gaze and uncharacteristically sought reassurance.

"You missed me?"

"Yes, I missed you, as you have declared to have missed me," She reaffirmed. A crimson blush peek over his collar and she asked,

"What troubles you sir?"

"That my utterance was audible," he said, now feeling foolish.

Clearly he had not meant to speak aloud, and his discomfiture was evident. She, however, had been both pleased and touched at his declaration. Elizabeth, known to sometimes speak what should only be thought, understood how he felt. Unfortunately too much had been said to now ignore it. She had already acknowledged it with a reply. To ease his discomfiture she spoke again.

"We are adults, betrothed and hold each other in affection. Why in a little over a week we will share more than sentimental words sir. Let us not dwell negatively on words expressed with honest feeling. You declared to have missed me, and I have returned the compliment. Is it that you are shocked to hear that I have missed you Mr. Darcy? Maybe you would prefer I did not voice my emotions, but refrained from doing so, perhaps taking my example from Miss Bingley?" she teased.

Darcy knew she would never falsify her feelings to placate him; it was not her nature. Therefore, her words must be genuine and heartfelt.

"Indeed madam, I am pleasantly surprised, and welcome any and all affection that you offer me Miss Elizabeth," he replied, and smiled broadly.

The urge to take her in his arms and shower her with kisses engulf him. Hoping to expand on the conversation in a more pleasurable way, Darcy chanced,

"I wonder Miss Elizabeth, might you be inclined to brave the December chill and accompany me in a turnabout the gardens, to continue this debate?"

Knowing they would be afforded some privacy there, Elizabeth was intrigued as to what he had in mind; she was just about to accept his offer when her mother burst in.

"Oh Mr. Darcy, I just heard, such terrible news; poor Mr. Wickham dead, and before he could make my dear girl a bride! How fortunate that you should come to her aid. I cannot bear to think what would have happened to her otherwise. Lizzie ring for Hill to bring us some tea. Sit by me Mr. Darcy for I have many questions and Mr. Bennet was most unobliging." She patted the seat adjacent to her own. "Run along now Lizzie, Mr. Darcy is waiting," she said, effectively dismissing Elizabeth.

Elizabeth and Darcy exchanged rueful smiles. Yes, he is waiting, she thought but tis not for a dish of tea. Elizabeth closed the door behind her to the strains of Mrs. Bennet lamenting Wickham's demise.

# CHAPTER 20

**T**wo days before the wedding Mrs. Bennet called Elizabeth into the parlour. Sitting in her preferred chair, she bade Lizzie sit next to her. Elizabeth could see samples of material, and receipts for goods clutched in her hand. It appeared she could not completely escape the business of wedding planning.

"Now Lizzie, I know we agreed I would make all the arrangements and decisions for your wedding, but I thought you would want to know how diligently I have beavered on your behalf," She finished with a sniff.

Elizabeth had taken her father's council and agreed to whatever her mother wanted, thus keeping her from interrupting either Elizabeth's, and more importantly Mr. Bennet's usual routine. It had worked well until this morning when she had insisted Elizabeth show some interest. With the exception to her wedding gown, Elizabeth had happily let her mother make all the decisions. Truthfully, she knew her mother would ignore any advice or objections she offered.

Elizabeth listened assiduously while her mother shared the details of the menu, course by course, before moving on to her trousseau. She detailed every garment, and matched it with either a receipt or sample. Elizabeth sighed; her mother had obviously forgotten that she had insisted Lizzie check each item for their fit, and comfort when she sent them from Brighton. After two hours of smiling sweetly and nodding where expected, Elizabeth felt stifled, and her cheeks ached from smiling. Seeing her mama pause, she took the opportunity to say,

"Mama, I knew by leaving the arrangements to you they would be in the most capable of hands. Your skill and knowledge of all things needed for such a celebration, far exceeds anyone else's in my acquaintance. I will enjoy my wedding day knowing each oyster or lark is the finest to be had, my clothes the most stylish, and the decorations the most beautiful. It was exceedingly thoughtful of you to remove this burden from me, and I will take pleasure in the fact that all will run smoothly, because of you."

Hearing herself speak these words Elizabeth realised her gratitude was indeed earnest.

"Well yes, that was of course my aim," Mrs. Bennet replied.

Though she did feel a tinge of embarrassment at the compliment paid her. In truth, she had enjoyed it immensely; it had filled her days and brought back vivid memories of her own joyous wedding day.

"Also I am well versed in the art of negotiation and you are not as yet Elizabeth. I have needed it with many of the tradesmen too. Once they knew how deep your father's pockets were in regard to your nuptials, some tried to increase their prices three-fold. I was most severe on them," she said with a wag of her finger "I reminded them I have five daughters to wed, and if they wanted our continued custom they must adjust their prices accordingly," she added indignantly.

Lizzie smiled and nodded in acknowledgement of her mother's efforts, then went to rise and make her exit. Unfortunately, her mama had not finished and began to address her again.

"And so, you may be confident that everything that can be prepared in advance has been so. Even your trousseau has been packed in readiness for its journey north."

"Mr. Darcy will be pleased to hear this, I will tell him with all haste," said Elizabeth and she again tried to take her leave.

"Hold your horses missy, I have yet to relay the delegation of accommodation to you," came her mother's sharp reply.

"All the guests have been assigned appropriate accommodation." She said with a triumphant flourish "Mr. & Mrs. Gardiner will of course stay at Longbourn, and then they can assist in any last-minute preparations. Mr. & Mrs. Collins, detestable man that he is, will stay at Lucas Lodge with Charlotte's family. Do you know Lizzie" she said leaning nearer to whisper "I am told Mr Collins has informed Lady Catherine of his attendance by missive only, do you not find that strange?" she asked.

Elizabeth wondered how her mama knew these things, for the Collins had yet to arrive in Meryton. It was probably her aunt Phillips, who was unofficially acknowledged as the town gossipmonger.

"Now whose next, oh yes Mr. Darcy's family; The Earl of Matlock and his wife Lady Abigail, will of course stay at Netherfield, as will their son Richard. I believe he is to be Mr. Darcy's groom's man. Mr. Bingleys sisters' and Mr. Hurst arrive today, and Caroline Bingley will relieve Miss Darcy as hostess, until Jane becomes mistress of course. All the other guests are only day visitors," she finished with a flourish.

Everything was indeed ready, and she could now look forward to the ball, which Sir James Lucas has insisted in hosting. Sir James took all the credit for the union between Elizabeth and Darcy, for he had first introduced them at the Meryton assembly. Although many a mama, including Charlotte's own, were decidedly displeased at the outcome of this introduction. Elizabeth escaped to the garden for a few minutes solitude, before the serious business of dressing for the ball began.

*************

Elizabeth felt tense as they approached Lucas Lodge. Darcy had insisted that she rode with him and Georgiana. She was pleased at not having to endure the overcrowding of the Bennet carriage, and she must get used to traveling with Darcy, but still, the closeness of him tonight made her uneasy. His dark, penetrating eyes rarely left her face. She had tried to make polite conversation with them both, but Georgiana was too excited at the prospects of attending a real ball, and Darcy was unwavering in his attention and replied only curtly. As they pulled up to the entrance, the footman jumped down to help the ladies out of the carriage, but Darcy brushed him aside and completed the task himself.

Once inside and relieved of their cloaks, Darcy admired Elizabeth's gown. The under layer was pure white and reached the floor, where her matching slippers peeped out. The sheer over layer was decorated with small silver flowers and leaves, intricately woven into the fabric. Her dark locks were in the Grecian style with silver headed pins holding it in place. She was stunning; he was under no illusion that he would be the envy of every man here tonight. He glanced around the room, and then frowned; there were too many people, too many men. The prospect of other men coveting his fiancé was extremely distasteful to him. He must also be circumspect over Georgiana. As she was not yet 'out,' Darcy should have refused her plea's to accompany them, but he saw no harm in her attending a small family gathering. Of course she would not be able to dance with anyone other than Richard and himself, but she was content with this arrangement. Her delicate features glowed with excitement, and it made her look younger than her sixteen years. The delicate gown of lemon, with small green vines growing up from the hem, suited her perfectly. He would have his work cut out this evening, ensuring the wellbeing of both his ladies. As usual, Darcy was dressed impeccably; with his waistcoat complimented Elizabeth's dress perfectly, embroidered with a pattern of silver knots.

Sir James and Lady Lucas greeted them; offering felicitations on their upcoming nuptials, and then Sir James bade them enjoy their last night as single people, and he winked at Darcy. It was kindly meant, but inappropriate with two unwed females at his side. Sir James had a tendency to put into words, sentiments that should remain thoughts, but his jolly demeanour showed it was said in jest, and not with malice. Charlotte and Mr. Collins welcomed them next, and Darcy's brow furrowed again. He offered the clergyman the curtest of nods in acknowledgement of his greeting, then swept the women into the ballroom. Elizabeth was mortified that he had let Mr. Collins presence affect him so. She alone understood the reason behind his action, yet to others it would appear as though he had been excessively rude. She would have to remind him that his actions now reflected on her too.

It turned out to be more than the intimate gathering she had been led to believe, but at least most of guests were friends or family. Spying Colonel Fitzwilliam, she hoped he would ask her to dance, they had enjoyed a warm friendship when both in Kent.

Elizabeth watched as Georgiana gently disengaged herself from her brother's arm, and went to talk to Elizabeth's younger sisters, who were now standing with Maria Lucas. She felt a pang of envy at how carefree and happy they seemed, and longed to join them as they laughed and chatted together. Six short weeks ago she could have done just that, she thought ruefully.

Elizabeth and Darcy would be expected to open the dancing, but she knew he did not care for such frivolities. Charles had once told her 'Darcy never lifts a hoof, even though he is most proficient in all aspects of the dance.' A sigh escaped her as she realised if Darcy did not take her to the floor, she could accept no other man's offer. It would be an unpardonable breach of protocol. No, she must resign herself to enjoying it vicariously. Slyly glance at her escort, yes, he was *still* watching her, only now his piercing stare was accompanied by a smile. As the musicians struck up the cords for the minuet, he bowed and asked,

"Miss Bennet, may I have the honour of the first dance?"

Elizabeth was taken aback by his offer, and for a moment words failed her. Her surprise must have registered on her face, and she stumbled over her reply.

"I did not, that is, I did not think that.....yes, I thank you."

Darcy raised both brows in a questioning pose, and then held out his hand. She placed her hand in his, and mutely they walked to the dance floor. Uncomfortably conscious that all eyes were upon them, Elizabeth realised every step, every expression would be scrutinised by the people assembled. With Darcy's intense dislike for large gatherings, or being the centre of attention, she felt more than a little nervous. The music started and they performed the customary salute before meeting, circling, and returning several times as the dance dictated. Fellow revellers slowly joined them, and Elizabeth observed Darcy's shoulders relax, happier to now be one of many. As the dance continued she realised Charles was right, Darcy was indeed an excellent dancer, and conducted the steps with an easy air.

"Sir you dance with an abundance of style and grace, why do you dislike it so?" She asked playfully.

"You are mistaken Madam. I do not dislike dancing; I enjoy it a great deal. It is that I find it difficult to secure a partner that meets my standard," Darcy said honestly. "I recall the first time I saw you dance, it was with the imbecile Collins. He was out of time, and trod on your slipper dislodging a flower."

Elizabeth remembered how mortified she had been at Mr. Collins ineptitude, and that she had to constantly correct him.

"I did not realise you had observed us sir, or that you had noticed the state of my slippers. I am surprised you would concern yourself with such trifling matters. Do I meet with your exacting standards Mr. Darcy?"

As the dance drew them together, Elizabeth caught her breath. Darcy's gaze seemed more intensified, and she felt as though his penetrated stare had somehow pierced her very soul. Taking both her hands, Darcy held them over his heart and replied with quiet, yet devastating passion.

"From our very first meeting Elizabeth my eyes have followed only you. There is not one moment when in each other's company, that I cannot recall the gown you wore, the style of your hair or who your partner was. For every smile, I remember the time and the place. Every word, every glance you have ever bestowed on me, kind or otherwise, they are all indelibly committed to my memory. Not one heartbeat have I forgotten."

Elizabeth felt spellbound; his words exposed the depth of his love, and they washed over her as an embrace. She had longed for such love, a passion that even after possession, it was not sated. They stood motionless while all around them danced.

"Come Darcy, you must not monopolise Miss Elizabeth in this fashion, I believe she is promised to me for this dance."

As the fog of emotion cleared, and reality returned, Darcy became aware that the dance had ended, and the musicians were still. They stood alone on the dance floor, being silently observed by the rest of the guests. Realising it was Bingley who had come to their rescue, Darcy turned and muttered,

"Thank you Charles, maybe the next one."

Without words, but still in possession of her hand, Darcy led Elizabeth from the ballroom onto the deserted terrace. The biting December air enveloped them, but neither felt it. Stopping at the veranda's edge, Elizabeth took hold of the stone balustrade. The impact of his words still reverberated around her mind. She had read about such powerful loves, in the books of poets and Master Shakespeare, never dreaming she could be the recipient of such herself. She had always professed this would be the only thing that could induce her to marry, but now she had found it, she could not in all honesty, say she returned the sentiment. Oh, she wanted to, so very much she wanted to, but her feelings were unclear even to herself. If she professed to love him and it was false, it would mean heartbreak for them both. No, it was better to stay silent until she was sure. Again the immenseness of Darcy's declaration washed over her, the power of his all-consuming love saturating every fibre of her being, and she began to tremble. She tightened her grip on the rail lest Darcy mistook her shaking for shivering, but too late. He slipped off his coat and draped it around her, his warm hands lingering on her shoulders. Hesitantly, she covered them with her own, and then leant back on him for support.

"I did not know," She murmured.

His warm baritone voice whispered close to her ear,

"You did not know what Elizabeth? How those months apart were torture for me? How I risked my friendship with Charles in order to reunite him with Jane? Or maybe you are referring to Lydia, and the sacrifice I was willing to make to restored her to her family. That I have openly disregarded my family *and* society, by choosing to marry for love? Tell me that you know how my heart burns with a passion so violent, that you are the very air that I breathe. Surely you must know Elizabeth; all I have done, I have done for you, only you."

The anguish in his voice deafened her to propriety, and she turned and sought his lips with her own. She wanted to kiss away all the pain her family had caused him, to thank him for helping Lydia and Jane, and to fill the void of his absent family. And as their lips met, she felt his arms slide around her waist, drawing her still nearer. His acceptance of her imperfect family brought tears to her eyes, and unable to restrain them, they silently slid down her cheeks.

Her kiss was bitter-sweet in so many ways Darcy thought, as the salt mingled on their lips. This was not the response he had hoped to provoke with his declaration. The uncertainty of what lie behind her actions was nothing short of agony. He longed for her caresses to be given with love, but suspected they were in gratitude. But for now he would take whatever she offered. Hopefully she would come to love him in time, for he could not, would not, live without her by his side.

Elizabeth, unable to hold back the sobs any longer, tore her mouth from his and buried her face in his coat. Darcy comforted her with soft words of reassurance, until finally Elizabeth managed to regain control of her emotions. Then Darcy lifted her chin to look into her eyes.

Beautiful limpet pools of the darkest brown, still glistening with tears. He un-tucked his neck cloth and used the end to dry her eyes, knowing Fletcher would admonish him for it later. Concerned they had been gone too long already, Darcy tenderly stroked her hair, and then her cheek, before offering his verbal reassurance.

"My love is constant Elizabeth. I will wait a lifetime if that is what it takes, but for now, I fear we must return. You are promised to Charles for the next dance, are you not?"

Retrieving his coat from her shoulders, he quickly shrugged himself back into it. He had not meant to cause her such distress, and was heartily ashamed of himself for revealing the extent of his love in such a way. Sighing, he knew there was little hope their actions had gone unnoticed, but they must return.

Elizabeth was also disinclined to return to the frivolity of the dance. Instead, her mind was focused on easing Darcy's pain, whilst trying to sort out her own feelings. The last thing she wanted to do was make merry, and engage in meaningless chatter. Darcy's tender embrace was far more alluring at this moment. Instead, she gave him a weak smile, and placed her hand on his arm. Silently, they turned and walked back inside.

# CHAPTER 21

Once through the glass doors and back into the heat of the crowded ballroom, they both forced a felicitous countenance. In an instance, Bingley was at their side.

"Miss Elizabeth," he bowed, "I believe you promised me this dance."

He held out his hand and smiled warmly. Gratefully Elizabeth accepted and took his hand.

As they walked onto the dance floor, Darcy watched them with a frown. How easily Charles brought a smile to Elizabeth's lips, in contrast to the effect he had on her. He would give anything to be like his friend, easy in company and with a ready compliment for all. Before he could slip deeper into torment, a hand touched his shoulder, and a familiar voice said,

"The devils take you Darcy, you are the luckiest man alive, but who would know it with such a face upon you!"

Instinctively Darcy knew it was Col. Fitzwilliam.

"Indeed I am cousin," he replied without losing sight of Elizabeth, as she circled around Bingley.

"It is true her sister would pass as the beauty of the family, but Elizabeth has so much more to recommend her. She is still a very handsome gel, but with her wit and liveliness, together with her compassion and intelligence, she is by far the better prize," the colonel observed.

"She is all you have said, and more," Darcy confirmed, his eyes still trailing her.

"Much more," Fitzwilliam chuckled before he continued sombrely, "I'll wager she will give you a fine ride Friday night cousin, and for that, I envy you."

He slapped Darcy on the back and moved away. Puzzled, Darcy turned and watched him retreat to the other side of the dance floor. They had shared numerous experiences and opinions over the years, about many things and many people, but they had always respected the boundaries of society, never besmirching the character of anyone, that the other might care for. How strange for Fitzwilliam to make such a crude comment about the woman he was to marry. It was quite out of character for Richard to be so derogatory; he was usually all politeness, and charm, where women were concerned. Turning his attention back to the room, he searched for Elizabeth. Finding his heart's desire ensconced with Jane and Bingley, he was content she was secure and felt free to find his other charge. At first her whereabouts eluded him, until a group of pubescent females parted, and he spied Georgiana seated within their circle. From the degree of laughter coming from her attendants, she had obviously imparted something of great mirth. It lifted his heart to see her smile again. This past year he had watched Georgiana's slow recovery, from the abuse she had suffered at the hands of Wickham. For a time she had seemed so fragile, he had feared for her wellbeing. Indeed, the past four weeks she had rallied greatly, and was nearly returned to her usual self. Could it be that his engagement to Elizabeth was the cause of her recent recovery? Smiling to himself, he mused that there appeared to be no end to the happiness Elizabeth would bring him.

Satisfied Georgiana was safe and did not need his presence, Darcy turned to check Elizabeth was still holding her composure. He spied Charles and Jane, but could not find his love anywhere. He looked around the room, anxiously scanning betwixt the crowd for her. He began to move towards Bingley, to enquire of her whereabouts, when a movement caught his eye. It was Elizabeth, disappearing through the salon door at the end of the hall. She was not alone. Before the door closed, he had time to see that her hand rested on the arm of a gentleman. Striding purposefully down the room, Darcy ignored all hails to his person. On reaching the portal, he stopped, unsure of what action to take next. Elizabeth would not ignore propriety to wander off alone with just any man. Maybe it was a relative he had not yet been introduced to. Turning back, he scanned the room to see who was missing, but with everyone either dancing or circulating, it was impossible for him to gauge who was absent. Pacing before the closed door, he could only conclude they wanted privacy for some reason. Should he wait outside for her in a nonchalant manner, and then feign surprise when they emerged? Should he enter and plead ignorance of their desire to be alone? This was ridiculous he cursed, as Elizabeth's intended he had every right to be at her side.

Deciding he must do something, he opened the door with stealth, barely enough for him to peer inside. A ragged breath caught in his throat, and he staggered back to find support against the wall. His thoughts ran amok as he tried to digest the scene he had just viewed. Heads almost touching, her hands held in his, both resting over his heart. Elizabeth was looking up into his face with open affection, speaking soft words. Fortuitously neither had observed him, and he quietly closed the door again. Darcy tried to rationalise the scene he had witnessed. It could have been words of congratulations, but then why the need for privacy? No man should be speaking to *his* Elizabeth alone, but her father, it was inappropriate and unpardonable. Closing his eyes he drew in a deep, calming breath. Darcy admitted it was far too intimate a moment to be anything so casual. Why, had he not thirty minutes ago held her thus and proclaimed *his* love. He must conclude it was also words of endearment they shared, and even before this thought had fully formed, he experienced the pain of betrayal pierce his heart. Unsure of what his next action should be, he fought the urge to burst in on the lovers. He wanted to thrash him to within an inch of his life, to tell Elizabeth she was for him, only for him; but he could not.

Confronting them would serve what purpose? Such an action would mean the loss of both of them to him. His own eyes had not deceived him as to the tenderness of the moment they shared. Searching wildly for an immediate solution, he concluded that, with some forbearance, he could tolerate the loss of one of them, but not Elizabeth, never Elizabeth. No, he could see only one course of action. For now, he would do nothing. The wedding would go ahead. Rather Elizabeth at his side as his wife, than to be called so by another. He may have to be a cuckold husband, but it meant he must deny himself the thing he desired the most, to join with Elizabeth physically. He could not share her body, not even once! To see the disappointment register in her eyes, as she imagined another while in his embrace, or worse, in his bed, was more than even he could bear. Those damn fine eyes, he cursed as he made his way through the crowd, stopping only when he reached the refreshment table. Taking not one, but two glasses of the rum punch, he drained them both. Straightening his back, he replaced the scowl on his face with his usual languid mask, and then turned to face the room.

It was not long before they emerged, and as they did so, he saw Elizabeth wipe away what he must surmise was a tear, before hurrying to the ladies retiring room. As a hawk watches its prey, so Darcy followed his adversary. The footman handed him his cloak and hat, and he exited the lodge. As he waited for Elizabeth to return, Darcy realised he must play ignorant of the previously witnessed event. He did not want to be the one to drive her to the arms of his rival. Once they were married, he hoped she would honour her vows, in appearance at least, of a happy and dutiful wife. As she approached him, he smiled. For now he must concentrate on getting through the remainder of the night.

All who observed the guests of honour that night, would have said they enjoyed the evening immensely. Only the two of them knew it was a facade. Neither could conquer the turmoil of their thoughts, and as everyone departed for their respected homes, Elizabeth begged a headache and asked to return in the family coach. She needed to think on what Darcy had shared with her earlier, and now this sudden, unbidden declaration of devotion from another! She must not be distracted or swayed by Darcy's presence, while she unravelled her feelings for him.

"Sir, I know it has been your custom to join me on my morning walk, but I fear we must both abandon that pursuit tomorrow. There are still several things I must do in preparation for my departure to Pemberley. Due to the shortness of time, it must be done tomorrow. Therefore, our next meeting will be before the minister. Till then, I bid you goodnight Mr. Darcy," she said.

And with a deep curtsy and a brief smile, she offered him her hand.

I understand quite well madam, he thought. He wanted to shake her and say, Gods teeth Elizabeth, what must I do to make you love me?! Twice I have bared my soul, and offered you my heart, yet still it lies unclaimed. Instead, he forced himself to remain calm and smiled.

"As you wish madam; until Friday at ten then."

And he bowed over her hand, and then strode to his own coach to settling Georgiana in her seat. He glanced back, hoping to catch a last glimpse of Elizabeth, but she had already gone.

# CHAPTER 22

That night, sleep eluded Elizabeth as she lay curled up in her bed. Two major events had occurred tonight, and she needed to keep them separate, for one was her future, and the other was not. Firstly, the unexpected declaration from Col. Fitzwilliam had come as a complete shock. She could not deny they had enjoyed many pleasant hours walking together when in Kent, and the conversation had flowed with ease, but she had never thought him a serious suitor. With no fortune of his own and being the younger son, he must marry for money or title, it was expected of him. Elizabeth must put aside his heartfelt words of love, and encourage him to find another. She was relieved Darcy had not been witness to the evening's events, after all Darcy and Col. Fitzwilliam were like brothers. It would be unthinkable for her to come between them, or to tarnish their mutual bond of trust and respect. Elizabeth suspected the Colonels feelings had been inspired by a longing to enjoy marital harmony, rather than actually being in love with her. She determined he would survive her rejection.

Now free to concentrate on Darcy's declaration, she repeated his words aloud, 'Not one heartbeat have I forgotten.' Could she say the same? As she tried to remember all their encounters, it brought forth more painful memories than expected. Her mother was often rude and obnoxious in her treatment of Mr. Darcy, even though he was a guest in their home. Then there was her father's ineffectiveness as head of the family, shutting himself away in his library at every opportunity. Lydia and Kitty's unruly, and decidedly flirtatious behaviour with the militia was reprehensible, and which had then culminated in Lydia's shameful elopement with George Wickham. While poor Mary, overlooked by all, took every opportunity to sermonise. And let's not forget Mr. Collins, whose appalling behaviour in their short acquaintance made her cringe. His outrageous behaviour at the Netherfield ball, his clumsy proposal to her at Longbourn, and his overbearing smugness at the parsonage, it was too much. Dear Jane she could not fault, but the rest of her family made her blush with shame and embarrassment.

Jane's future happiness and Lydia's rescue had been achieved at the hands of Darcy, with little aid from any of her own family, save the Gardiner's. Even she was not blameless in her dealings with Darcy. From the very start, she had misread his character as proud, when in fact he was actual shy. She had accepted Wickham's duplicity with no proof but her own prejudice. Even she had slandered Darcy most shamefully, when he had first proposed. How could it be that he still loved her? And yet he did. In her circle of acquaintance, he was without and equal, he truly was the best man she had ever known. Could it possibly be more than gratitude she felt for him? Might it actually be love? Oh, how should she know which it was, love or gratitude. Who knew falling in love would be so complicated? With little more than a day till her wedding, she felt as confused and miserable as ever. Turning her face into the pillow, she sobbed until sleep and exhaustion claimed her.

It could not be morning already, Elizabeth thought sleepily, but she could definitely hear people abroad in the house. Suddenly there was a loud banging at her door, and Kitty was calling her.

"Lizzie, Lizzie wake up you are needed downstairs, quickly Lizzie."

Now wide awake, Elizabeth hastily put on her slippers and dressing gown, and then opened the door to face an excited Kitty.

"What has happened?" she asked, but Kitty turned and walked towards the stairs.

"Kitty!" Lizzie hissed in a low tone.

"A visitor for you," was all she replied before running ahead.

A visitor at this late hour, it must be Darcy she thought. Only he would have the nerve to rouse the whole house in the middle of the night. She slowed her step; let him cool his heels awhile. How very typical of him to do something like this, no doubt he wanted to speak to her about his cousin behaviour. Well, he would find her sorely tempered, she thought as she walked past her parents to the parlour door. Taking a deep breath, she turned the handle and entered.

"Miss Bennet," said a stern female voice from the shadows.

"Lady Catherine?" Elizabeth said, her incredulity evident as she curtsied to Darcy's aunt.

"You cannot be at a loss as to why I am here," Lady Catherine boomed as she stepped into the light.

"You are mistaken madam; I am quite unable to account for the honour of your visit."

"I will not be trifled with Miss Bennet. I am here after receiving Mr. Collins letter, informing me he had left

Rosings to attend *your* wedding, and to Mr. Darcy no less!" Her ladyship's disbelief was evident in her tone.

"I have come so you can deny it in person."

"I cannot, Lady Catherine. The information you have received is, in fact, quite true," Elizabeth was pleased to confirm.

"It is obvious to me you have somehow entrapped my nephew into making you an offer, and he is too much of a gentleman to revoke it. I, on the other hand, hold no such scruples." She said as her eyes darted over Elizabeth's face.

Elizabeth cocked her head to one side, and raised her brows at this statement, but she remained silent.

"Your family will lose this house when your father dies, and then what is to become of all you Bennet females, answer me that?"

"I am sure Mr Darcy..." but Lady Catherine interrupted,

"I am a very wealthy woman Miss Bennet, and *you* are not. Darcy has been promised to my daughter Anne, since they were in their infancy. It was his mother's dying wish and mine also. However, I am willing to settle five thousand pounds on you, if you do not make it to the church," she offered flatly.

A vast sum of money Elizabeth knew, but she had no intention of breaking her engagement. When compromised, Darcy had offered his protection, and she had accepted it, she would not throw it back at him now.

"That is indeed a fortune ma'am, but I am afraid what you ask is quite impossible."

"Very well then, ten thousand pounds, but Darcy is to be left at the altar. You must never see, or speak to him again. That way, he will soon seek us out at Rosing, and do as I bid, he will marry Anne. Do you agree?"

"Madam, you are incorrect if you assume I withhold my consent to elicit additional funds, and I must again decline your generous offer."

Elizabeth said this with as much politeness as she could muster. In truth, she was incandescent with rage at Lady Catherine's assumption that she could be bought, or that she would treat anyone, let alone Darcy, in such a manner.

Changing her tactics, Lady Catherine rounded on Elizabeth with a more personal attack.

"Do not think his family or friends will accept you. I will ensure every door of the 'Ton' is closed to you. For who are you gel, who are your mother and father? You have no fortune, no connections, nothing to recommend you. A fortune hunter, that is what you are Miss. Bennet, I am not deceived. Are the shades of Pemberley to be thus polluted, I think not!"

What a truly vile specimen of humanity this woman is, thought Elizabeth. As Lady Catherine spat her insults out at Elizabeth, her face had contorted to resemble an ugly gargoyle. How could I ever have thought Darcy and her were alike? The notion of inflicting such pain, and humiliation on Darcy and Anne, meant nothing to her as long as she got her own way. And now to come here, and insult her in such a manner was inexcusable. After such an attack, Elizabeth now made no effort to hide her contempt for the older woman.

"How dare you come into my home at such an hour, and insult me, and my family, with your attempt at bribery! I love Mr. Darcy, and he loves me, and we *will* be married. He is a gentleman, and I am a gentleman's daughter, so far we are equal. If my want of connection or lack of fortune does not concern him, it can be nothing to you. As for excluding us from society, well that will be no hardship to either of us I assure you madam. But if you can be that cruel, and unfeeling towards Georgiana and Anne, then I pity you. Now, you have insulted me in every way possible, and I must ask that you do not intrude on my time, or my family's hospitality any further. Your carriage is waiting."

Elizabeth opened the parlour door, and stood aside.

"And this is your final word?"

"It is."

"I have never been treated thus. Unfeeling gel that you are, I send no compliments to your mother, you deserve no such attention."

As she watched Lady Catherine hurry out the front door and into her carriage, Elizabeth caught a glimpse of Anne. Wrapped in layers of blankets against the cold air, clearly wishing she was anywhere but here. Poor Anne, she thought I would rather my imperfect, but loving mother any day. Closing the front door as the carriage pulled away, Elizabeth suddenly felt exhausted. Turning to go back to bed, she found her path blocked by her family; all eyes turned to her. They had obviously heard every word of the encounter, and were probably mortified at her treatment of Lady Catherine. Then there was the money. Sighing, she wondered how she could justify refusing ten thousand pounds. Her mother was first to break the silence.

"Well, bearing a title clearly does not make you a lady. What an obnoxious woman, and to leave her sickly daughter in the carriage on a night such as this. Well, it shows no breeding at all if you ask me. Come, everyone back to bed. You heard Lizzie we have a wedding to attend."

Mrs. Bennet began shooing everyone back upstairs. Relief washed over Elizabeth at her mother's surprise words of support, and she rushed forward, throwing her arms around Mrs. Bennet's neck and kissing her cheek while saying,

"Oh thank you mama, thank you."

"Yes well, do not forget Lizzie, when you are married to Mr. Darcy we will all be relying on you when your poor father dies. I am not implying that you hasten to the grave Mr. Bennet, just that it is a relief to know we will be taken care of when the time does come, that is all I am saying. Now, goodnight everyone goodnight Lizzie."

And they all returned to their rooms.

Elizabeth was elated. Her mother had her faults, but she was a fierce protector where her children were concerned. And tonight, that protection had come at a cost of ten thousand pounds.

Back in her bed, Elizabeth revisited the words she had exchanged with Lady Catherine. Defending Mr. Darcy, and their marriage, had felt so right, so natural. Had her feelings for him changed? No, not really changed she concluded, but grown and evolved, becoming clearer. Gratitude does not make your heart race at the thought of being with someone, nor does it make you feel sad or alone when they are absent. And when Darcy smiled at her, and she felt that fluttering in her stomach like a butterfly, all the while thinking he must surely see how wildly her heart was beating at his nearness... No, this was not gratitude, though she was grateful to him and for so many things, this was love. She loved Darcy. Even now, just thinking of him made her heart race. Tonight's confrontation had lifted the mist of doubt, and given her a clear view of her heart. Pulling the covers about her shoulders Elizabeth closed her eyes, only now sleep eluded her for a very different reason.

# CHAPTER 23

The morning of her wedding dawned, and as consciousness slowly returned to Elizabeth, she realised the smile from the previous night still curled the corner of her lips. Lifting her arms high, she savoured an early morning stretch before opening her eyes. The winter sun seemed lazy to rise, and she could barely make out the furnishings of her room. She pulled the blankets up around her shoulders, and deciding to enjoy their warmth for a few more minutes. Soon the hustle and bustle of the day would begin in earnest, and there would be little time for rest then. Elated that she finally had clarity in regards to her feelings for Mr. Darcy, she could not wait to stand at his side and speak her vows. And now she could recite them with a clear conscience and a full heart.

Elizabeth's mind wandered over the events of the evening of the Lucas ball. It had given her much to ponder on while completing the final wedding preparations yesterday. In truth, the day was a blur of busy hands and happy thoughts. Darcy's heartfelt revelation amidst the dance floor filled her with joy, leaving the other more unwelcome conversations to pale in comparison. Fitzwilliam's untimely and unbidden declaration, followed by Lady Catherine's insufferable diatribe in the early hours of the morning, could not mar her mood. However, she could not deny that it had been an eventful night, but Elizabeth was happy with how she had served each encounter, even Darcy's. She was excited and thrilled at the revelation it had heralded, and now wished she had not cried off from their usual walk yesterday, so eager was she to share her feelings.

When Col. Fitzwilliam begged her for a word in private, she had assumed he wanted to bestow her with cordial felicitations on her impending nuptials, and had willingly been guided to the small salon. Being Darcy's cousin, it did not cause her undue alarm when he closed the door behind them, and then drew her deeper into the room. Stopping afore the fire, she had turned to him with a warm smile, innocent of his intent. It was when he raised her hands to his lips, and placed a lingering kiss on each, that she realised the folly of her actions. Then speaking with urgency the Colonel began.

"Miss Elizabeth, I beg your permission to speak freely," he implored, and without leave to continue went on,

"When we parted that last day in Kent I had no idea Darcy was about to make you an offer, indeed, he had cautioned me not to lose my heart to you. He said such an alliance would be insupportable, due to your lack of fortune and want of connections. Against my better judgement, I heeded his warning and took my leave. After I had returned to London I realised my mistake. Before I could return, Darcy arrived and told me you had accepted him. I found his words incredulous after what he had advised me. I could not resume my duties to their fullest for my mind was elsewhere, and my heartbreak was complete. You see, my affection for you is more than that of a brother."

Renewing the grasp on her hands, he then declared,

"Miss Elizabeth, I cannot let you marry Darcy!"

As if Elizabeth were not already stunned by the Colonel's words, this last statement came as a slap in the face. If any other had uttered these words, she might have thought they spoke them in jest. But this was Darcy's closest male relation, his friend, his confidant. From boyhood to manhood they had shared a special bond, one that had stood the test of time, separation and yes, even war. Although she could not deny, while in Kent she had developed a tender regard for the Colonel, even flirted with him a little, it was inappropriate for him to address her in this manner now. Elizabeth formed his name on her lips to begin her reply, when he began to speak once more.

"I do not mean to deny either of you happiness, but before it is too late I must ask, is there any hope that you could yet return my sentiment?"

Elizabeth saw the look of beseechment, tinged with desperation in his eyes, and was sad to be the cause of it. Realising he would now suffer the pain of disappointed hopes, she chose her words with care.

"Dear Colonel Fitzwilliam, I am honoured that you would consider me worthy of your affection. If the right moment had arisen in Kent, and you had declared the depth of your feelings then, I would have considered your offer most seriously."

The sting of tears, still fresh from her encounter with Darcy, rose once more and threatened to fall. Causing injury to anyone was abhorrent to her, but she must make it clear that her affections lay elsewhere.

"I am content in my promise to Mr. Darcy. My heart is fully engaged."

Then to soften her rebuff, and offer him hope for his own future happiness, she continued,

"In time, you will find the right girl who will fill your heart, as Mr. Darcy does mine, and she will bear your name with love and pride. Come now; be happy for me and let us never speak of this again. Your cousin will never know these words we have exchanged," she coaxed.

She could not bear to look at his crestfallen countenance, so she reached up and brushed his cheek with her lips. Turning away to leave, she barely managed to reach the door as the first tear broke free. Dashing it away with the back of her hand, she made her way to the room set aside for the ladies. Elizabeth knew she must compose herself before returning to the dance floor, if she was to avoid a barrage of questions from Darcy. Dipping her handkerchief in the cold water, she dabbed her face with it. Surveying the damage, she decided the slight flush on her cheeks could be explained away. She returned to the main room and hoped to reach Jane before Darcy reclaimed her. At present she felt ill-equipped to face his scrutiny. The rest of the evening had been a blur, and she returned home with her family

Elizabeth took it as a good sign that she had seen neither Darcy, nor the Colonel yesterday.

The soft tapping at the door brought her out of her reverie, and she quietly bade her sister enter.

"I knew it would be you dear Jane."

"Lizzie may I get in with you," Jane asked rhetorically, "I can scarce believe it is your wedding day. Are you not excited?"

"I am Jane, finally I am," she said with a wide grin. "You know, I have not always loved Mr. Darcy as I do now, but I do love him so very dearly." Elizabeth beamed. "I fear my false impression started when he declined to dance with me at the assembly, and then called me barely tolerable. Had my pride not been wounded by this remark, would I have taken such heed of Wickham's bitter words? I have always considered myself to be a good judge of character, but I have been guilty of prejudice for no other reason, than an inconsequential slight."

"But you do not think ill of him now Lizzie surely?"

"No indeed! He is the best man I have ever known Jane. When I stand at his side today and recite my vows, I will speak them from my heart. Oh Jane, how wonderful and mysterious is this feeling of love!" Elizabeth threw off the covers and jumped from her bed, twirling about the room.

"Oh Lizzie, it is the most exhilarating feeling is it not!" Jane agreed.

Jane sat up and leaned closer to Elizabeth, who now stood at the side of the bed. In a hushed tone, she confided to Elizabeth,

"Sometimes, when Charles and I walk out, we hold hands, and I have even let him kiss me. Are you very shocked Lizzie?" Jane asked, blushing furiously.

Elizabeth returned to the bed, and taking Jane's hands enthused,

"When your lips touched, did your body feel on fire Jane? I swear my whole body tingles when he touches my hand. It is so different to what I have observed pass between mama and papa. When they kiss I see no passion, affection yes, but nothing more. When Mr. Darcy kisses me, I feel a heat in my veins I cannot describe. If our kisses are so different from our parents, I am hopeful that the marriage bed will be too."

"Lizzie!" You must not speak about our parents and the marriage bed together!" Jane scolded.

Then after a moment's contemplation, she leant closer and whispered,

"What do you mean, different Lizzie? What do you know of the marriage bed?"

Elizabeth hesitated, unsure if she should repeat her mother's pre wedding advice, but she decided as Jane was also betrothed, there could be no harm in forewarning her.

"The night of the Lucas ball, before Lady Catherine arrived, mama came to my room. She spoke of my wedding night, and divulged what I am to expect. It sounded most unpleasant, and if true I wonder there are two of us, yet alone five," Lizzie said with an indignant bluster.

"What did she say Lizzie, can you bear to repeat it?" Jane shyly asked.

Elizabeth straightened her back and folded her hands, mimicking her mother.

"I am to complete my toilet, then go and lay in bed with my nightgown pulled up to my knees. There I am to wait Mr. Darcy's pleasure," Elizabeth stated flatly.

"When he comes to me, he will climb atop of me, pull my gown up about my waist, and then pierce me with his sword."

At these last words, Jane gasped.

"I should expect some pain, but must lie still until he satisfies his desire. Then he will alight from my person, and return to his room. Once alone I may wash him from my body and then retire," imparted Elizabeth flatly.

"Oh Lizzie, it sounds awful, I am sure I will not like it. How often must we endure this assault?"

"Mama said at first it would be nightly, but as time goes on it will lessen to only a couple of times a week. Then once with child, it will cease until after the baby is three months old, more if we are lucky. I had thought it would be as pleasurable as the kissing," she sighed.

Seeing Jane's look of horror at what must befall them on their wedding night, Elizabeth tried to reassure her and make light of it,

"Oh Jane, do not look so sad; it is only what all women have had to endure, and you do want children do you not?"

Jane nodded and smiled.

Unannounced, Mrs. Bennet came bustling into the room and immediately scolded them,

"Come away now Jane and get yourself ready, only then may you return to assist me with Lizzie's hair. Be gone girl," she repeated.

Jane gave her sister a rueful smile before scurrying out of the room.

"Hill is bringing up your hot water as we speak Lizzie, and once you have bathed Cissy will come and help you dress. Jane and I will dress your hair; Cissy is not experienced enough in the new fashions from town. I will not be shamed in front of Mr. Darcy's relations, so do not linger in the tub and call me when you are ready Lizzie. Oh, and I believe your Aunt Gardiner would have a word with you if there is time. Hurry girl get out of that bed, you must not be late today of all days."

With that Mrs. Bennet went off to oversee some other aspect of the preparations.

Hill shut the door and Elizabeth slipped into the warm water. It was a ritual she enjoyed every morning, and although some frowned on her habit of daily bathing, it was a pleasure Elizabeth would not forgo. She assumed Mr. Darcy bathe daily also, he always smelt clean and fresh. His hair was soft and had a shine of health and vitality about it. Unlike some of her father's friends, whose hair looked as though they had greased it from the kitchen! Elizabeth shuddered at the thought of running her finger through such a matted wig. There was much she did not know about Mr. Darcy she thought. Slowly, Elizabeth drew the soapy clothe up her left arm and around her shoulder, before crossing over her neck and down the other side. Bathing could be so pleasurable, she thought. A fierce blush rose to her face, and she giggled. What would the Reverend Muir think of her if he knew she was daydreaming about sharing her bath with her husband?

## CHAPTER 24

The hive of activity that had dominated the Bennet household for the last few weeks, had now transferred to the church adjacent to Longbourn. All the guests had been ushered in and shown to their seats, while Darcy stood before the high altar, with Col. Fitzwilliam at his side. Occasionally the Colonel would tug at Darcy's waistcoat, or brush an invisible speck from his coat, in an effort too busy his hands and mind. Darcy, annoyed with this intrusion to his concentration, slapped his hands away each time, until he finally turned to Richard and said,

"The devil man, leave me be. Fletcher has done his job to perfection."

"I'm pretty sure you are *not* permitted to curse in church old man."

Fitzwilliam joked, but it was lost on Darcy. His eyes had returned to the doorway. His only thought, would she come?

The Bennet carriage had been outside the church for a good five minutes, with no sign of its occupants alighting. Mr. Bennet, his elbows resting on his knees, joined hands with Elizabeth. The duty that was before him was dreaded by all fathers, to give one's daughter to another man. Mr. Bennet was no exception in this. First though, he must share a secret with his favourite child.

"I cannot pretend I have not dreaded this day for the last one and twenty years Lizzie. I knew someday another would claim my place in your heart, and take you from my side. Though in watching you and your young man together, I am convinced he will do well by you. It makes it a little easier I must confess. And while in the mood for confessing, there is something I need to share with you my dear. These many years I have let it be known that my estate is barely profitable. Well, that is not strictly true. Since your mother first told me she was with child, I have squirreled away a portion of the annual profits, and have managed to build a small dowry for each of you girls."

Mr. Bennet paused and chuckled. The look of surprise on his dear Lizzie's face was quite amusing. He released one of her hands, and gently closed her open mouth before continuing,

"I believe yours will be a long and happy marriage Lizzie, but if it is not, you will have enough funds to see you to the end of your days. Now, three thousand pounds is not a fortune, but if you live a quiet life it should be sufficient. Only your Uncle Gardiner and my lawyer know of this."

Elizabeth's eyes were now wide with amazement. Mr. Bennet smiled.

"Now before you utter a word let me explain. The reason I did not give it as your dowry is twofold. Firstly, I wanted you to marry for love, which I am convinced you are doing. Secondly, I wanted you to retain control of this legacy. You understand my meaning behind this Lizzie?" he asked.

Eventually Elizabeth found her voice,

"I think I am too in shock to fathom it papa, will you enlighten me?"

"I was once turned from my chosen path, by a pretty face and my obligation to duty. Your mother is still a handsome woman, and I love her well enough. I would say we are content after a fashion, but it is not what I would want for you. If you find yourself genuinely unhappy Lizzie, you will have the means to be independent, to start again." He squeezed her hands as if to make a point. "However, if as I suspect, you enjoy a life of connubial bliss, it will remain in trust for my grandchildren, of which I am sure there will be many," he chuckled.

Elizabeth was stunned. The belief commonly held by all, was that the family estate provided a comfortable living, but nothing more. Now to be told it brought in a much larger income than reported was quite a revelation. Did her mama know the estate's true worth, and more importantly, did Charlotte or Mr. Collins?

"I understand papa, and I am both surprised and grateful. I hope to invest it for your grandchildren" she replied as a faint blush stained her cheeks.

"Come then Lizzie I think we have kept your young man waiting long enough" But he could not let her go before telling her, "I will miss you child" and he bent forward and kissed her tenderly on the cheek.

The organist began playing, and Darcy watched the church doors open. There stood Mr. Bennet, with Elizabeth at his side. She had come. Relief washed over him, and he allowed his body to relax a little.

Moving into the aisle, he watched as they made their way towards the altar. Elizabeth looked radiant in her gown of silver, with her dark curls adorned with tiny red rose buds. Darcy wondered if anyone had noticed that it perfectly matched the one in his buttonhole.

He had sent word to Pemberley, instructing Watkins to raid the hothouse for some of his prized blooms, knowing they would be the perfect accessory for Elizabeth's hair.

She looked radiant, Darcy thought. He would be the envy of all the men gathered, especially his cousin. He looked at his approaching bride, and as Elizabeth met his gaze, she bestowed him with a dazzling smile, making the breath catch in his throat. Just days ago he would have been euphoric that such a smile was for him, but not now. He returned a slight smile and gently inclined his head. As the Reverend Muir began to speak, Mr. Bennet placed Elizabeth's hand into Darcy's, and the service began. When the time came for the preacher to ask if there was anyone who knew of any just impediment, as to why they should not be joined in holy matrimony, to speak now or forever hold their peace, Darcy held his breath. Would Richard speak out and claim her for his own? Would Elizabeth deny him and turn to Fitzwilliam? What seemed like an eternity passed before the ceremony resumed. Unbeknown to Darcy, Elizabeth also suffered such thoughts, willing the Colonel to stay silent. Then separately, but together, they breathed a sigh of relief. Fitzwilliam had held his tongue. The vows were spoken; the rings exchanged, followed by the words they both waited to hear.

"I therefore proclaim that they are husband and wife. Those whom God has joined together, let no man put asunder."

It was done.

Darcy was relieved, not the feeling he expected to experience on his wedding day, but surprisingly it felt good. While Elizabeth was bursting with happiness, she was married to the man she loved. True, it had been a gradual realisation, but she was convinced it would be a love of the most powerful kind, both passionate and enduring.

After signing the register, they proceeded through the throng of well-wishers. Eventually they arrived at Darcy's carriage, which had been decorated with mistletoe and holly. They were both surprised when Mrs. Bennet stepped forward, and ushered Charles and Jane into the carriage with them. There seemed to be a shortage of transport, she muttered. Although Elizabeth had hoped to speak to Darcy before the ceremony, but there had been no time. She resigned herself to the fact that it now seemed it would have to wait until after the wedding breakfast.

Netherfield looked magnificent. The staff had twisted garlands of evergreen, holly, and mistletoe around the door frames and banisters. In the main room set aside for dancing, dozens of candles sat in scented water, illuminating and heating the room with a sweet fragrance. The musicians had rehearsed for hours to ensure the entertainment went smoothly, and a feast was set out in the dining hall, where several footmen stood ready to serve thee guests. As the guests arrived and the celebrations got underway, Mrs. Bennet bathed in the glow of self-satisfaction, having received several compliments on accomplishing so much, in such a short time.

All too soon it was time to leave. Darcy came to escort Elizabeth to the carriage, and she was surprised when he informed her they would be going directly to Pemberley. He had even arranged for Georgiana to return to London in the care of his aunt and uncle. Elizabeth was puzzled; they had agreed the journey to Pemberley would be easier if they rested the night at Airwhile house, and then made an early start the next morning. This new plan meant they would spend their first night as husband and wife at an inn.

"I see no need to tarry in London madam, and lose a day's travel," he said "and besides, Fitzwilliam can escort the ladies and uncle home before re-joining his regiment," he informed her stoically.

Elizabeth quickly found Georgiana to say a tearful farewell, while reassuring her they would meet anon at Pemberley. She had been shocked when Darcy had told her of their change of plans, but even more so when she saw him mount his horse. He would not be riding in the carriage with her? Abashed at his demeanour, she said nothing; she settling herself down for the journey ahead, and drew the blankets tightly around her legs, resting her feet on the hot bricks.

After travelling for nigh on four hours, they finally stopped at a large roadside inn called 'The Haystack.' They would only partake of some refreshment while the horses were changed, Darcy had said. The swaying of the carriage had helped Elizabeth fall asleep for part of the way, but now she felt refreshed and hungry as she alighted from the carriage. Expecting Darcy to be there to assist her down, she was surprised when James the footman, offered his hand.

"Thank you James, but where is Mr. Darcy?"

"I believe the master has gone to the stables. He wanted to check the condition of the new steed's madam, and leave instructions for his four to be returned to Pemberley. Is there anything else you require Mrs. Darcy?" he asked.

Elizabeth froze; that was the first time she had been called Mrs. Darcy. How strange it sounded. Realising she would never again be Miss Bennet brought a mixture of feeling. For the loss of her carefree life, she felt sadness while for her new role as mistress of Pemberley, and wife of Mr. Darcy brought only excitement. 'Mr. Darcy' she mused, I cannot call him that now that we are married. Making her way to the inn, she tried to think of an appropriate term of endearment. Should it be William as Georgiana preferred, or perhaps Fitzwilliam? It certainly would not be Fitz as many of his male relations called him.

"This way ma'am, Mr. Darcy bid us keep the best and most private dining room for you. Young Nelly is at your service"

The innkeeper tugged his forelock and made a clumsy bow. He was a rather rotund individual, and whilst losing his hair, he seemed of a jolly disposition. Elizabeth noticed there were only a few other travellers, either eating, or warming themselves by the fire.

"Elizabeth."

On hearing her name, she glanced over her shoulder and saw Darcy standing behind her. He took her by the elbow and propelled her to the back room. Then he turned her to face him, and slowly undid the ribbons on her bonnet. Somehow she knew he would be studying her face, his eyes sweeping over her every feature, as if to burn them to memory. Suddenly he spun her back around, and in one fluid moment dashed her clock from her shoulders. Unsure of his mood or intentions, Elizabeth nervously awaited instructions. He pulled out a chair by the fireside table, and beckoned the serving girl over. Elizabeth obediently sat down.

"Please bring Mrs. Darcy a dish of beef stew, some bread and a jug of wine."

"Nuffin for you sir?" the young girl asked.

"A brandy, bring the bottle," and he waved her away.

Elizabeth looked at him in puzzlement. Something had clearly upset him. In truth, he had been out of sorts since they had exchanged their vows. Oh he had been all civility and politeness, when greeting the line of guests and well-wishers at the wedding breakfast, but since the first dance, he had scarce spoken a word to her.

Sitting in the chair he held for her, Elizabeth tried to lighten the mood and playfully said,

"I believe we must have some conversation sir, a very little will suffice."

These words she had first spoken to him at the Netherfield ball, and she thought it might amuse him to hear them repeated. He merely took the seat opposite her, and said nothing.

She thought it was his dislike of large gatherings that had tainted his mood during the wedding breakfast, but clearly not. Since they had left Hertfordshire, Darcy had become cold and aloof, as when they first met. The state of marriage was new to them both Elizabeth realised, but surely this was not how newlyweds behaved? Where was the congenial and passionate man of the last six weeks? No, something had gone adrift, and until he confided in her, she had no other option but to endure it. If he desired conversation, she would engage, if he teased her, she would return in kind, and if it was silence he wanted, she could oblige in that too.

I cannot let my guard down, Darcy thought. It was torture for him not to take Elizabeth in his arms, to bruise her lips with his kisses. Only then he could purge himself of this pent-up passion, which ravaged both his body and soul. He had longed for the day he could call her wife, yet the very word made a mockery of him. The sooner they were at Pemberley the better; at least there it would be easier to put some distance between them.

Elizabeth ate her meal in silence but for thanking the young serving girl. Although she had shared many meals in the company of Mr. Darcy, this was the first time she had felt self-conscious. Having taken the chair opposite her, Darcy then proceeded to watch her intently, moving his gaze only to top up his glass. It was quite disconcerting for her, having someone scrutinise every morsel she put in her mouth, every sip of her wine. Finally, Elizabeth could bear it no longer.

"Sir, are you not hungry after such a long ride? May I not ask the girl to bring you a bowl of stew, or if you prefer some bread and cheese?"

"Thank you madam, I am content with my liquid supper," was all he replied.

His shifted his gaze to the fire, and Elizabeth continued eating. Putting the last bit of bread in her mouth, she gave a sigh, relieved that she had finished her meal. In an instant Darcy stood, knocking the chair over as he rose,

"I am sorry if my presence is not to your liking madam," he hissed.

He then strode to the door, pausing only to turn and say,

"We rest here the night, but be ready to depart at first light," and then he was gone.

Elizabeth looked at the door in astonishment, then back to the chair; instinctively she rose and set it right. What had induced such an outburst? Lost in her own thoughts, Elizabeth failed to notice the innkeeper enter. Startled, she looked up when he said,

"Your trunk is in your room Mrs. Darcy and Nellie will be with you directly; she will show you the way."

True to his word the young girl arrived just a moment later.

"Guvnor said to show you to the best room miss. You're in luck, it was only vacated this morning so it has freshly linen too."

Nellie smiled, picking up her skirt, and led the way.

"Thank you Nellie. You are very happy; do you enjoy your work here at the inn?" Elizabeth asked. She hoped her words had masked her shocked expression at Darcy's outburst.

"Tis hard work and no mistake, but gents like your husband make it easier."

Puzzled by her answer, Elizabeth asked her how so?

"The gentleman gave me a thrupence to make sure I took good care of you, and he gave the guvnor a crown to make him sweet to the idea. He said 'anything Mrs. Darcy asks for is to be delivered, anything," she replied rendering a good impersonation of Darcy. After the last half hour in his taciturn company, Elizabeth was astonished that he had bothered to ensure her comfort. Nellie opened the door to a spotlessly clean and surprisingly large bed chamber.

"Does my husband's room adjoin mine, and do you know where he is?"

"No miss, he only took one set of rooms, and at present he is in the bar. I warned him the folk in there were local field workers, not refined like you are miss, but 'e paid me no mind."

Seeing Elizabeth's look of alarm, the girl reassured her,

"Don't you worry miss, the guvnor will look after 'im, he won't let any of the lads step out of line."

So, he had taken only one set of rooms; she must assume he intended to join her, though it was not where she had expected to consummate their union. As she waited for Nellie to bring her hot water, Elizabeth undressed and looked around. It was quite a large room for an inn, with an equally large bed. She wondered what her mother would make of this situation, for there appeared to be nowhere for Mr. Darcy to retire to after they had joined. When the girl came back with a pail of steaming water, she also carried Darcy's outer clothes, his tail coat and neckcloth, which she placed on a chair with care.

"I brought these up miss so they don't get stolen or soiled."

Then she poured half the buckets contents into the pitcher and half into the bowl.

"And what is their owner doing?" questioned Elizabeth.

The girl chuckled; she had watched as the handsome young man easily integrated himself with the locals, putting them at their ease with his knowledge of crop rotation, and field irrigation. He further rose in their esteem, when he accepted the challenge to arm wrestle, even though he was a fair way to being in his cups. She recalled the look on old Groggin's face, when Darcy slammed his hand into the table for a second time. He admitted defeat and slapped Darcy on the back in good humour.

"He still be making merry with the regulars miss," Nellie replied with a smile.

Elizabeth's toilet was soon complete, and she now sat alone to awaited Darcy's arrival. As the room grew darker, Elizabeth turned to look out of the window. The moon was high, and the sky was awash with twinkling stars. She tried to stifle a yawn, but sleep was encroaching on her and she no longer had the energy or will to resist. As she climbed beneath the blankets, she thought what a long and eventful day it had been. Thankfully, sleep found her quickly.

"Mr. Darcy sir, the sun is up and the carriage is packed, and your lady is abroad in her room."

Muffled words filtered their way into his consciousness, and as he lifted his head to acknowledge them, a searing pain ripped across his brow. Raising both hands, he cupped his head, which did nothing to ease the intense throbbing.

"Water," he begged, before saying, "Bring me a flagon of ale too if you please innkeeper."

His voice was husky and his throat felt parched. The drink had been strong, but on an empty stomach it had taken its toll with speed, and now he was to suffer for his arrogant foolhardiness. Darcy followed the innkeeper's directions and went outside. With careful aim, he headed for the pump over the horse trough. Beckoning to a young stable lad, he jabbed a finger towards the water pump, indicating his need for assistance. Whilst the lad pumped the handle, Darcy hung his head and let the cold liquid revive him. With the effects of his enthusiastic over-indulgence still felt in his head and stomach, he arranged for Nellie to retrieve his clothes, while he made his way to the stables. The journey would have to continue at a slower pace than yesterday he realised, less he lost his balance in the saddle, or more embarrassingly, the contents of his stomach in a ditch.

Elizabeth was not surprised she would again be riding alone. Nellie had informed her of Darcy's activities last evening, with a note of admiration in her voice. She was both puzzled and annoyed, that he had not come to her at bedtime. It was certainly not what either her mother, or aunt Gardiner had told her to expect on her wedding night, to sleep alone. Nor from her past encounters with Mr Darcy, had she thought events would unfold as they had. So much for Darcy telling the inn keeper to give her anything she desired. A convivial husband in her bed chamber was what she desired, but apparently that had been unattainable last night.

Elizabeth thanked Nellie and climbed into the carriage. Her most pressing task now, was how to restore harmony between her husband and herself.

# CHAPTER 25

With the slowing of the carriage Elizabeth drifted awake. She stretched and rubbed her eyes, stiff after being asleep in one attitude for so long. She suddenly realised they were stationary, and so lifted the curtain to see where they were. Standing on the other side looking in, was Darcy. He was dust-covered from his ride, but the hint of a smile played about his face. Taking this as encouragement, Elizabeth beamed back at him. His languid look quickly returned, and she gave an inward sigh. Nothing had changed. He opened the door and held out his hand whilst saying,

"This is the best aspect to view Pemberley from for the first time. I did not want you to miss it madam."

Accepting his hand, Elizabeth stepped from the carriage, unprepared for the spectacular vista that lay before her. *She* was to be mistress of *all* this? The setting was undeniably superb; the house was large and stone built, sitting on its own rise, with a lake to the front which was traversed by a stone bridge. To the rear she could see the hint of both formal gardens, and wild meadows leading to a wooded slope. Adjoining the house was what she suspected was an Orangery or hothouse. And finally she could see a vast expanse of beautifully manicured lawns. She had never seen a place more naturally situated and in harmony with its surroundings.

"Tis breath-taking sir, truly breath-taking," she offered with all sincerity.

Overjoyed by Elizabeth's reaction to his home, Darcy momentarily let his emotions break through.

"Then you approve?" he asked with a broad smile.

"Oh very much so, I do not think any structure could be more pleasingly situated sir."

"At the risk of sounding like Mr Collins, it boasts over 200 rooms!"

Elizabeth laughed, and hoping to prolong their easy banter and tease him,

"And do you akin yourself to Mr Collins and Rosings, to lecture me on the cost of each window and fireplace sir?"

"Pray do not inflict such a mantle upon me madam, I fear we may be overheard and taken in earnest," he replied happily.

Turning back to admire the view, they stood silently for a few minutes more, then Darcy helped Elizabeth back into the carriage and on to Pemberley.

They stopped at the steps front entrance, and Elizabeth peered out. The staff had lined up to greet her, and she felt a little apprehensive at the prospect of meeting them all. However, this was their way of honouring her, and she was touched by their kind gesture. Darcy assisted Elizabeth from the carriage, and gently guided her towards a middle-aged couple standing in the centre of the waiting servants.

"Elizabeth, may I introduce you to Mr and Mrs Reynolds, my butler and housekeeper." Turning to the retainers he said, "May I present my wife, Mrs Elizabeth Darcy."

The couple stepped forward, bowed and curtsy, then welcomed her to Pemberley. As they ascended the steps, Darcy inclined his head and greeted each person by name, while she smiled and nodded, accepting their felicitations. As they reached the front door, Darcy paused to let Elizabeth look around the atrium before following her in. As she gazed around her face lit up with delight. It was suitably grand for such a building, decorated tastefully and for comfort, with an appropriate amount of splendour without being ostentatious.

A maid stepped forward, bobbed and took their outside clothes then quietly retreated. Shyly Elizabeth looked to Darcy for guidance, who in turn spoke to the waiting housekeeper.

"Mrs Reynolds, I will show Mrs Darcy to her rooms, and then we will take tea in the small parlour in an hour. A bath is in order first I think?" and he looked to Elizabeth, who nodded in agreement, "Yes, so hot water if you please. Also I would be obliged if you would assist my wife for today. I take it you have arranged some candidates for her to interview, as I asked?" Mrs Reynolds nodded.

He took Elizabeth's arm and together they climbed the central staircase. They walked half the length of the corridor on the second floor before Darcy stopped.

"These are your rooms, I chose them for their proximity to mine, but if you are unhappy with their location, there are several more suites you may choose from."

He opened the door to let her enter, alone at first, and then followed a few minutes after. He stood behind her and clasped his hands behind his back, lest he temptation to pull her into his arms. He was afraid of her response if he did so. Instead he stood proud, taking time to admire her slender neck.

"You may of course change anything you wish, I have purposely not redecorated, so you could have the pleasure of making it your own."

Elizabeth took a few steps forward till she gained the centre of the room. It was so spacious she could hardly believe it was for one person, let alone her. The main feature was the oversized four-poster bed, placed in the centre of a long wall, opposite the large ornate fire-place. Beautiful curtains hung from the canopy, embroidered with delicate flowers in pink, yellow and blue, with tendrils of green winding up from the hem. There was a good half dozen plump pillows, encased in snow white covers, and a white embroidered eiderdown over the blankets. She imagined Darcy laying there, his dark hair in stark contrast to the white pillows. She suddenly felt very aware of his presence behind her, and a rose tinge crept up to stain her cheeks. Elizabeth hastened to put a few steps between them, hoping he had not noticed. The room boasted two sets of tall windows that looked to the rear of the house, with views over the gardens, meadow, and distant wood. It was a delightful room, light, pretty and feminine. Elizabeth loved it, just as it was.

"It's perfect," she said a little breathless, "would you mind very much if I changed nothing?" she asked.

Darcy was enjoying a daydream of his own, but in his vision it was Elizabeth that was reclining on the bed, her arms open in a welcoming pose. Her words brought him back to reality with a jolt, and he too coloured a little, before replying.

"As you wish; remember this is your home now Elizabeth, and within reason you may change whatever you wish."

She nodded her acknowledgement and moved to another of the three doors in her chamber. Darcy opened the door and said,

"Through here is your dressing room."

About half the size of the bed chamber, it was perfectly equipped with all a lady needed to complete her toilet. Plenty of storage cupboards for her clothes, a dressing table and a comfortable chair. But for Elizabeth the beautiful, white roll topped bath was the most importantly piece of furniture. It too was a lovely room and needed no alteration. Then Darcy entered and went straight to the side door. Here he paused, as if deciding whether to divulge its purpose or not, then in a clipped tone he said,

"And this room is your private nursery, should we ever be blessed with children."

He opened the door to show her inside, but quickly closed it again. Somewhat perplexed that he was giving her no time to examine or explore the room, she walked over and opened the door again. It was empty. Then Elizabeth recalled that Darcy had lost his mother when his sister was born, and presumably it was Mr Darcy's father that had moved Georgiana to the wet nurses room. She closed the door quietly, and returned to the main chamber. There was still one room that they had yet to explore. Elizabeth guessed it led to her sitting room, and walked over and opened the door. It was decorated to please both male and female occupants. Her gaze lingered on the fire surround, and she smiled. The white marble hearth was adorned with naked nymphs, and to coin a phrase favoured by Mr Bingley, she thought it was charming. She walked to the opposing door and made to open it, but as she turned the handle she heard Darcy shout,

"No!"

But it was too late, she had entered. It was obviously a man's bedroom, decorated in hues of blue, red and brown. There was a large desk situated under one of the windows, and a painting of Pemberley hung on the wall. Elizabeth thought it was a perfectly pleasant room, for a man, and was about to voice her approval when she felt Darcy's hand on her arm. Gently, but firmly, he guided her back from whence she came.

"As you have discovered madam, this door leads to my bed chamber. You may lock it from your side, should you so wish."

He indicated the key in her side of the lock.

"I am glad you are pleased with the rooms I have selected, they were my mothers, and although they are attended to every week, they have remained unoccupied since her death."

Seeing the look of horror cross Elizabeth's face, he quickly added,

"Of course the bed and linen have been newly acquired for your arrival. I will leave you now. I will return to escort you downstairs in an hour."

He gave a curt bow, and then Elizabeth found herself alone. Considering their past encounters, Elizabeth was surprised that Darcy had not wanted her to enter his bed chamber; indeed he had often professed a desire to never let her leave it. What had changed to make him act so cold and unfeeling she wondered.

As Darcy left Mrs Reynolds entered, and immediately began laying out fresh clothes for Elizabeth. As she began to undress Elizabeth thought how puzzling Darcy's words seemed, '*Should* we ever be blessed with children,' and then the strange remark about locking the door. Why *would* she refuse him entry?

**\* \* \* \* \* \* \* \* \* \***

Darcy arrived to collect Elizabeth promptly one hour later, and although she gave him a shy smile, they proceeded downstairs in silence. Entering a small salon, Elizabeth looked around in admiration. Beautifully decorated in lemon and gold, it seemed light and airy, with large double doors leading to an impressive veranda. Only now did the true size of her new home dawn on her, and she felt more than a little daunted at the prospect of running such a grand house. There were so many servants to get to know, their names and their duties. Of course her mother had trained her well, and she knew all that a mistress needed to know, but Pemberley was no Longbourn. Casting a sidelong glance at her, Darcy noticed the frown upon her brow. Wisely, he understood her change in circumstances must be a cause of concern for her, and spoke to reassure her.

"Elizabeth, I realise you must be concerned about managing a house such as Pemberley, but Mrs Reynolds has been doing it for years, quite successfully. She will guide and assist you, until you feel ready to take on the mantle for yourself."

She nodded gently, but still her brow was furrowed.

"In truth, Pemberley is such a well-oiled machine, there will be little for you to actually do, but the level of your involvement is for you to decide." Darcy continued.

Elizabeth slowed her steps then turned to him. His countenance was unreadable, yet somehow Elizabeth now felt easier. How intuitive of him to surmise her feelings of apprehension, and to then address them so completely. This was the Darcy she had come to love, thoughtful and sensitive to her needs.

"I will give you a tour of the main parts of the house before dinner. I expect it will take you a while to become accustomed to living in such a large dwelling. Do not be afraid to ask the servants if you need assistance. Also, Mrs Reynolds has detailed floor plans in the hall leading to her parlour. I understand she uses them to familiarise new staff. I am sure she will welcome you making use of them."

This time there was a smile to accompany his words, albeit only briefly. Elizabeth thanked him for addressing her concerns so perfectly. Happy to have allayed some of her fears, he called for tea to be served. For the next thirty minutes they conversed on the house and grounds, punctuated with awkward silences. How did we come to this, she thought sadly?

As soon as tea was finished, Darcy offered his excuses and made his way to the library, leaving Elizabeth on her own. After spending the best part of two days cooped up in the carriage, she decided some fresh air was what she needed. Perfect, she thought, what better place to start her exploration than the lovely gardens. She slipped out the doors and looked around. The beautifully carved stone veranda ran the entire length of the house, only interrupted by three sets of steps leading to the formal gardens. Although the sun was giving off little warmth, Elizabeth was so eager to be outside, she ventured out in only her shawl. It was hard to believe that one man could own so much, and even harder to believe she was now its mistress. As she wound her way around the immaculate lawn paths, a movement caught her eye. It must be one of the groundsmen she thought. Eager to know the staff as well as Darcy, she went to seek them out. She must take every opportunity to acquaint herself with all the member of the household, it was expected of her. As she neared them, she saw it was an old man. He was dressed in several layers of clothes, topped off with a thick padded jacket. He was bent over a mass of spindly sticks, inspecting the pruned shrubs.

"Good afternoon, do you tend all the gardens here Mr...?" she asked.

"Watkins madam and that I do, with the help of fifteen youngsters," he chuckled as he tugged at his cap before pulling it back over his brow.

"Goodness, it takes that many people to tend one property?"

He straightened up to get a better look at the new mistress, then took the clay pipe from between his uneven teeth and said,

"Yes ma'am, not counting the tenant farms, the park land rangers, the gamekeepers and the villages of Kympton and Lambton to name but a few. There be over thirty thousand acres to Pemberley grounds miss. We use double that number in the spring and summer for planting, then come harvest time it's all hands to the fields." He paused to puff on the empty pipe.

"Did you make use of the rosebuds?" he asked.

"Oh yes, they were beautiful and greatly admired. You sent them, did you not?" Elizabeth asked, a little embarrassed in case her assumption was wrong.

The old man puffed up his chest with pride at her kind words. Ay, she'll do very nicely for the young master, he thought.

"I did, at the masters request madam. Well you best make your way back now; those clouds look heavy with snow. Besides, I can see young Molly Weaver approaching. Mrs Reynolds probably sent her to guide you back to the house."

And he put the pipe back between his teeth, and returned to his work. Elizabeth smiled. She liked his directness, even though he had completely dismissed her to return to his work.

As Elizabeth set off to meet the approaching maid, she glanced up at the sky. The clouds looked black and menacing, so she hurried her pace. The house was aglow with light and smoke was curling from the chimneys, hopefully a warm welcome was waiting inside. Suddenly a movement at one of the windows caught her eye, the lone figure of a man, his arm resting on the window rail. He appeared to be watching her. Realising he had been detected; he stepped back and was gone. The maid's hail of 'Mrs Darcy' pushed it from her mind, and she hurried to meet her as the first flakes of snow began to fall.

As Darcy realised Elizabeth had seen him, he stepped back into the shadows. He cursed at having been caught watching her, but he was like a moth to the flame. He could not resist the light, even though he knew it would burn him. Throwing himself down in his desk chair, he surveyed the pile of correspondence and invitations that he should be beavering his way through. But he was in no mood to work; he preferred to wallow in self-pity at his own misfortune. Newly married he should be basking in contentment and happiness, his desires, sated and his future set. Instead he had never been so miserable in his life. How did we come to this, he thought?

# CHAPTER 26

Elizabeth went down to dinner a little early, so that she might have time to locate the dining room unaided. She had spent some time with Mrs. Reynolds after her walk. As they scanned the plans of Pemberley, Mrs. Reynolds pointed out the route from Elizabeth's chambers, to other areas of the house. Whilst doing so, they passed the time talking about the history of the house and family. Elizabeth found it fascinating, and quite enlightening. It also gave her a clearer insight to Darcy's character, one she was certain he would never have revealed himself. Mrs. Reynolds had cared for Mr. Darcy since he was four years old. Then, when his mother had died in child-birth with Georgiana, it was to Mrs. Reynolds he'd turned. At the time, Darcy was twelve; she revealed her sorrow as she witnessed first-hand, how Darcy had been forced to take over the running of the estate. His father had become withdrawn, taking no interest in the life, or his children.

She also revealed details of how Mr. Wickham had wreaked havoc on both families, and many of the villagers too. Young Mr. Darcy had made sacrifices to confine, and repair the damage, often as great expense. Each time ensuring the image of Wickham his father believed in, was not tarnished. Then his own good father had died five years ago, and she again stepped in to help him, especially with Georgiana. This enabled him to devote the time needed to rebuild the estate. In regard to Georgiana, he had borne all the responsibility for raising her, cloaked in the mantle of both father and brother. Yes, Darcy's burden of responsibility had been heavy indeed, and Elizabeth felt she understood him better for knowing it.

After only one wrong turn, Elizabeth managed to find the dining room, and she took a seat by the fire to await her husband's arrival. As she soaked in her bath, she had done a lot of thinking. Her conclusion was she was weary of suppressing her natural spirit and good humour; all this sobriety and aloofness was most taxing and unpleasant. Besides, it was almost Christmas, a time for joy and to celebrate. She would no longer play his game, but would return to being her convivial self, and hope Darcy followed suit. Elizabeth cast a glance at the mantel clock; it read ten minutes before the hour. It was better to be early, she knew how much Darcy disliked tardiness, especially at meal times.

Darcy had done little work and much thinking, while sitting in his library. He knew things could not continue in this vein, and had decided to savour, what remaining time he had with Elizabeth. Wallowing in self-pity in this morose manner was unproductive, and reminded him of how he was before Elizabeth came into his life. For the harmony of the household, he would be civil, attentive and entertaining. It was only his heart that needed guarding. Nostalgically, he thought of the night in the glasshouse at Longbourn. Closing his eyes, he rested his head on the back of the chair and recalled how it felt to wrap his arms around her. He could almost taste those soft lips, feel the sensation of her body as it moulded to his own. He recalled her slender waist, and the inviting curve of her hips. Abruptly he sat up and opened his eyes, as he felt the unmistakable stirring of arousal. Cursing that he allowed his thoughts wander in that direction again, he picking up a previously discarded letter and began reading.

Eventually he realized he was wasting his time and made his way to his chambers. He hoped along soak in the tub would clear his head. He rang for Fletcher and began to disrobe, while he waited for Tuppence to bring up the water. A few strides passed that door, and he would be at Elizabeth's room. Was she in her bath, or perhaps changing for dinner? He walked to the shared sitting room door, and placed his forehead against it. Everything he ever desired in a wife lay beyond this portal. She was *his* wife, in *his* house, and he had the *right* to take her as he willed. Yet he could not. He must resist; he would not have the willpower to drink only once of her sweet nectar. Frustration broke free, and he banged his fist on the door. Damn Fitzwilliam and damn Elizabeth too.

When he entered the dining room some time later, there was no sign of the angry, frustrated man who had sat in his bath until the water turned cold. He was surprised to find Elizabeth already waiting for him though.

"Good evening Elizabeth, did you manage to find your way here unaided?"

"I did, thank you. I took your advice and spent the afternoon with Mrs. Reynolds. I found our conversation both enlightening, and instructive. We went over a few of the plans too, ones that would afford me the most benefit."

"How did you find Mrs. Reynolds?" Darcy asked.

"I like her very much," she said warmly.

"I am pleased you have had a pleasant and productive afternoon. Are you hungry, shall we call for dinner?"

He gave her no time to ask how he had spent his afternoon, and so Elizabeth nodded and placing her hand on Darcy's arm. He escorted her to her seat then took the chair opposite. Darcy had instructed the servants to remove several of the central panels, from the usually vast dining table. He hoped the less imposing setting, would encourage their conversation. His direction had been proved correct, and they enjoyed a pleasant meal of soup, followed by venison, and a delicious lemon sorbet. The deer was from the estate herd, while the wine came from his vineyard in Italy. To round the meal off, they were served with some tasty homemade cheese and biscuits. The conversation had flowed easily to start with, and on a variety of subjects. The possibility of a white Christmas, how did Elizabeth like Derbyshire, and finally their smooth, but speedy journey north. During the latter topic, Elizabeth had decided it was not prudent to reveal that she was aware of his escapades, while at the Haystack Inn. Finally, they seemed to run out of safe pleasantries to converse on, and a stony silence resumed. As Elizabeth toyed with her cheese, Darcy divulged some news that took her completely by surprise.

"When I called on your father, the day after the Lucas ball, he informed me that he has arranged for your two younger sisters to return to the school room."

"He what?!" was Elizabeth's first instinctive words, before quickly composing herself to continue in a more ladylike manner.

"Do I understand you correctly sir, my father is withdrawing Lydia and Kitty from society?"

"Yes, that is my understanding, perhaps for a year, maybe two. He concluded that after recent events surrounding Lydia, she was in need of further instruction on how to act, *in* society, before being *abroad* in it. Catherine is to go too. Although I understand she is a full two years older than Lydia, she has a tendency to mimic her, in both words and deeds. I agreed with his decision wholeheartedly. I believe he has also made arrangements for her future, when she returns from her additional schooling."

Elizabeth was astounded at how calmly he imparted such a revelation. He had known three whole days, before revealing this news, and then did so in a cavalier manner over the cheeses!

"When and where are they going, did he share this with you also?"

Elizabeth tried to mask the sarcasm in her voice, but was unsuccessful. It was incredulous that her father had informed Mr. Darcy of his plans, but had not seen fit to tell her, his own daughter. More worryingly, did her sisters know, she wondered? Undoubtedly they would both benefit from further instruction on how to conduct themselves when in polite society, but could her father have not hired someone to do so at Longbourn?

"He did as it happens."

Darcy did not understand her outrage. Indeed, when Mr. Bennet had asked him what he thought of the idea, he had not only approved it, but had actively encouraged him to put the wheels into motion, as quickly as possible.

In his opinion, society would benefit greatly from the temporary absence of the younger Bennet gels.

"They will be going to a highly respectable finishing school in Bath. One I recommended actually. My understanding is they will repair there directly after the Christmas and New Year festivities are concluded. After which, I understand your father intends to encourage Lydia into courtship with one of your neighbours, Johnson I believe. It is all arranged," he finished flatly.

It seemed that Mr. Darcy and her father had become firm friends, friends that enjoyed sharing confidences, and in only a few weeks. While it was not a bad thing, she certainly did not want them to collaborate where she was concerned! So the girls would be at Longbourn until mid-January she concluded. That would give her enough time to write to Jane, and receive a reply. Unfortunately, Darcy's disclosure soured all attempts at further conversation. Darcy, conscious of both their discomfiture, instructed the footman to bring his coffee to the library, he then excused himself. Elizabeth waited a few minutes to be sure he would not see her, then hurried to her chamber to write to Jane.

*Pemberley*
*Derbyshire*
*December 21st 1811*

*My Dearest Jane,*

*I hope this missive finds you and all my family in good health.*

*I am pleased to confirm our safe arrival at Pemberley, and after only three days travelling. It is far grander than even I could have imagined. The housekeeper's floor plans have aided me greatly, as I try to navigate my way around. Mr. Darcy informs me there are in excess of two hundred rooms, so you can understand how easy it is to get lost. It is decorated in a grand fashion of maybe ten years ago, but somehow it seems appropriate for this house. I have learnt from the head gardener, Watkins (the one who sent the flowers for my hair) that Pemberley also boasts over thirty thousand acres. Is that not very grand indeed my dear Jane? Mama will be most impressed! And Jane, it is quite in harmony with its surroundings and nature alike. I long to explore it more, weather permitting. When you visit, I hope to have discovered some of the special places I have heard Mr. Darcy refer to. Then I will be able to share them with you and Charles.*

*On a serious note Jane, I have just discovered that papa intends to withdrawn Kitty and Lydia from society. They are to be send to board at a school in Bath, is this correct? How have they taken such news? I fear father will not only have Lydia's wailing and moaning to deal with, but also mama's, for she is sure to oppose such an action. Write soon and tell me all, hold nothing back I implore you.*

*I must hasten if this is to catch the morning post.*
*Your loving and affectionate sister,*
*Elizabeth Darcy.*

Reading it over, she decided she was right not to mention her father's plans for Lydia's betrothal, unsure if Jane would yet be party to this information. Folding the letter, Elizabeth melted the dark red wax and pressed her new *ED* stamp firmly in it. Casting a glance at the clock, she decided there was enough time before she retired, to take the missive to Mrs. Reynolds. It could then be despatch on the morrow. She only hoped that the dusting of snow they had earlier, would not become more substantial before she got a reply.

# CHAPTER 27

Bedtime drew near, and Elizabeth wondered if Darcy would finally come and join with her. She finished her toilet, and let Mrs. Reynolds help her into her nightgown before brushing her hair. After bidding the housekeeper goodnight, Elizabeth propped herself up in bed and waited. I have been married two full days, yet still I am a maid, she thought. What should she do, what was expected of her? Events had not unfolded as she had been led to believe, and now she was completely confused. Her mother had imparted her version of expected marital duties, but her Aunt Gardiner had told her something completely different, yet neither had come to fruition. Suddenly, she remembered the gift from her aunt, and slipped out of bed to retrieve it. There in the drawer, was the parcel of brown paper Madeline Gardiner had gifted her. Lifting it out carefully, she placed it on the top of the chest of drawers. Slowly she unfolded it, revealing a neat bundle of plain white cotton cloth. Concealed within this layer was another garment. Opening it with care, Elizabeth exposed a nightgown and robe made of the sheerest gossamer material, she had ever seen. When held up to the light, she could almost see her hand through the two layers of material. The nightgown was held in place by two silk ribbons, one tied at each shoulder, and a thin belt for the waist. Her first thought had been it was indecent, surely worn by ladies of ill-repute. But after talking with her Aunt Gardiner about what to expect on her wedding night, she felt emboldened, and accepted the gift. Elizabeth had whispered to her aunt what her mother had told her, and Madeline Gardiner had been shocked.

"Dearest Elizabeth, from my personal experience, nothing could be further from the truth. I am sorry if this has been your mother's destiny though, I would have thought differently of Mr. Bennet. Perhaps it is not so, and she was merely embarrassed at having to discuss such matters. However, without being too indelicate, let me tell you what I know of the matter."

Taking Elizabeth's hand, she chose her words with care as she elaborated.

"When a man and woman truly love each other, what passes between them in the marriage bed, can be both an exciting and pleasurable encounter. If your husband has some experience, as all men tend to, he will be able to touch you and bring forth sensations that you will never have felt before. He will kiss and caress your whole body Elizabeth, and be not afraid to do the same for him."

Elizabeth looked down as a crimson blush stained her cheeks, recalling how she had already enjoyed Mr. Darcy's touch. Not once but on several occasions, thus bearing out her aunt's words.

"He will take and give, great pleasure as he explores your body my dear, and Elizabeth you must learn what pleases him also. The 'sword and piercing' your mother mentioned are true, if a little dramatic. The first time there will be a little pain, but it will pass quickly, and never be experienced again. After that the journey of exploration, and fulfilment should be mutually satisfying. Go to your husband my dear, with open arms and an open mind. The marriage bed is not just to beget children Lizzie; it can be a playground of adult fun, a place to share intimacies and secrets with your loved one, your husband."

Mrs. Gardiner paused for a moment, thinking of what she had purchased for her niece. It was an expensive and risqué gift, but clearly she would receive no such item from her mother. Maybe she should have a similar chat with Mrs. Bennet? Though passed childbearing age, she might yet enjoy her husband's company in the bedroom. She continued,

"So, my wedding gift to you is a similar creation my mother gave to me. It is risqué I admit, but when you wear it, it will fan Darcy's passion, until he burns with desire for you, mark my words."

"Well, here it is," Elizabeth said aloud as she shook it out, "a nightgown to seduce and inflame my husband desire."

He seemed to need no such allurement before we married, she thought sadly. If he comes to me tonight, he will find me ready and most willing. She shivered as she slipped the gown on, and moved nearer to the fire. Beautiful as it was, it was not very practical on a cold December night. As the darkness marched by, she was determined to stay awake, but her idle brain was making it more and more difficult. Elizabeth decided a book might aid her vigil; she pulled on her robe, and made her way to the library.

The candlelight made the house look different, but she quickly found her way, and with a single turn of the handle, entered Darcy's inner sanctum. It was an impressive room that was split into two sections, each having several comfortable chairs and tables. At one end there was a grand fire-place, with the remnants of a dying fire still burning. At the other end sat Darcy's magnificent, oak desk. In the middle of the room, a tall bookcase jutted out, almost touching the richly decorated ceiling. Darcy had proudly boasted to her, that the library contained over twenty thousand titles. Also he could indulge in his love of solitude here. He found the aroma of the leather bindings, one of his most-comforting smells. It was clearly his favourite room in the house. It had taken several generations to amass its contents, and seeing the row upon row of books, Elizabeth could easily believe it. She looked forward to spending many happy hours in here, curled up in one of the big chairs, lost in the works of Shakespeare or Byron. It was the perfect place to find something to keep her awake, maybe a lively play by the bard, or a rousing canto from Dante's 'Divine Comedy.'

The only light in the room came from the weak glow of the dying fire. Elizabeth held the candle closer to the spines, thus enabling her to make out the words. Spying a small leather-clad book with no visible title, she placed the candlestick on the nearest table, and pulled it from its resting place. How intriguing she thought, eager to discover its worth. It was certainly well-worn, though the leather was still pungent. It deserved further investigation she decided.

Darcy sat motionless, afraid his vision would disappear. Night after night, he had dreamt of Elizabeth coming to him, to confirm their love as only a man and woman could. Tonight was no different. He must have drunk deeply for his apparition to appeared so real; When she turned to set the candle down, its light illuminated her features, and he realised it was no dream. Frozen, he held his breath, afraid she would hear his heart pounding, as it thumped against his ribs. He watched mesmerised, as she ran her hands over the soft leather of the book. Then something fell to the floor. As Elizabeth turned to look where the belt had fallen, he perceived the sheerness of her gown. The hint of her breasts and the curve of her hips, beckoned to his senses. The impact of such a vision caught him unaware, and he drew in a sharp breath. Knowing his presence had now been announced, Darcy realised he must say something.

"Not tired Elizabeth?" he said, trying to hide the desire in his voice.

Elizabeth was startled at the realization that she was not alone, but thankfully it was Mr. Darcy and not a servant. His chair was tucked into a recess by the fire, but Elizabeth could see he was dressed in only his breeches, boots, and shirt, which was open at the neck. She fully appreciated what a fine specimen of masculinity her husband was, and his remaining clothes did nothing to hide the rippling muscles concealed within. She observed the half empty glass in his hand, and correctly surmised he'd been drinking. Remembering the gown she had donned before coming downstairs, Elizabeth felt conscious of her state of undress, but she neither retrieved the belt nor pulled her robe together.

"On the contrary sir, I was looking for a volume to revive my flagging spirits," she replied honestly.

"Well, you have plenty to choose from in here madam," he paused to determine what she held, before continuing,

"Although I believe that particular volume is not suitable for a virgin maid."

Piqued by his words her spirit rose, after all she was still a virgin by his design. Had she not waited these past three nights for him to come to her? She could not let his comment pass unchallenged; Recollecting his earlier comment, and that actions spoke louder than words, she closed her eyes and lifted the book to her nose. She let the pleasant aroma of old leather invade her senses. Peeping through lowered lashes, she could see he had moved, and was now perched on the edge of his seat. No longer was he holding the glass, instead his hands were gripping the arms of his chair. Elizabeth lowered the book to her breasts, held his gaze, and boldly replied,

"I think this will suit me quite well sir."

For a moment, she thought he had not heard her, but in the next instant he rose from his chair, and closed the space between them. Taking her by the shoulders, he shook her until her dark curls scattered in disarray. His gaze was piercing, but she could not fathom if it was with anger, or desire. Either way, his presence and touch made her heart race.

Slowly, so as to leave her in no doubt of his intention, Darcy bent his head and took possession of her lips. He capturing her mouth and forcing her to accept his exploration, as his hands slid under her robe. Elizabeth let the book tumble to the floor; she brought her arms up and entwined her fingers in his hair, pulling him closer.

She felt she wanted more, and with naive urgency she arched her body against his. The taste of the brandy he had imbibed earlier, transferred to her as he plundered her mouth again and again. Elizabeth relished the heat from his palms, as they travelled to her hips, pulling her lower body into contact with his. He awoke a craving in her wherever he touched, burning its way through her body, radiating from her thighs and beyond. Darcy could not deny it; his desire for her was unmistakably evident. He tore his mouth from hers, and began to trail kisses down her neck, and shoulder. Everywhere he touched left her body throbbing, aching for more, and she cried out,

"Oh Fitzwilliam,"

Instantly he was still, and then in a voice as cold as steel he spat,

"No madam, it is your husband!"

# CHAPTER 28

Thrusting her away with more force than he intended, Elizabeth was propelled backwards into the bookcase, and fell to the floor. Darcy looked at her crumpled form, and fought the urge to pick her up and beg for forgiveness. He longed to fold her in his arms and smother her with kisses, to tell her he was a fool, and would take whatever morsel of affection she offer. But this was one time she would find him no gentleman. Turning his back on her, he strode to the table snatched up the decanter of brandy, and then slammed the door as he left.

Elizabeth lay slumped on the floor. What just happened, she thought? Finally, they seemed to have reconnected, were one in thought and desire, and now this. Pulling her robe together, she searched the floor for the belt, but her unshed tears blurred her vision. To have been thus rejected after welcoming his attentions, was more than she could bear. Although un-witnessed, her humiliation was complete. No longer trying to stifle the sob that had risen to her throat, she buried her head in her hands and released her tears of despair.

Back in his room, Darcy threw himself into the chair by the fire, lifted the decanter to his mouth, and took a large gulp. As some of the amber liquid escaped and trickle from the corner of his mouth, he felt the familiar warmth turn to a burn, as the rest slid down his throat. He had been certain when she entered his inner sanctum, that she had purposely sought him out. Her attire spoke of her intention to seduce him, and he was only too willing to succumb to her wiles. Fitzwilliam! He spat. In the heat of her passion she had called the name of her lover, probably unconsciously done, but done all the same. Plus the remark about the book, had he not told her it was unsuitable for a virgin maid? Yet she had quite brazenly told him, it would suit her well! Her implication was clear; the book was acceptable because she was no longer a maid. Again he raised the glass vessel to his lips, and ignoring the burning that ripped at his throat, took another series of gulps. Oblivion could not come quickly enough.

Exhausted, Elizabeth got to her feet and wiped her face on the hem of her robe. She wrapped it tightly around herself, and secured it with the wayward belt. Uncertain of her strength, she gingerly walked to the table and retrieved the candlestick. Assured that she was steady on her feet, she quickly exited and made her way back to her rooms. Once the door was safely closed behind her, she rested against it and let out a long sigh, grateful that no-one had seen her. What had she done that she should incur such disdain, and anger from him? Was it because she had invaded his privacy by going to the library without first seeking his permission? Surely not, for he knew of her love of books and reading; indeed she had spent many hours ensconced in the library at Longbourn with her father. She even recalled that Darcy had once said, 'for a lady to be considered truly accomplished, she must improve her mind with extensive reading.' No, it could not be that. Did he disapprove of her attire then, thinking it unsuitable for his wife? She walked over to the full length mirror, opened her robe, and looked at her reflection. While the material was sheer, it was not transparent, more translucent she thought. While it gave a hint of her figure below, it was by no means on display. When he first glimpsed the nightgown beneath her robe, he had pressed his suit most ardently, and she had welcomed his advances; indeed she was eager to participate. No, it could not be the gown or her reaction to his advances.

Setting the candle down on her bedside table, Elizabeth took the robe and gown off and threw them on a chair, then donned a simple shift before climbing into bed. She extinguishing the candle and stared the glowing embers in the hearth. Absently, she pulled the covers up to cocoon herself in them, and then went over the incident, detail by detail. It was when she murmured his name that he flung her from him.

Fitzwilliam, for that was what she had decided to call him, the name his beloved mother had chosen for him. She did not want her affection associated with any others. Georgiana called him William or brother, while his male friends like Mr. Bingley, or close relatives such as Lady Catherine simply called him Darcy. The odd person such as Lord Byron or Richard used the horrible acronym Fitz, which she disliked intensely. Suddenly the realisation hit her. Fitzwilliam! It was when she had called him Fitzwilliam. He thought she was calling for Richard! Throwing the covers back Elizabeth sat up, her mind racing. Did he know of his cousin's declaration? And if so, who had told him, for it was not her, she had kept her promise of secrecy. It must have been Richard, the day before the wedding. It would certainly explain why Darcy had acted with such indifference towards her. But if Richard had confessed all that passed between them, why was Darcy so angry with her? Perhaps it was because she had not been the one to tell him. Elizabeth could not believe he would betray her so readily. When she rejecting Richard offer she had done it with compassion and thoughtfulness, conscious not to wound his pride or trample his feelings. Agitated by the turn of events she jumped from her bed; this must be remedied and at once, she thought; they could not start their married life with this between them. Snatching up her thick robe from the chair, she made her way through her sitting room to Darcy's door. Once there, her courage failed her. He had clearly imbibed heavily while brooding in the library, and she guessed once he had gained his rooms, he had continued thus. Elizabeth decided it would be unwise to confront him while he was in such a state, and turned to retrace her steps. First thing tomorrow she would make a clean breast of it. Once more huddled up in her bed, Elizabeth still found sleep elusive.

*********

Darcy slept dreamlessly, more unconscious than asleep, but when he roused in the morning, it appeared he had at least made it to the bed. However, he had not managed to undress or gain the covers. He was sprawled on top of the mattress, with the counterpane tangled between his legs. He tried to sit up, but the thumping in his temples forced him to merely prop himself up on one elbow. 'This is getting to be all too familiar' he thought, and where the devil was Fletcher? He tried to shout for him, but only a rasping sound came forth, his mouth and throat dry from his over indulgence the previous night. Rubbing at his eyes with the back of his hand, he gingerly swung his legs to the floor, and tested their capacity to hold him. Ascertaining they would, he slowly made his way across the room, only to be stopped by the sound of crunching underfoot? Looking down, he saw shattered glass scattered across the floor, radiating from the fireplace. The memory of him hurtling the empty decanter into the dying flames, came back to him, and he felt heartily ashamed of himself, and his lack of self-control. He was reluctant to call for Fletcher again, knowing he would have to deal with either a look of quiet disdain, or a fatherly lecture from him. But unless he was to shave himself, he would have to endure one or the other.

The next morning Elizabeth made her way to the breakfast room, but with no thought of food in her head. However, she arrived just in time to see the footman clearing away Darcy's place setting.

"Has Mr. Darcy finished breakfast already? Do you know where he is?" she asked.

"Yes ma'am, fifteen minutes ago. He was dressed in his riding clothes," he informed her.

Elizabeth was perplexed that she had been thwarted in her attempt to put things right between them. Having missed him now meant she would have to wait even longer to resolve the matter. She decided to make good use of her day, and asked Mrs. Reynolds to introduce her to the indoor staff. She spent a few minutes with each of them, until only Fletcher remained.

Now Fletcher knew a good deal about the new mistress, and although not one to gossip, since his return to Pemberley he had passed on a few interesting snippets during the servant's meal times.

"Let me tell you this," he said as all eyes to turn to him. "When Lady Catherine tried to bribe the mistress with the offer of ten thousand pounds," and he paused for effect, "she demanded she abandon the master at the altar, thus forcing him to turn tail and scurry back to Miss Anne. Well, Miss Elizabeth Bennet sent her packing in no uncertain terms. Told her flat that they were a love match, and no amount of money could buy her off. Her ladyship said she had never been spoken to in such a manner."

A ripple of undistinguishable words of approval fluttered around the table before he continued.

"Our new mistress is a lady of breeding, and I like her very well," he finished with a flourish.

He stood before Elizabeth and gave a low bow, then they exchanging a few words of welcome and thanks. Fletcher reminded Elizabeth of her father, his face a little craggy with lines, and his thinning hair all but grey. This man is as close to Mr. Darcy as any, she thought; surely he will know the answers to my questions.

"Mr. Fletcher, I understand you have been with Mr. Darcy since he came down from Cambridge?" she asked gently.

"Just Fletcher madam, that is correct. I have served the young master as valet these last seven years, and his father before him."

"He has spoken to me of your expertise in knot tying; I understand he is the envy of all his friends due to your skill."

Fletcher gave a humble smile, but his chest puffed up with pride.

"I wonder do you know when he is expected back from his ride today?" she asked, knowing he would assist Darcy to change from his riding clothes.

"Mr. Darcy has gone on a tour of the south perimeter madam, and is not expected back before supper. I believe he wants to survey as much as possible before the snows come," he answered, touched that she was missing the master already.

"He will not return for luncheon or afternoon tea?" she asked.

"That is my understanding ma'am. Cook usually prepares them a cold repast, plus there are several tenants out that way to give the master a dish of tea, or a bowl of hot soup. He'll not go hungry," he said with a chuckle, thinking her concern was for Darcy's stomach.

"Is that wise? The weather is so cold, and Mr. Watkins said heavy snow was imminent?"

"The master always checks the whole estate when he has been away for any length of time, and be assured I dressed him for inclement weather madam," he replied.

Well at least he is not avoiding me she thought. Elizabeth remembered to thank Fletcher, and then made her way to Mrs. Reynolds room, where they went over the menu for the evening meal. Mrs. Reynolds offered her a list which detailed the required skills of her new Abigail, and then asked if there was anything else she wished to add. Elizabeth looked over the list; select and co-ordinate outfits and accessories, style hair, sew clothes, clean jewellery, care of shoes, gloves, bonnets, etc. It was a comprehensive list, and Elizabeth could think of no additions, and so she happily approved it. These were her first instructions as mistress of Pemberley, and she had no-one to share her joy with. So this was how it felt to be homesick.

Darcy made his way to the library with stealth; he had no desire not to speak to anyone, least of all Elizabeth. His mood was foul and taciturn, and the only company he wanted was his own. When he entered the library he saw the little leather book, still where it had fallen last evening. He picked it up and flicking through a few of the pages, until he came to a few familiar lines.

*And they who carefully survey will find*
*Each part is fitted for the use design'd*
*The purest blood we find if well we heed*
*Is in the testicles turn'd into seed:*
*Which by most proper channels is*
*transmitted*
*Into the place by nature for it fitted:*
*With highest sense of pleasure to excite*
*In amorous combatants the more delight*
*For in this work nature doth design*
*Profit and pleasure in one act to join*

The book, Aristotle's Complete Masterpiece was attributed to the great philosopher Aristotle, but was not actually penned by him; among other things it described the act of love, and the bliss of the matrimonial bedchamber. In fact it was a rare first edition, published in England in 1684. All the Darcy men had been given it to read before putting its teachings into practice, and although he had no reserves about a married woman perusing its pages, it was, as he had stated to Elizabeth, unfit for the eyes of a maiden. He tossed it onto a pile of paperwork on his desk, and then sat in his desk chair, letting his head rest back. Had Elizabeth known what book she had chosen, or was it as he now suspected a random selection? Knowing Elizabeth, the lack of any outward title would have piqued her inquisitive nature, driving her to peek inside its covers. Running his hand through his hair, he sighed heavily. It had felt so right when he held her in his arms, savouring her willing response as his hands travelled over her slim body. Damn! He thought, he must stay firm in his resolve, he did not know if he had the strength to reject her a second time. The only solution he could see was to remove temptation. He would wait until the festive season was over, and then join Georgiana in London for a few weeks. He could then send Georgiana north to keep Elizabeth company, while he journeyed abroad.

Elizabeth dressed with extra care that evening. If she was to straighten this mess out with Darcy, she needed to make certain his mind was focused on her words, not her attire. At the last minute she decided to add a piece of lace to cover her décolleté, just in case it was her nightgown that instigated last night's outburst. When she walked into the dining room, she was surprised to see Darcy already there. Standing before the fire with his legs astride, and his hands locked behind his back, he looked devastatingly handsome. As she met his gaze, Elizabeth felt her heart flutter with a mixture of excitement, and anxiety. She longed to be held in his strong embrace again, and at the risk of sounding wanton, in his bed too. But until all was resolved between them, there seemed little chance of either. Taking courage, she walked to the seat nearest to Darcy, sat down, and waited. She hoped Darcy would initiate a conversation, but when he also elected to remain silent, Elizabeth opened with a safe enquiry.

"How was your day sir? Did you attend to all that you hoped?"

"Thank you, yes. I have made a start on my rounds and will continue tomorrow. There are a few minor things that need attention, and Peebles will action them directly," he replied politely. Elizabeth was encouraged.

"That is good news indeed sir," she replied with a smile.

Elizabeth was not one to suffer from attacks of the vapours, but she could most certainly attest to not feeling herself. A whiff of Mrs. Bennet's salts would have been most welcome at that moment. Realising delay was pointless; she went directly to the subject.

"I wondered if we might speak in private sir," her voice giving way to a slight quiver.

"We have nothing of a private nature to discuss madam," Darcy replied staring straight ahead.

"Sir, you give me no choice. I wish to speak of the events of last evening." Elizabeth said insistently.

Darcy shot her a burning glare of anger, before returning his eyes to the front.

"Very well madam, if you insist," he said coldly.

With a slight nod of his head, Darcy dismissed the waiting footmen. Once alone, he turning and glared at her, his eyes burning with anger and declared,

"I realise you have led a rather different, and often lax existence at Longbourn, in comparison to what is observed here at Pemberley madam, but the facade of a harmonious existence is to be maintained in front of the servants at all times, is that understood?"

Turning to face the fire, he grasped the mantel and kicked at the burning logs with venom. Shocked at his rebuke, Elizabeth stared at his back momentarily before defending her actions.

"That is unfair sir; did I not ask to speak to you privately but a moment before?" she asked, "If you had acquiesced to my request..."

Darcy cut her off mid-sentence.

"There is nothing, nothing, you can possibly have to say to me about the events of last evening, I would wish to hear," he hissed, "The utterance of your lovers name was more than enough madam. Now, if you will excuse me, I find my appetite has deserted me."

He strode from the room, purposely ignoring Elizabeth's pleas to stay, to let her explain.

Elizabeth sat alone, bewildered at Darcy's unreasonable behaviour. A mixture of emotions racing through her mind, anger that he had given her no chance to explain, dismay that her worse fear had been confirmed; he thought Richard was her lover. And finally disbelief that he did not trust her. If he would not let her speak on the subject to explain, how could his misapprehension ever be resolved? Elizabeth sighed; clearly there would be no resolution tonight. How she missed Jane and her ready words of comfort.

Darcy made his way to his favourite room in the house, his inner sanctum, his retreat. In this room he had spent many happy hours with his parents, reading, playing games or debating something they had read. It was where he did his work, his reading, and of late, his drinking. He poured himself a large glass of port, and then retrieved the small book. Taking to his favourite chair in the alcove by the fire, he was assured no-one would disturb him. He would not be surprised if Elizabeth packed her trunks and returned to Longbourn. His treatment of her since the night of the Lucas ball had been un-forgivable. He had been wrong tonight too; he should have let her offer up her excuses, maybe it would have helped. He longed to wipe from his mind the vision of Elizabeth's hand in Richard's, but unfortunately it was seared in his memory. Sir Walter Scott's 'Marmion', 'Oh what a tangled web we weave, when first we practice to deceive,' seemed to lend itself perfectly to her situation. He reasoned that to conquer his emotions, he must first let her confess. Maybe then they could come to some arrangement. Draining his glass, he opened the little book at random. The page described how a couple should think happy, pleasant thoughts during coitus. This would ensuring any child conceived from their union, would be fair of face. As the alcohol mellowed his mood, he chuckled at such an archaic notion. Only one hundred years ago such ideas were thought to be fact. Such falsehoods belonged only in storybooks, he mused. Refilling his glass, he tossed the book back on to the table. Would he ever have a child of his own he wondered? It seemed unlikely now. He could not ask Elizabeth to surrender to him just to beget an heir. And it was unthinkable for him to force himself on her, although he knew such practices went on. Now completely despondent, he once thought life without Elizabeth would be unbearable, but at the moment, life with her was just as torturous. Draining his glass, he reached for the decanter again.

# CHAPTER 29

Elizabeth rose early again the next morning, intending to explore the grounds a little more before breakfast. Knowing Darcy would have left hours ago, she did not expect to see him until the evening meal. She also hoped to use this time apart to solicit Fletcher's help. Mulling over her plan as she descended the stairs, Elizabeth was startled to see Mr. & Mrs. Reynolds standing in the atrium afore a huge, potted tree. They took a few steps back and appeared to be admiring it. How strange, she thought. Hearing her approach Mr. Reynolds turned and bade her good morning, then disappearing down the hallway. Mrs. Reynolds curtsied and asked,

"Good morning Mrs Darcy, I trust you passed a restful night?"

"Good Morning Mrs. Reynolds, yes I did, thank you. Forgive me, but why has a tree been brought inside?" she asked.

"It's from the estate ma'am. Every year Mr. Darcy and his steward ride out and select a tree for the house. This one has taken thirty summers to grow. Tis a fine example, is it not?"

"Yes indeed, but for what purpose Mrs. Reynolds?"

Full of curiosity, she walked around the huge pot, inspecting the magnificent specimen and its decorated container.

"Well ma'am, when Mr. Darcy went on his grand tour, he spent the festive season with cousins in Vienna. Traditionally they bring in a tree on the eve of Christmas, and cover it in decorations. The master admired the notion very much, and decided it would be the perfect tradition to start here at Pemberley. When Miss Georgiana was a youngster she would help me with the trimmings, but the last few years she has elected to spend Christmas in town. But she decorates the Airwhile House tree very well madam. Nowadays I usually pick the newest serving girl to help me; helps take their mind off feeling homesick. It is hard work, but the outcome is quite prodigious."

Elizabeth was fascinated with the idea, and although she did not want to deprive anyone of the prospect of helping, she longed to participate.

"I would not wish to divest anyone of a welcome opportunity, but would you think it very presumptuous of me if I offered to be your assistant? I should like to immerse myself in the household traditions very much," she offered shyly.

"Why not at all madam, that would be most gracious of you, besides we have no new girls this Christmas. I'll get Tuppence to retrieve the boxes. Once you have finished breakfast we can make a start."

Elizabeth was pleased to have something to occupy her, it was many hours until Darcy would be home; and she would still had ample time to enlist her accomplice. After enjoying a slice of toast and honey, she quickly drank a dish of tea, and returned to Mrs. Reynolds. The housekeeper was sitting on a stool next to a table on wheels, and all around were empty boxes. The curious looking table was laden with an array of objects. There were small wooden animals from the nativity, dozens of brightly coloured paper flowers tied into small posies, and a rainbow of coloured ribbons stitched together to make bows. Then she found painted walnut shells threaded on a ribbon to look like bells, and dried orange peel and cinnamon stick tied in to small bouquets. Next Elizabeth spied a piece of soft white linen neatly tied with a pink ribbon. Picking it up, she carefully unfolded the cloth. Inside was a string of paper dollies, clearly decorated by the hand of a child, and wrote on the hem of one of the dresses it said; Miss Georgiana Darcy December 25th 1800 aged 5. Elizabeth was touched that a man like Darcy had kept something so delicate, and sentimental. She hoped that one day contributions made by her children would be added in a similar fashion.

Finally she came to a beautiful red velvet box. After removing the lid, she found five small silhouettes nestled inside. Each attached to thick white card, with a border of gold leaf. They ensemble was completed with a red, velvet ribbon to hang them by. Elizabeth quickly recognised one as a younger Mr. Darcy. The second one, a chubby cherub, she deduced must be Georgiana. Retrieving another two, a man and woman, she decided they must be Darcy parents. Elizabeth picked up the final one and studied its features. It was of another young man, and she realised it was the likeness of George Wickham. A wave of sadness washed over her. Although she no longer had any feelings for him, she could not help but think of a life wasted. How different his life could have been, had he followed her husband's example. He might have been a respected clergyman with his own parish, a family and a future to look forward to. Instead he lay in the cold dark earth of the cemetery, that he might have called his own.

"These are what we use every year ma'am. We space them as evenly as possible around the tree. I will start hanging them and maybe you would like to follow?"

Elizabeth watched as Mrs. Reynolds hung a few of the ornaments on the tree, and then tried to follow her example. Tentatively at first, but her confidence quickly grew as the housekeeper praised her efforts. Lastly, the silhouettes were placed on the front of the tree in a pleasing group, but Elizabeth reconsidered including Wickham's one. After the events of last year with Georgiana, and then Lydia, she thought it prudent to just hang the family ones. Mrs. Reynolds nodded her approval as she returned it to the box.

Within the space of two hours, the tree had been transformed from a single block of green, to an array of colour and light. The final touch was the small candles of bee's wax, which they had placed in special holders on the sturdier branches. With the candles alight, there seemed to be a warm feeling of celebration and happiness in the air. Elizabeth stood back with Mrs. Reynolds, and the two ladies admired their efforts with pleasure. It was wonderful, and she could certainly understand why Darcy had instigated the tradition.

"Now madam, you take yourself off to the master's library. There's a good fire burning in there, and I will bring you some luncheon. You need to keep warm now the snows falling. I'll just get Tuppence to clear these boxes away. Then the master will get the full effect of our efforts when he returns."

"Tis an unusual name Mrs. Reynolds, Tuppence, is it a family name?" she enquired.

"No madam, no-one knows his real name, nor his age for that matter. He says no-one cared enough about him to give him a name, poor mite,".

"How did he come to be here at Pemberley then?"

"Oh that's the masters doing, rescued him from London two years ago."

"I know so little of my husband's past Mrs. Reynolds; I would be very interested in anything you can share with me," Elizabeth asked.

Mrs. Reynolds studied Elizabeth's face for a moment. She knew her master and the staff at Pemberley better than any other, and it had not escaped her notice that the master and his new wife had yet to share a bed since they arrived. She understood that his demeanour was sometimes mistaken as proud and taciturn, but it was not a true statement of his character. Although she strictly forbade gossip of any kind, she knew Elizabeth needed some help understanding her new husband. So she smiled and said,

"Would you like to hear the story of how Mr. Darcy brought Tuppence home?" Elizabeth nodded.

"Master William was riding in Hyde Park, when he saw a fellow gentleman beating a bundle of rags, or so he thought. It was not until he drew closer he realised it was a child, a young beggar boy. His clothes were filthy, and hung from his skinny body in tatters. Wrapped in his arms was a puppy, which he was trying to shield from the gentleman's whip, instead, taking the brunt of the beating on his own back. Well, Mr. Darcy jumped from his horse and took hold of the gentleman's arm, to forestall him from raining any more blows upon the lad. He'd bought the dog to do tricks to amuse his friends, but would not perform. Savage brutality over something so trivial saw Mr. Darcy's anger complete. He demanded the man relinquish his ownership of the animal immediately, and then duly recompensed him with a guinea. The master thought to make the pup a present for his sister. Imagine his surprise when the boy refused to part with him. He stood up and thanked Mr. Darcy for rescuing them both, then said he could not give the animal up as he had no notion of the master's character. Then he offered to buy him. He said he could not match the guinea, but was willing to part with everything he had, which was Tuppence. The master was impressed by the boy's integrity and bravery, and asked where he had leant such traits. Father Dominic, the boy replied. Well, Master William went and spoke to the good father, who told him the boy had no family or friends of worth, but he was honest and a fast learner. So Mr. Darcy offered him a home at Pemberley. There were conditions of course; he has to attend school, work on the estate to learn a trade and be a good Christian. He does all that was asked of him and more. He is apprentice to Mr. Watkins, the head gardener."

Mrs. Reynolds paused to look at Elizabeth. She knew her master would not brag of his good deeds, but she could. She was as proud of him as any mother could be.

"Several estate workers have come to Pemberley in a similar fashion. People rarely leave Pemberley. Mr. Darcy is the kindest, fairest master there is, and all the staff and villagers are completely loyal to him."

Elizabeth was spellbound by the story, and when Mrs. Reynolds finished the tale she asked,

"And the dog, what became of the dog Mrs. Reynolds?"

"Oh, that little pup is now the beast Master William calls Trafalgar, and he is the most loyal of us all." she chuckled.

Elizabeth had listened in silence, in awe of her husband's actions. There were few men who would have bothered to stop a street urchin receiving a beating, let alone offer him a home. She hoped Mrs. Reynolds would share other stories from Darcy's past with her. She suspected he would be reluctant to boast of his kind deeds to anyone, especially her. She had sorely misjudged him, and on so many levels too. Thinking him proud and aloof, when he was shy and reserved, accusing him of having a selfish disdain for the feeling of others when clearly he was quite the opposite. The more Elizabeth discovered about Darcy, the stronger her love became. He truly was the best man she had ever known.

"Mr. Darcy is reluctant to speak of past events, so I am most grateful to you Mrs. Reynolds, for sharing this with me. Already I have a much better understanding of him."

"I am not one to speak out of turn Mrs. Darcy, but as mistress of Pemberley there are things you should know. Every servant's history is one of them."

"I understand, and thank you Mrs Reynolds."

Elizabeth returned to the library, taking a seat by the fire again. Soon a young maid brought in a tray, and set down a bowl of warm vegetable soup, and a plate of thick, crusty bread. It was delicious, and after she had finished it she sipped her hot chocolate. With a full stomach and a warm room, she quickly succumbed to her bodies desire to sleep. The click of the door latch woke her as the maid left with the tray. Although groggy, Elizabeth could still hear their voices through the door. First the maid spoke,

"She must be plumb worn out Mrs. Reynolds, fast asleep in the chair she is. Probably all the night-time activities catching up with her," followed by a girlish giggle.

"That is quite enough of that Molly Weaver; the mistress has had a tiring journey and no time to restore herself. Now get below stairs with that tray and make sure no-one disturbs her," the housekeeper scolded, "I'll give her an hour or so before I offer her some tea," said Mrs. Reynolds.

Then turning back to the maid she added in a motherly tone, "Go on girl, and get about your work."

Elizabeth was now wide awake, and decided she had an hour to explore the room Darcy loved without interruption. She wandered along the rows of books, taking in some of the titles. Only now did she appreciate just how diverse a collection it was. She found books on farming and architecture, poetry and plays, religion and theology as well as all the classics. Shakespeare, Homer, Galileo, Dante, Plato and many more, each category in its own section of the library. If she lived to be a hundred she should never be able to read them all, she mused. Then her eyes moved to a large shelf where the family bible rested. Elizabeth was astonished to see it was a rare King James I original edition, written in the fifteenth century. She hoped Darcy would make time to show her it, to introduce her to his ancestors. It would be a family's who's who, with all the details held in its front pages, birth, baptism, marriage and finally deaths.

At the end of the room stood a rolling staircase to reach the uppermost shelves, and nestled in a corner stood a tall set of drawers. Each drawer was filled with cards, each card detailed one book. Never had she seen such an organised library, but then this was Darcy she reminded herself. She made her way to the beautifully carved desk by the window; his desk. Pausing, she ran her fingers along the edge of the well-loved surface, whilst imagining him sitting there attending to matters of business. She felt quite mischievous as she gently lowered herself into his chair. She admired his choice; practical yet comfortable. Its high cushioned back had a slight curve to fit the contours of the spine, and the seat was covered with soft brown leather, with extra padding for comfort. Where each leg met the carpet stood a carved lion's foot. It was a beautiful piece of furniture, just like its owner, strong, welcoming and a pleasure to look upon.

Sitting on top of the desk were two silver trays, a round one that held a number of cards left by callers, and a square one that contained a variety of envelopes to social events. Apparently Darcy was a little behind with his correspondence. The silver ink well and goose quills were sitting in the middle edge, leaving the centre space clear for use. Either side of the desk was a tier of four small drawers, each with a brass lion's head as a handle. Elizabeth was curious as to what a man like Darcy would keep in them, and innocently opened the top drawer to observe its contents. There she saw a few spare quills, a knife for sharpening them, a small glass bottle containing ink and a little box of sand for blotting. Moving to the next drawer, she found the Darcy seal, sealing wax, some small candles, wax and tallow, and a few tapers to take a flame from the fire. Next had sheets of cream writing paper in a variety of sizes. Moving down she found a copy of the new Samuel Johnson dictionary, which amused Elizabeth immensely. She could not imagine Darcy having to searching for the right word; they seemed to flow with ease when addressing her... The next drawer held a box of expensive cigars from London's finest tobacconist, along with an ornate wooden box containing Darcy's personal blend of snuff, although he rarely partook of either.

Having worked her way down, Elizabeth came to the final drawer. When she opened it, she was surprised to find it contained nothing. Bending down she felt right to the back. As she did so, her finger caught on something. A button! With just a little pressure, the front of the base sprung open. A secret compartment! How mysterious and exciting she thought. Inside she found a book, bound in leather and thick with pages. Her curiosity was certainly piqued now. Glancing around to make sure she was truly alone, she carefully lifted it out. The outer cover was devoid of adornment, giving no clue as to its contents. Imagining it to be in a similar vein as the book she selected last evening, she opened it. Elizabeth stared in disbelief at the words before her. On the first page in bold script it read, Fitzwilliam Darcy, 1811. A Diary! It was Darcy's diary! Elizabeth closed it and held it to her breast. She could not possibly read his diary, his inner most personal thoughts. Could she? It was beneath her, contemptible to even think such a thing. But then again, it might give her some clue as to his understanding of the events that occurred at Lucas Lodge, in which case it would be beneficial to them both. Having rationalised her actions with her conscience, she lowered it to her lap, let it fall open randomly, and began to read.

# CHAPTER 30

## Thursday 24<sup>th</sup> October Rosings

*My aunt has remarked that she cannot understand me paying her a second visit in one year. I can hardly tell her I only planned my return, after learning Miss Elizabeth was going to be visiting her friend, the newly married Mrs. Collins. She married my aunt's new parson, a fellow I cannot like for he is a practised sycophant. Elizabeth has not changed since I saw her last; a little more tanned if anything, probably from enjoying her morning walks, but it does not detract from her looks. How refreshing to find a woman who is not afraid of exercise, indeed her figure is slender and supple for it. I have no doubt Caroline Bingley would not agree with me. Richard has accompanied me to Rosings, but I find I resent every smile she bestows upon him. Would that I found it so easy to converse with my heart's desire……*

Elizabeth realised she was reading the entries from just eight weeks ago, when she arrived for her visit with Charlotte. Knowing she would not have time to read every entry in full, she skimmed over the mundane items and read only what pertained to her.

## Tuesday 29<sup>th</sup> October Rosings

*I have resisted the pull of the parsonage for as long as I can. On seeing Miss Elizabeth here last night, when they came to dine with my aunt, I knew, despite my struggles, she held my heart still. The months spent in town trying to convince myself I could put her from my mind, have been a futile waste of time. I now realise how Charles felt about Miss Jane Bennet, and wonder where they might be now but for my interference, however kindly meant. Does he dream of her as I do Elizabeth? I dreamt of her again last night; she came to me and declared her love. I embraced her and un-pinned her hair, then let myself caress its silky tendrils...*

Blushing at the words describing his dream she moved on.

## Friday November 1st Rosings

*My aunt was typically rude to her guests tonight; I care not what she utters to the imbecile Collins, or indeed his wife, which is most ungallant of me I know, but to treat Miss Elizabeth in the same manner is untenable. Yet what could I do but hold my tongue? If I defended her, would not my affections have been revealed, and I am not yet ready for all to know. I am decided though; they are to join us for tea on Sunday after church, and I will seek some time alone with Elizabeth that I may declare myself. These past weeks we have enjoyed intimate walks, and fluid conversations. No doubt she is anticipating my proposal, and I feel assured of a positive reply. When she looks at me with those expressive eyes, and the corners of her mouth turn up in playful jest, I want to fold her in my arms and take possession of those oh so tempting lips......*

*P/s I have warned Richard to steer his thoughts away from Miss Elizabeth. I know he was on the verge of making her an offer. He has returned to Town, but I will make my peace with him after Elizabeth and I are betrothed.*

## Sunday November 3rd Rosings

*It is done and done badly. I have compromised my beloved. Elizabeth was unwell and did not join us for tea, so I went to the parsonage. Knowing her to be alone, I sought her out. I asked Miss Elizabeth to do me the honour of becoming my wife, and to my surprise she refused me. I fear she holds me in contempt for my misguided intervention with Jane and Bingley. We exchanged some excessively harsh words in the heat of the argument. She told me I am arrogant and conceited, that I am not a gentleman, and that I am in fact, the last man on earth she would consent to marry. Yet as I looked into her eyes, filled with fire and indignation, I thought she had never looked more beautiful. I could not help myself; I was blind to her words of rejection, and drew her into my embrace and kissed her. Not once but several times. It was at this point that the toad Collins came upon us, and to prevent her reputation being ruined, I told him Elizabeth had accepted my proposal. A falsehood I know, yet I feel she is not so set against me as she protests, for the tentative response I felt was willingly given. I would have preferred her to come to me with love in her heart, but I hope in time she will find some regard for my affection.*

## Monday November 4th Netherfield

*I have ridden on ahead of Elizabeth to seek Mr. Bennet's consent, before a letter from the imbecile Collins is despatched, and completely damages my chance of a positive reception. I will seek an interview with him tomorrow. I am heartily ashamed of myself. My loss of control yesterday was inexcusable, and I have put my beloved Elizabeth in the position where she has to accept me. However, I do not regret tasting her soft cherry lips, and her naive response promises there is much more to be discovered. I am determined it will be only six weeks until we are wed, and have set a date for the 18th December in my mind. Then we can spend Christmas at Pemberley before we set off on our honeymoon, Italy I think. Besides I have already waited too long to have Elizabeth at my side.*

*Charles has kindly agreed my use of Netherfield for as long as I need it. I have not confided in him as to the nature of my business in Hertfordshire, and wonder if he knew my purpose, would he be so generous?*

### *Tuesday November 5th Netherfield*

*I rode to Longbourn early this morning, and sought out Mr. Bennet. His shock and surprise at my request, was nothing compared to his disbelief that Elizabeth has accepted me. Their disdain for my presence was barely masked, yet who can blame them. I have done little to ingratiate myself with my future in-laws, something I must work on and rectify with alacrity. Elizabeth is due to return tomorrow, but I will have to forgo being here to meet her, I have pressing business in town that cannot wait. I will, however, see her in the evening, as I have accepted Mrs. Bennet invitation to dinner.*

Elizabeth smiled. She remembered how vexed she had been by his absence. But her ire had been brief, for Mr. Bingley followed him in, and Jane's face shone with happiness and anticipation.

## Thursday November 7th Netherfield

*I have decided I must, due to the way our engagement came about, offer Elizabeth the opportunity to be rid of me. Bingley and Miss Bennet are also to be wed. I have confessed all, and he has forgiven me, yet still he asked for my blessing! Since taking Charles under my 'wing' at Cambridge, we have forged a strong friendship, but I fear I have yet to instil in him the importance of running his own life, as well as being master in his own home. I do not think Caroline or Louisa Hurst would have enjoyed as much mirth at the expense of the Bennet's, if he took a firmer rein on his family. We are to ride to town tomorrow, to inform Charles's sisters of his betrothal, but will be gone only a day. I will speak to Elizabeth on my return from Pemberley. I do not know what I will do if she decides to accept my offer, but it must be done. My conscience demands it! If the worst happens and she releases me, I cannot stay here. Maybe I will travel overseas; Byron heads for Italy shortly, and has asked for my company, perhaps I will agree.*

## Saturday November 9th Netherfield

*I spoke out of turn to Elizabeth today, and needing to explain my reasons why, I journeyed to Longbourn in the dead of night. It was to give Elizabeth a letter regarding my dealings with GW, and God help me, I was on the brink of damnation for what nearly passed betwixt us. I seem to lose all control when she returns my kisses with those sweet lips. When she draped her arms about my shoulders, and caressed the nape of my neck, I felt transported back to the library at Pemberley, and we are consummating our love again and again. I must try to control myself, and cease using any excuse to take these liberties. Elizabeth is a gentle woman, naive to the world of carnal knowledge. How am I to win her love and convince her I am a gentleman, when I act as a rake?*

Elizabeth blushed scarlet as she recalled the event to which he referred.

## Tuesday November 12th Pemberley

*Fool! I must put right what I have omitted to do. I must make a proper proposal to Elizabeth. One she will be able to recount to our children with pride and affection, rather than the actual events that lead to our betrothal. I would not have them think their father a beast that was unable to control his baser instincts. Though, each time we are together, I am convinced I am gaining Elizabeth's affection and trust. She appears to welcome my attentions, and responds with a sweet innocence that only fuels my desire. I cannot rest at night; Elizabeth fills my dreams. Last eve I dreamt we were in the library at Pemberley, and she came to me, her hair abandoned and in her night attire. She began to undress me as I sat before the fire, savouring deep kisses, until we ended up tumbling to the floor. It culminated in us exploring each other's bodies to fulfilment. I long to hold her in my arms at night, and wake to find her still beside me in the morning. I have retrieved mother's ring from the safe, and will ask her for a second, and final time, to be my wife.*

*Georgiana is eager to make Elizabeth's acquaintance, and knows that I imparted to her the events of last year. Thankfully she was not vexed with me, but said she wanted to start her relationship with Elizabeth with openness and honesty. How proud I am of Georgiana, no longer a child but a young woman.*

## Saturday November 16th Netherfield

*To my immense relief, Elizabeth has not rejected me; instead she has confirmed our betrothal, and now wears my ring. I am sure Mother would have approved of my choice, as does Georgiana. She tells me she likes Elizabeth very much, and I understand the admiration is mutual. I find the events of the last few days have given me a feeling of euphoria. I thought I knew happiness in the past, but nothing compares to how I feel now.*

*Before I left for Pemberley, I agreed a financial arrangement with Mr. Bennet. I will fund any extra cost of the wedding he incurs, and have arranged a line of credit for him to draw upon. He has assured me he will keep this arrangement strictly between the two of us. Although I do not doubt he has the funds for such a venture, I am acutely aware of how expensive female attire and trivia can be. I have only to look at the receipts from Georgiana's modiste to remind me.*

## Sunday November 24th Netherfield

*Church was an ordeal today, but knowing that my beloved was at my side helped me keep my composure. All eyes were upon us, and my aversion to gatherings of un-*

*familiar's was at a premium. Her hand on my arm calmed me greatly.*

*P.S. I thought the Revd. Muir glanced often in the direction of young Mary Bennet. He is unwed, and she is of a studious nature. Maybe there is a match to be made which would suit all. I must mention it to Mr. Bennet.*

Skipping several entries, Elizabeth read on

## Tuesday December 7<sup>th</sup> Netherfield

*I cannot deny my sadness that Elizabeth has yet to declare any regard for me. I know she enjoys my attentions, for she comes willingly into my embrace. We frequently share stolen glances, and sometimes I think I see affection there, but I cannot let myself imagine it, not until I hear her speak the words. I am bewitched by the captivating Miss Bennet, and December 18th cannot come soon enough.*

*P/s Wickham has convinced Miss Lydia to elope with him. I cannot let Elizabeth be tainted by his actions. Richard and I are on his heels, and this time he will marry the girl, silly though she is. It pains me greatly though, that I must call him brother after they are married. However, I will endure anything for my beloved...*

Having been made aware of their true association, Elizabeth understood Darcy's abhorrence to this, and what he was willing to endure for her. Thankfully, providence had stepped in.

## Thursday December 12<sup>th</sup> London

*Wickham is dead. I cannot write more of it now. I have arranged for him to be buried with his parents in the Pemberley parish of Kympton, it seems only fitting. Lydia is restored to her family, and seems unchanged for her ordeal. No word of the unsuccessful elopement seems to have emerged, and her reputation remains untarnished. Would that she has learnt her lesson, but I fear not.*

*Only six days until my wedding. Richard informed me the mama's of the Ton are already in mourning at my loss to the marriage market. I do not know if he speaks in jest, but I thank the Lord for Elizabeth, after God, she is my saviour.*

## Saturday December 14th Netherfield

*We are to attend the Lucas Ball in two days, and I am full of anticipation at dancing with my beloved. We have only danced once before, and the conversation was completely blighted by Elizabeth's misconceptions of me due to Wickham's lies. This time I am convinced it will be more enjoyable.*

*I long for the night of our wedding, and would not normally write of such, but my dreams are becoming too painful to bear. The other morning I had to send Fletcher away until I had reined myself in. They are often of a similar vein, the library, a fire burning, and Elizabeth offering herself to me with words of love. I know in reality it will not be so, but in time I hope...*

## Monday December 16th Netherfield

*I can barely put pen to paper. I had hoped, in time, Elizabeth would grow to love me; I know she holds me in some regard, and though this would be, for now, enough. Tonight though, my hopes have been shattered. I observed Elizabeth and Richard disappear into a private room, unaccompanied. Curious, I followed them. What I witnessed I can only describe as a lovers tearful farewell. Have I been blind all along? Did more pass between them when in Kent than I am aware of? Thankfully they were unaware of my presence, and believe me ignorant of the facts. If Bingley suffered such pain when he thought Jane did not return his affection, then I am aggrieved at having caused it. The reality of a broken heart is excruciating.*

Elizabeth's breath caught in her throat as she realised she had falsely blamed Col. Fitzwilliam, for confessing all to Darcy, but it was worse. He had witnessed it for himself. Why had he not asked her for an explanation? But she knew the answer already. His damn pride she silently cursed.

## Tuesday December 17th Netherfield

*At Elizabeth's behest, I have not called on her today; instead I have spent some time with Mr. Bennet. He asked my opinion on withdrawing Lydia and Kitty from society. He intends to send them away to school. He would have them less silly, and more in the mould of Jane and Elizabeth. I have agreed that the girls, and society, would benefit from this plan and encouraged him whole heartedly. Although I am unsure how Mrs. Bennet will take the news. He also told me that my assumption of last month was right. Mary is to be courted by Revd. Muir.*

*I know I cannot live without Elizabeth in my life, and if I am to be a cuckold husband, at least it will be with Richard. I cannot stay angry at him, for who can blame him for falling under the spell of such an angel as she. Good grief, I find myself sounding more like Charles everyday....*

## Thursday December 19th The Haystack Inn

*We are married. Yesterday I took myself a wife, and last night I imbibed to excess purposely, so as to avoid my overwhelming desire to consummate my union with her. Elizabeth is mine, but in name only. So this is what they call hell on earth!*

## Friday December 20th Pemberley

*Today we arrived at Pemberley, and Elizabeth seems genuinely pleased with my home. All the servants assembled to greet her; I hope she was impressed with the warmth of her welcome. Finally, I have my beloved with me at the place I feel the most at ease. Had it been but a week earlier, I am sure my heart would have been bursting with happiness, instead it feels leaden. I cannot let things carry on in this vein, and must decide what to do. But, what am I to do?*

## Saturday December 21st Pemberley

*My fear of becoming a sot is preferable to going to my wife. My wife, how I have longed to call Elizabeth that;*

*however, I will not indulge myself in her embrace while she longs for the arms of Fitzwilliam. I cannot ask her, and it is clear she is not disposed to tell me what transpired between them. My only escape is to ride out early, work until exhausted, and then find solace at the bottom of the bottle. Yet my longing is more acute than ever, and my dreams are so vivid, I swear I can feel the warmth of her body next to me. It is a blessing we are alone.*

## Sunday December 22nd Pemberley

*I am broken in body and spirit. The worst has happened. Elizabeth, while in my embrace called out the name of her lover. I am now certain that she cannot love me, for her heart already belongs to Fitzwilliam. This ache in my chest is as much a physical pain as any I have known, and yet I know no cure, but one, which is denied me. I cannot bear the agony of seeing her daily and not make her mine. I will stay until the New Year, and then visit Georgiana for a spell. I will then join Byron and his party on the continent; I know not when I will return.*

Elizabeth closed the two halves together, and stared down at the book nestled in her lap. Only now did she understand his all-consuming love for her. The pain she had previously caused him, paled in comparison to the depth of his agony now. He believed Richard and her to be lovers, torn apart by duty and honour. If she had made more of an effort to confide her newly discovered regard for him before the wedding, maybe this would never have happened. Wishing she had resisted the temptation to read his private words, Elizabeth placed the book back inside its hiding place and pushed the false bottom shut. Why had he not tackled Fitzwilliam that night at Lucas Lodge, or even the next morning, she wondered? It would appear Darcy had not seen her reject his cousin, and had, therefore, misconstrued the situation completely. Elizabeth knew it was imperative she action her plan tonight, or risk losing him forever. However, it would not be prudent to be discovered at his desk either, lest her intrusion is revealed. Checking all was in its place she went to leave. Suddenly a dreadful realisation hit her. What if she was unable to convince him of her love, if he chose to believe what he mistakenly witnessed, or thought it offered fraudulently? She must act with all haste. Opening the door she peeped out, confirming the passage was deserted, she made a dash for the stairs.

Having gained the safety of her rooms Elizabeth threw herself on the bed. The trickle of tears that had begun to fall turned into full sobs as she gave way to her despair. What if having grown to love Darcy, most ardently, he now no longer loved her?

After several minutes Elizabeth sat up, wiped her face and gave herself a mental shake. Darcy had fallen in love with a lively and spirited girl, someone who was not afraid to tease him or speak their mind, not a watering-pot. In one area at least, her prying had given her an insight into what he desired the most. If this was to be her last chance to convince him of her love, she must hold her nerve and deliver his fantasy. Elizabeth washed and dried her face before hurrying downstairs.

"Ah Mrs Reynolds, I am in search of Fletcher for a word in private, may I use your parlour?" she asked

"Of course madam, I will send Fletcher to you directly."

Elizabeth sat in the housekeeper's chair and waited for Darcy's valet. Presently, a bold knock came on the door, and she bade him enter.

"Good morning Fletcher, I trust you are well?" She enquired nervously.

"I am madam thank you," he replied with a deep bow, curious as to why he had been summoned by the mistress of the house.

"Mr. Fletcher, I know you have been with Mr. Darcy for a number of years, and, therefore, would I be correct in saying you know him well?"

"Yes madam, I would agree with that statement," he said still puzzled.

Fletcher had an air of authority about his person and having the ear of Mr. Darcy put him at the top of the pecking order amongst the servants, after the Reynolds of course. Elizabeth was embarrassed by what she now had to lay before him, but she needed an ally, and it *must* be Fletcher.

"Good. Then you must agree that there has been a considerable change in his mood and habits since we returned to Pemberley?"

"Yes ma'am and not for the better," he answered honestly.

"Fletcher I am going to trust you with a tale. My hope is you will assist me in my endeavour to restore Mr. Darcy to his former visage," "If not better" she added under her breath.

Elizabeth knew Darcy trusted this man implicitly, and she must do the same if her plan was to have a favourable outcome. As she imparted the events of Lucas Lodge, and what had transpired between them last evening, she could not meet his gaze, acutely aware of the deep blush that stained her cheeks. Finally, when she had completed her narration, she raised her eyes, and saw that Fletcher's brows were drawn together in a frown.

"You do not seem shocked or surprised by my tale Fletcher."

"Madam may I speak freely," and he continued before she could reply,

"You are correct; Mr. Darcy has not been himself of late. Normally I would not break a confidence, but you should know that when the master has imbibed a little too freely, he is apt to be quite liberal, and verbal with his thoughts."

Elizabeth raised a brow and nodded for him to continue.

"I had gleaned a little of the events leading to his morose mood while going about my duties. In unguarded moments, he has professed you should 'trust him and confess all.' Then he would take you in his arms and shower you with his forgiveness in the most," and pausing to clear his throat before finishing "physical of ways."

Elizabeth felt the renewal of the colour to her cheeks,

"Let me assure you Fletcher, and *all* the servants at Pemberley, my affections *are* engaged to their fullest in regards to Mr. Darcy. Now, we have to set about clearing up this mess, will you help me?"

"I am your most obedient and trusted servant Mrs. Darcy," he said bowing low while holding her gaze.

"Excellent. Then this is what we must do...."

# CHAPTER 31

Darcy walked to the stables with leaden steps. He had again imbibed too freely last night, and was now the recipient of a thumping headache, but he knew he must be gone from the house before Elizabeth was abroad. She had tried to speak to him last evening, but his pride had won the day, and he had angrily rebuffed her attempt to explain. His pride was one of the traits she had based her refusal on when he had first proposed, yet here he was hiding behind it again. It would not do, he thought, kicking at the ground.

His steward was waiting to ride out with him, but Darcy was in no mood for company. In one smooth move he mounted his horse, and kicked his heels into Nelson's flanks, racing out of the yard towards the woods. Darcy urged the thoroughbred on faster and faster as he headed to the trees. His destination was a small secluded clearing, where an array of wildflowers bloomed each spring. In its midst was a fresh water spring that wound its way down to feed the lake. At this time of year you could find patches of winter heliotrope and yellow jasmine. It was a favourite place of his, and when duty permitted Darcy would go there to think, or while away a pleasant afternoon. He'd envisioned sharing it with Elizabeth, thinking she too would appreciate its beauty and tranquillity. As he neared his destination, he slowed Nelson to a trot and eventually a walk. Both rider and steed were covered in mud and sweat from their exertion. Darcy dismounted and retrieved a large carrot from his coat pocket, having picked it up from the kitchen before he left. He dropped the reins and walked over to a group of low rocks. Finding his favourite stone, he eased himself down to sit on it, picking a jasmine bloom as he did so. He gave it a shake to dislodge the dusting of snow from its petals; tomorrow the snow would be thick on the ground. He twiddled it between his finger and thumb, then pulling at its yellow petals, saying, "She loves me, she loves me not, she loves me, she loves me not, she loves me." With one petal remaining, he gave a derisory huff, and pulled it from its resting place muttering "she loves me not" Looking down at the now naked stem he sighed, "Even nature conspires against me."

Having secured her acceptance of his proposal, not once but twice, Darcy thought that Elizabeth had finally begun to love him. She no longer acted like a trapped animal when in his embrace, but responded with a naive passion that made him ache to teach her more. The image of Elizabeth and Richard standing close together, again invaded his thoughts, and he threw the wilting stem to the ground. *Had* she refused an offer from Richard while at Rosings and now regretted it? Maybe it was because he could not offer her the power or prestige that came with being Mrs. Darcy. No, he knew Elizabeth well enough not to lie that at her door. Was it that her affection for Fitzwilliam had only emerged after she had given her promise to him? Unlikely he thought, considering he had given Elizabeth the opportunity to recant, and she had declined. Could it be she was under pressure from her parents to continue with the engagement? Their match had certainly enhanced the other sister's prospects. He gave a heavy sigh; he could not fathom it. Having made his decision to remove himself to the continent, he must also give Elizabeth the chance to say her piece. Perhaps then he would feel less betrayed, and the healing of his heart could begin.

After several hours pondering the situation, and to the detriment of a large patch of jasmine, his stomach and the dwindling light, told him he had passed the day away in idle torment. One minute feeling the injury against himself at the hands of Elizabeth and Fitzwilliam, the next full of self-loathing for not having the strength or courage to step aside so the lovers could be together. Realising he must make haste and return if he was to change before supper, Darcy called to Nelson. The evening repast, the only meal they shared together, was like a sadistic pleasure. It caused him unbearable discomfort to be so close to her, remembering their recent encounters, while knowing he could not forgo sharing her company, regardless of how much it pained him. Walking the final few steps to meet the ever patient Nelson, he mounted and made his way back to the stables.

Entering the house through the salon doors, Darcy hoped to slip upstairs before being noticed. Turning into the atrium, he was surprised to see the tree was finished. Slowly, he completed a circuit, taking in any new decorations, and looking for old and familiar ones. Mrs. Reynolds had out-done herself this year, he thought. It looks amazing; so balanced, so bright and cheerful glowing in the reflected candle light. It was her best effort yet.

"Does it please you sir?"

Darcy spun round to see Elizabeth standing a few paces away. She looked adorable in a lemon dress, which complimented her dark hair perfectly.

"It is delightful madam," he answered with genuine warmth.

"I am glad you approve, I enjoyed myself immensely…."

"You did this? But I thought Mrs. Reynolds ….."

Elizabeth, thinking his words were said in reproach bristled in her reply.

"Oh, fear not sir; Mrs. Reynolds instructions were quite comprehensive, and I followed her direction in all areas, all but one." She walked over to a small wall table to retrieve the red velvet box.

"I hope I have not been too presumptuous sir, but I must own to making the decision to omit this particular decoration. Of course I will understand if you feel it should be included."

She handed him the box that contained the likeness of Wickham, and watched his expression as he lifted the lid. Darcy stared down at its contents and released a weary sigh. An array of emotions played across his face. Elizabeth stepped closer

"Your decision sir?" she asked softly.

Darcy knew adding the ornament would bring no harm to him or his family, as the real Wickham had, but the memory of past incursions were still fresh in his memory. He wanted no unsavoury memories to mar any happiness they may be able to salvage during the Christmas festivities.

"I think for this year at least, it is best returned from whence it came," he replied solemnly, then in a barely audible voice he added, "I thank you for your thoughtfulness Elizabeth," and he held out the box for her to return to the drawer.

"Thank you sir," she replied taking the item. She then offered him a deep curtsy, with her eyes lowered.

Darcy could not bear to see her acting so subserviently, and said in an exasperated tone,

"I am neither your father nor am I your master Elizabeth, I am your husband; you do not have to call me sir."

With a defiant tilt of her chin, and a flash of daring in her eyes, she replied,

"Well sir," emphasising the latter, "as things stand between us at present, I cannot call you husband, nor employ any of the familiarities that are afforded a wife."

Darcy quickly closed the space between them and retorted sardonically,

"As we exchanged vows before a minister I beg to differ, *you are my wife Elizabeth!*" and now Darcy emphasised the latter phrase with a raised brow.

"You are of course correct *sir*," again Elizabeth paused after calling him sir, "in the eyes of the law, and the church we are married. But in my eyes, I am as I was when I resided under my father's roof, and went by the name of Miss Bennet."

Darcy was fully aware to what she was referring, and opened his mouth to deliver a harsh set down. But as he looked into her defiant eyes, he knew what she said was true, and of his doing. Expelling his held breath, Darcy turned and made for the stairs.

Looking down at the red box in her hands, Elizabeth blinked to forestall the tears from falling. The onset of Elizabeth's plan had been to goad Darcy into voicing what name he preferred her to use, and then there would be no repetition of the previous disastrous events. But it seemed her scheme had fallen flat at the first hurdle. Brushing away a stray tear, she too turned to climb the stairs. Only Darcy was still standing there, watching her. Raising her chin defiantly she waited, expecting a rebuke to be delivered.

He studied her face intently for a moment, and the fact that she was crying had not escaped his notice. Turning his back to her, he said wearily,

"You will call me William, Elizabeth." Then he continued upstairs.

A smile spread over her face as she returned the box to the drawer. Happier now, she followed him upstairs to change for dinner.

Elizabeth closed her eyes and leant her head back, resting it on the rim of her bath. After their earlier exchange she was encouraged that her plan might succeed, convinced Darcy still had feelings for her. Methodically Elizabeth went over each detail in her mind.

Fletcher would ensure there was a roaring fire burning in the library, and plenty of wood to keep it so. He would also procure a few extra cushions and blankets, discreetly placed near the hearth. On the table, only one, half-filled decanter would be set out, thus ensure Darcy could not imbibe too heavily. Once Fletcher had dressed

Darcy for dinner, he would feign illness, asking to retire early. Darcy would of course agree, and then be in no hurry to return to his chambers. Fletcher would position a chair under the stairwell, hidden from view, ensuring no unexpected interruptions or prying eyes. Finally, Elizabeth would dismissed her maid, with instructed to wait until summoned in the morning. All eventualities had been thought of, she hoped.

Fletcher gathered a few amusing books that would keep his spirits from flagging, he could also use them to cover his eyes should their plan be successful. He had no desire to witness the master carry his bride off to their marriage bed dressed only in her night-clothes.

Seated in the smaller dining room, Elizabeth and Darcy ate their meal in relative silence, only conversing when the servants were present. Elizabeth began her prepared narration, knowing she must lay the foundations before he excused himself, and retreated to the library.

"I find your tradition of decorating a tree for the festivities quite charming, are there any other Darcy traditions I should know about?" she asked pleasantly.

Surprised by her enquiry, he took a moment before replying cordially.

"A gift is sent to each of my tenants, usually a small hamper.. Something appropriate for each family, usually food and household items. The children are each given a toy. We have a list for both boys and girls, and it is rotated every five years. Also, we hold a New Year's Eve party for all that are able to attend, young or old."

"Including the children?" Elizabeth asked.

"Of course including the children, they are under my care too are they not? Besides, it helps to put names and faces together, which benefits the whole estate."

Elizabeth was again reminded of the weight of her husband's responsibilities. She could see how this might give him the appearance of being of a studious nature, when in fact she knew him to be quite personable. Also, it explained how when they first arrived, he was able to greet everyone by name.

"And gifts William, do family members exchange gifts also?"

She cast him a sly glance after using his name for the first time, wanting to observe his reaction. She was not disappointed. Darcy almost dropped his cutlery at her utterance. A smile tugged at the corners of his mouth, although he made great play on chewing his food, and emptying his mouth before replying,

"Yes, Elizabeth," he emphasised her name, "we also exchange gifts. Is it a custom you followed at Longbourn?"

"It is, William, we would exchange our gifts on Christmas Eve, giving Christmas Day over to celebrating the birth of our Lord."

"Then we are in accord," he said with a smiled.

Elizabeth returned his smile and nodded her agreement.

Again they lapsed into silence, neither wanting to risk disrupting their new found harmony. Darcy wondered if Elizabeth had a present for him. He had secured Elizabeth's present while in London several weeks earlier, when still under the illusion she could love him. The diamond and ruby compilation, nestled in a black, velvet lined box, sat in the safe. As for her gift to him, he had only ever wanted one thing, and now that seemed unattainable.

Once the meal was complete, Elizabeth waited for Darcy to excuse himself as had become his custom, before returning to her room to prepare. Laid out on her bed was the nightgown and robe her Aunt Gardiner had gifted her. On the dressing table was a blood red ribbon to go in her hair. Mary was especially attentive tonight, tying Elizabeth's hair exactly as instructed. As Fletcher had advised Elizabeth that 'it may be some hours before Mr. Darcy succumbed to the effects of the refreshments, having a strong tolerance to alcohol' she settled down to wait.

It was after eleven before Fletcher tapped at her door. Mary repeated Fletcher's message verbatim,

"The master had acquiesced to Mr Fletcher's request, and when quite convenient would like your company madam."

Mary's last duty of the night was to relay Elizabeth's reply to Fletcher, 'ten minutes.' The excessive fluttering in her stomach made it hard to breathe, and Elizabeth hoped her courage would not fail her. Checking her appearance one last time, she took a deep breath, picked up the candle and exited her room.

How strange and quiet the house seemed now, devoid of all activity. Aware that the fabric and cut of her nightgown was created to induce an amorous reaction, Elizabeth hoped all the servants had heeded Fletcher's advice. With slippered feet, she made her way silently down the stairs. As she drew near to where Fletcher was on sentry duty, she paused and quietly called,

"I am passing now Fletcher."

On hearing their prearranged signal, he diverted his gaze, whilst offering up a silent prayer for her success.

Placing the candlestick on the nearest table, Elizabeth stood before the library door, her hand trembling as it hovered over the handle. Taking one final, calming breath, she smoothly turned the lever and entered Darcy's inner sanctum.

## CHAPTER 32

Elizabeth was pleased the glow from the fire provided enough light to gently illuminate the room. The flames flickered to and fro, casting shadowy patterns that danced on the walls. The ambience of the room was warm and inviting, just as she had hoped. She searched for Darcy, and found her hearts-desire slouched in a large easy chair in the recess by the fire. One leg was carelessly slung over the chair arm, and a half empty glass of amber liquid nestled in his hand. Devoid of his jacket and waistcoat, with his neck-cloth hanging loosely he looked at his ease. A stray curl rested on his brow, and he appeared to be quietly talking to himself as he gently swirled the brandy around his glass. He had never looked more handsome or more vulnerable than he did at this moment, and Elizabeth knew she would never love another.

Taking childlike steps Elizabeth slowly inched her way forward. Not wishing to startle him, she paused a few feet shy of his chair. Elizabeth untied her belt and she let her robe slip from her shoulders. The glow from the flames filtered through her nightgown, revealing the outline of her slender body. Standing before him, Elizabeth softly called his name.

"William."

Darcy lifted his eyes from the glass just enough to see a pair of slippered feet before him.

"Even in my dreams the siren calls to me, how am I to resist?" he mumbled.

Smiling at his own witticism, he closed his eyes and emptied the contents of the glass, then reaching for the decanter again. Elizabeth knew this might be her only chance to convince him of her true regard. Also aware she was no femme fatale in the art of seduction, she closed the space between them with trepidation, then silently knelt before him. Having surreptitiously gained knowledge of his deepest desire from his diary, she tentatively reached up and caressed his cheek, then gently drew the palm of her hand down his strong jaw.

Unsure if this was real or yet another of his drunken incarnations, Darcy set his glass down and shook his head. As if reading his thoughts she offered him confirmation.

"It is no dream William, I am here," she said, unable to hide the quiver in her voice.

Darcy seized her hand and placed a lingering kiss on the soft skin of her wrist then drew it to his breast.

"So you are my little vixen, but I must resist your many charms, for whenever I succumb reality encroaches, and once again I find myself alone." Closing his eyes, he rested his head on the back of his chair and sighed heavily, "Would that my Elizabeth desired me so."

Elizabeth realised Darcy still thought he was dreaming, and for a moment her resolve faltered. What if he accused her of taking advantage of his weakened state? Despite that possibility, she was willing to risk his wrath on the morrow, if only she could spend one night in his arms.

"William I have come to give you your gift."

"My gift?" he questioned, raising his head to gaze at her once more, before realising to what she pertained.

"Ah yes, 'tis Christmas Eve and we must exchange gifts," he said with a low chuckle.

Retrieving her hand, which Darcy released with reluctance, Elizabeth reached up and took the velvet ribbon between her fingers and slowly pulled. Darcy sat mesmerised as Elizabeth's hair cascaded down in a fluid, luminous curtain, the soft, lush curls coming to rest about her shoulder.

Was she inviting him to indulge himself he wondered? Again he shook his head as if trying to dispel the fog of alcohol from his senses. Hesitantly, he reached out to pluck at a stray tendril, and then raise it to his face. Inhaling deeply he detected the sweet scent of lavender as it rippled over his senses. Darcy allowed his eyes to roam over the vision of loveliness before him. From her sparkling eyes, to her moist lips which were parted expectantly, all encompassed in *that* gown. Finally, he realising she was actually here, and his heart began to pound against his ribs. He ached to pull her into his embrace and plunder her sweet mouth, to feel her respond to his desire as he had so long dreamt she would. Yet he dare not, fear of rejection held him ridged in his chair.

Seeing his uncertainty, she reached up and finished removing his neck cloth. Lightly she placed her hands on his chest and slowly moved them over the contours of his firm torso, shyly letting her fingers brush his nipples. Concerned Darcy would think her to forward, she glancing up to gauge his reaction. His breathing was shallow and his jaw was clenched, but his eyes told her it was desire, not anger he was experiencing. She had memorised his dream in its entirety, even going so far as to practice his seduction in the privacy of her chamber, but actually seducing one's husband was a shocking reality. Elizabeth's hands travelled back to the buttons on his shirt and she started to unfasten them, relieving them of their burden. Focused wholly on her task, she unconsciously tilted her head and moistened her lips.

Darcy knew he should put a stop to her ministrations; her touch was wreaking havoc with his self-control, but his desire and longing were too strong to resist. Unable to remain passive any longer, he pushed the chair back and knelt on the floor before her. He knew it was not the heat from the fire that seared through his veins and warmed him, but an all engulfing animal hunger to possess Elizabeth. His knuckles had turned white as he gripped the chair, but he was oblivious to the pain.

As she continued to unbuttoned his shirt, he reached up to entwine his fingers through her thick, luxurious curls, savouring their softness, before giving it a gentle tug, forcing her to tilt her chin up to face him.

So often had he dreamt of this moment, never daring to hope it would become a reality, but here she was of her own volition, beautiful, intoxicating, and offering herself to him? Would she allow him to taste her sweet mouth, to quench his thirst as only she could? Elizabeth met his gaze for a moment, and guessing his intention, lowered her eyes. She parted his shirt fronts, exposing his broad, muscular chest and the soft, dark curls of his chest hair. Slowly, Elizabeth began placing delicate feather kisses on his exposed skin, tracing a line from his neck to his shoulders, before tentatively delving still further.

Darcy's breath caught in his throat as Elizabeth let her moist lips brush against his nipple. The trail of fire she had ignited drove his desire beyond any man's endurance. Her naïve seduction had been more potent in arousing his desire, that the most experienced courtesan. He pulled her to him roughly, ensuring their bodies moulded together, thus leaving Elizabeth in no doubt of his desire for her. Grabbing a handful of her hair, he gently tugged her head back once more. This time there would be no escape; his self-control had been worn away kiss by kiss, now he would taste her sweet lips or be damned trying. Unable and unwilling to hold back any longer, Darcy took possession of her mouth with a savage urgency, invading and exploring every moist recess.

Elizabeth accepted his all-consuming kiss with no regret, and matched him with naive enthusiasm.

Dear God, he thought, can this be true? Does Elizabeth yearn for me as I do her? Hesitantly he ran his hands over the soft curves of her hips, still unsure of her reaction to such an intimate touch. Hearing her soft moan of pleasure, he explored further. Brutally aware that only the flimsy gown separated him from becoming one with his beloved, Darcy knew he was almost beyond the point of recovery, yet still he hesitated to take the final step.

Elizabeth relished the heat from his touch. It sent a pleasurable, yet unfulfilling ache to her most intimate area, creating a hunger for him she did not understand, but longed for him to satisfy.

Finally, Darcy knew he could resist no more, and in one fluid motion twisted them around until they sank to the floor. Looking down at her inviting smile and outstretched arms, every fibre of his being aching to fulfil both their desires. Seeking her verbal consent, he murmured with an undeniable longing in his husky voice,

"Elizabeth, are you sure this is what you want?"

Tangling her fingers in the soft curls at the nape of his neck, she pulled him closer until her warm breath caressed his cheek, and in a sultry voice said,

"Make me yours William."

After a year of dream filled nights, full of painful longing and subsequent denial, Darcy finally took Elizabeth as his wife.

Content, they lay folded in each other's arms before the library fire, with Darcy nuzzling at his wife's ear. Elizabeth had come to him willingly, and he had not been disappointed. Introducing Elizabeth to the pleasures of love-making had awakened a passion, and enthusiasm in her that has surpassed all his expectations. He had never known such longing as he had with Elizabeth, but neither had he known such satisfaction. Darcy suspected he would never be able to completely satisfy his desire to join with Elizabeth, but for now he was content. He tightened his grip around her slender waist, never wanting to release her again. His happiness overflowed, and he nipped her ear playfully.

"All my life I have searched for an Aphrodite to call my own. Had I realise she lived in the shires I would have journey there earlier," he teased.

Elizabeth, glowing in the aftermath of their lovemaking, tried to nestle even closer to her husband. Making love with William had been a wondrous experience. The effect on both her body and mind had been a revelation of biblical proportions. How wrong her mother was in her notion of coupling, and how very insightful was her Aunt Gardiner. Her future outlook of visiting the marriage bed had been drastically reversed. Although this first time had been a little uncomfortable, it was greatly compensated for by its concluding event. Elizabeth giggled and gave a sigh of contentment, her husband thought her a goddess. A compliment indeed, but she would be happy to be his wife, now true in every meaning of the word.

"That is a lofty pedestal to place me on my love, I would much rather just be your wife, especially if one of my duties will be to repeat our actions of tonight. Is it always so delicious?" she asked as she placed nibbling kisses along his jaw.

"With us it will be; my desire for you will never wain, and you will never be left wanting in any respect. You are everything to me Elizabeth; I will always love you," he said solemnly.

Realizing he had become still, and silent, she pulled back a little to look into his face. Gone was the passion and warmth she had basked in for the last hours, now replaced with the familiar tight lips, and furrowed brow. Concerned that her careless jest had offended him in some way, she spoke words of reassurance.

"My love, it was not a criticism, merely an observation. Tonight was more enjoyable and fulfilling than I ever expected, or indeed was lead to believe it could be. I am happy to be both."

"You will be my wife until I draw my last breath Elizabeth, and that is twice you have called me that. Do not say it if you do not mean it madam," he said in a clipped tone before pulling her once more into his embrace. He buried his face in her curls, then pleaded, "Dearest Elizabeth, tell me you mean it, do not rip my heart out after only one night. I could not bear it."

Elizabeth was aghast as she realised he still doubted her love. After joining with him so completely, she knew she must, with all alacrity, dispel any notions he still held in regard to his cousin. This new beginning must be built on mutual trust and respect if they were to build a life together. Unfortunately this would mean she must break her promise to Colonel Fitzwilliam. As Darcy had witnessed their meeting with his own eyes, and then jumped to the wrong conclusion, it could not be helped. Richard would understand. And after reading Darcy's diary, she already felt fortunate that he had not renounced on their engagement. Untangling herself from his arms, she struggled to sit up, whilst pulling at the blanket that covered her nakedness. Once comfortable and modestly covered, she looked down at her husband, lines of worry and doubt etched on his face.

"William, do you remember how you declared your love for me at the Lucas Ball?" he nodded and she continued. "Until that moment I thought you saw me as a drug you must have, an itch you must scratch. I thought, wrongly, that once you had done so you would turn into a typical husband of the Ton, seconding me at Pemberley while you found your amusement in town. I did not want to lose my heart to such a man. I was fighting falling in love with you so I would not be hurt. For such an astute man I am surprised you did not see it. After you declared how ardently you loved me, I felt free to acknowledge my own feeling, to let my love grow. I only intend to give my heart once my love, and that I have done joyously."

Darcy's face broke into a wondrous smile, and he began moving forward to recapture her in his arms, but Elizabeth held up her hand in denial.

"William, although it pains me to break a confidence, I find I must do so in order to set something straight between us. This time you must let me speak. If we are to embark on a life of what I hope is marital harmony, we have to discuss what transpired between the colonel and myself at Lucas Lodge."

Over the last few days Elizabeth had rehearsed her declaration several times, but had found no opportunity to deliver it. Now she must. Taking a deep breath she slowly began.

"I do not now, nor have I at any time in the past, held your cousin Colonel Fitzwilliam in any regards other than that of friend and now cousin."

She waited for his response.

Darcy mulled over her words, then in a tone of resignation said,

"Elizabeth if you tell me you have re-evaluated your feelings for Fitzwilliam I will believe you, but I feel honour bound to inform you I was witness to what transpired at Lucas Lodge. You cannot deny what my own eyes have perceived."

Elizabeth's heart ached over his misconception, and now pain. She took his hand in her own and held his gaze.

"Yes I know William, but you did not hear the words that we exchanged. It is true that your cousin declared to hold me in a higher regard than a sister, but I professed my love and loyalty to you, most ardently. I rejected him with as much kindness and compassion as I could. I am determined that his so-called feelings for me, spring only from a longing to have what we now share."

"But when we were last in here together, and I took you in my arms, you called out his name?"

"No William, I called out your name." Then she added playfully, "You are Fitzwilliam Darcy of Pemberley are you not?"

Darcy let her words sink in for a moment. She had loved him even before they were married. Then propping himself up on one elbow he asked,

"So you have never had romantic feelings for Richard, of any kind, ever?"

"No never. You alone have touched my heart."

"Then I have been an arrogant fool Elizabeth. There is no denying it; I have thought ill of you these last days, and let my pride get in the way of ending my agony sooner. Had I let you speak of it when first you tried, we might have resolved the matter days ago. I have wasted three whole days of being in your arms. Can you forgive me, dearest, loveliest Elizabeth?" He pleaded, the remorse evident in his face and voice.

"I can and I do. Now come, tis Christmas Day and I have not given you my gift yet," she said moving to rise.

"You have not?" he teased, "but I thought..."

And at his implication Elizabeth picked up a nearby cushion and threw it at him. With lightning reflexes Darcy caught her wrist, and then effortlessly executed a turn, pinning her under him.

"Mrs. Darcy, do you mean to inflict some kind of retribution on your husband's person, after being wed only a trio of days?" he enquired playfully.

Elizabeth wriggled until her hands were free, and then lifted her arms up to curl them around his neck. Looking deep into his eyes, she gently pulled his lips to meet hers and said softly,

"Most assuredly Mr Darcy, most assuredly"

# EPILOGUE

Having just celebrated their fourth wedding anniversary, Darcy and Elizabeth stood in the main hallway, admiring their handy work. This year the tree was even more magnificent than usual.

"And now the finishing touch," Darcy said.

He pulled a black velvet pouch from his pocket, gently removed its contents, and then handed them to Elizabeth.

"Oh, William they are beautiful, an excellent match to the others too," she gushed. "When did you have the boys sit for them?"

She ran her finger along the silhouette likenesses of their two sons. Darcy, who now stood behind her, placed his arms around her waist and chuckled.

"You know as well as I, they are not still long enough for anyone to capture their likeness, not in one go anyway. Do you remember when Byron and his friend came to dine last month? You were visiting Charles and Jane I believe?" She nodded.

"Well his friend was Auguste Edouart, a French silhouettist. Byron assured me he was the best, quite famous in his homeland apparently. Mrs. Annesley brought the boys down for a couple of hours; somehow he managed to make several good sketches."

Turning to captured her face in his palms he earnestly asked,

"Are you truly pleased my love?"

"Oh yes William, very much so."

She reached up to enjoy the taste of his lips for a moment, and then freed herself to go over to the tree.

Thoughtfully, she placed each of them on a branch between her, and Darcy's likeness. Returning to link her arm through his, they stood quietly for a moment. Then Darcy said,

"Perfect."

"Well almost, I feel it lacks something," she replied playfully.

"How so my dear?" he asked, sounding just like her father.

"Maybe this time it will be a girl, that way we may redress the balance a little, do you think?" she quietly murmured.

Darcy drew in a sharp breath; did he hear correctly, could Elizabeth be with child again?

"Elizabeth my love, am I to understand that we are to be blessed again?"

The smile on Elizabeth's face told him it was indeed true. He took her in his arms and lifted her into the air, spinning her around and around.

"William," she squealed with laughter.

"I am the happiest man alive," he said as he lowered her into his embrace.

"Truly Elizabeth, you give me more joy than any one man deserves. My dear, sweet, Elizabeth."

*******

Relaxing in the warm water of her bath, Elizabeth closed her eyes, and thought how fortunate she was. Apart from a brief period of discord some four years ago, her life both before and after her marriage had been truly blessed. All her siblings were happy and settled, as were her parents. And she and William were blissfully happy.

Mary had eventually married the easy-going Reverend Muir, and although wed three years now, they had no children of their own. It seemed they were not to be blessed in that way. Acknowledging their sorrow, and thankful for his own two sons, Darcy had financed a small children's refuge centre for them. Most of the children were fleeing the London workhouses, with a few others being orphans or foundlings. Often on the brink of starvation, and beaten with little provocation, they were grateful to receive some much-needed love and security. For the very young ones, they looked for foster homes, and for the older children, suitable employment. It was rewarding work, and lessened Mary's pain. As for Reverend Muir, he proclaimed it would bring salvation to all their souls.

Kitty and Lydia had done extremely well, during the two years they attended the Academy for Young Ladies in Bath. They became quite genteel, with only the occasional outbreak of hoyden-like behaviour.

On their return to Meryton, Mr. Bennet had insisted Lydia agree to a meeting with Mr. Johnson! It turned out that they liked each other very well, and after only a six month courtship, they were married. He enjoyed being a farmer, but being in his early twenties lacked practical knowledge. Darcy recognised his need for assistance after just a few conversations. To make his land work efficiently, Darcy had advised him on crop rotation, field irrigation, cattle husbandry and the importance of being a good landlord. Consequently he had increased his yield by almost two-fold. More money for Lydia to spend, Elizabeth mused.

Kitty had been introduced to a nice young gentleman, Davyd Benedict, at one of her Aunt Gardiner's soirees. He owned a modest cotton plantation in the West Indies, and though not of the same standing as Darcy or Bingley, his yearly income was sufficient to afford him a comfortable living. Having courted Kitty, and gained Mr. Bennet's consent to wed her, he purchased a small manor house near to Lydia. It had not been long before they too were married. He expressed an interest in expanding his plantation into sugar beet, so Darcy arranged a meeting with an agriculturalist from Jamaica. When he realised the expense would stretch his pockets, Darcy loaned him the capital. Already it was showing enough profit, for him to begin repayments to the Pemberley estate. With all of them prospering, children soon followed, with a son for Kitty and a daughter for Lydia. Her three younger sisters enjoyed frequent visits to Longbourn, where the cousins played happily with the children from the refuge. After a year of quiet solitude, Longbourn was again filled with laughter, and the noise of happy children. Mrs. Bennet was pleased to feel useful again, all the while declaring she was far too young to be called grandmamma.

Jane and Charles gave up the lease on Netherfield House, shortly after returning from their honeymoon. They both found being only three miles from Longbourn, too much of a temptation for Mrs. Bennet and her daily visits. On Darcy's recommendation, they inspected and then purchased, a similar property only ten-mile from Pemberley. Bingley was still the most congenial, and happiest of men she had ever met, more in love with her sister every day. They also had been blessed with children, twin daughters that were the image of Jane, but unsurprisingly with a shock of strawberry blonde hair like their father. Elizabeth was sure there would be many more Bingley children to come.

Her parents, now the only fulltime inhabitants of Longbourn, found that they were still quite fond of each other, even Mrs. Bennet's nerves had improved. The danger of her having to live in the hedgerow, as she had so often bemoaned in the past, had been removed. Charlotte, having already produced a daughter, was about to deliver her second child, when she was suddenly widowed. Mr. Collins, unhappy that Charlotte had produced a girl, was at the grave of his late patroness, Lady Catherine de Burgh, when it happened. He was bemoaning about the incompetence of his wife, and her inability to providing him with a son and heir, when he enthused too much and suffered a fatal heart attack. After his funeral, Charlotte produced the much wanted son, but now had no husband, no home and no income. Ever the gentleman, Darcy had stepped in and offered Charlotte a solution. He would purchase her a cottage in Meryton near her parents, and provide her with a comfortable allowance. In return, she would sign over all rights to the entail on Longbourn, which she had gratefully accepted. Although both properties would remain in Mr. Darcy's name, her parents and Charlotte were secured of a home for their lifetime.

Lady Catherine had died shortly after Darcy and Elizabeth's wedding. She had suffered an apoplectic fit, while venting her anger at Darcy's desertion of his duty to Anne. Anne, on the other hand, had flourished since her mother's demise, growing stronger every day. Having taken over the running of Rosings, she was now a wealthy woman in her own right. Then last year she had married her mother's lawyer, who had secretly been in love with her for years. He had even asked Lady Catherine's permission to court Anne once, but was rebuffed with scorn. On bearing a healthy son last year, she had followed the family tradition, and baptised him Fitzwilliam Darcy Richard Felix De Burgh. He would be called Felix after his father. They too were frequent visitors to Pemberley, and Elizabeth and Anne had become firm friends. Elizabeth chuckled, what would Lady Catherine say!

And then there was Georgiana. Elizabeth did not think having another sister would add to her life, but she had been wrong. Once Darcy and Elizabeth had sorted out their misunderstanding over Richard, she found getting to know her a great pleasure. Georgiana's confidence continued to grow, and the distasteful events pertaining to George Wickham, were but a distant memory. Elizabeth and Lady Matlock had given her a dazzling coming out ball, and when presented at court, even the king had commented on her beauty. Then she spent a season in London with her Aunt Matlock, attending balls, the theatre and every other social event possible. Many titled, and noble suitors wanted to court her, all of which she refused. She had already lost her heart, and with Darcy's complete blessing, she was married a few months ago. They were now settled in a beautiful estate a easy fifty miles away. Her husband was the second son of Lord and Lady Matlock, Colonel Richard Fitzwilliam, retired. He had inherited an estate from a distant uncle, and was now a respectable landowner. Both Elizabeth and Darcy had forgiven Richard years ago, knowing his declaration to Elizabeth was merely a hiccup on his road to true love. He had apologised profusely on their first meeting after their wedding, but now it was all forgotten and harmony between them was restored.

Although their road to wedded bliss had not started off smoothly, they had in each other, found their true soul mate. Darcy had stepped in and secured the future of everyone she held dear. He truly was the best man she had ever known. And this year was going to be special. Everyone had been able to accept their invitation, and was to spend the festive season with them at Pemberley. Elizabeth had no doubt it would prove to be a happy, and most interesting, house party.

THE END

9415810R00185

Printed in Great Britain
by Amazon.co.uk, Ltd.,
Marston Gate.